CATHERINE LESCAULT

Walter Idlewild

INTRODUCTION
Dr Andrew Watts
University of Birmingham, UK

ILLUSTRATIONS
Rocío De Juan Bayarri

Fårö
PO Box 2046
New York, NY 10022
info@LanguageAndPhilosophy.com

www.LanguageAndPhilosophy.com

Cover illustration: Liz Luisada, untitled (detail), 2016.
Courtesy of the artist and Klaus von Nichtssagend Gallery, New York
Book design: Ingrid Bromberg Kennedy, In-Grid Design
Logo design: Eva Megias

ISBN 978-0-9986226-0-6

For

Mike, Pat, Leil, and Giorgio

ACKNOWLEDGEMENTS

This novel would not have been possible without the enthusiasm and encouragement of the scholars at Harrison Middleton University. The author extends his appreciation for their efforts and insights, and wishes them the best of continued good fortune as they pursue their ambitious academic agenda. He also offers a hearty "Thank you!" to Gene Hult, whose editorial suggestions improved the text considerably. Finally, for vital assistance with Greek and Latin, a tip o' the hat to Dr David Butterfield, Lecturer in Classics at Queens' College, Cambridge, UK.

It was in that moment's flight between the picture and her canvas that the demons set on her.

— WOOLF

CONTENTS

PART 3: Art

INTRODUCTION

On the first day of February 1831, a new periodical launched in Paris under the title *L'Artiste*. As its name suggested, the publication aimed to promote new work in the arts, and to provide artists themselves with a means to share their ideas with a wider audience. Alongside illustrations, the periodical featured novellas and short stories by contemporary authors. The creation of *L'Artiste* proved especially timely for Honoré de Balzac. By 1831, Balzac had established himself as one of France's most popular writers, specializing in stories of everyday life which he set mostly against the backdrop of recent history. However, despite his growing celebrity, the novelist was still wracked with debts he had incurred in the 1820s, following his disastrous attempt at making his career as a printer and publisher. As Balzac became increasingly desperate for money during the summer of 1831, he decided to pour his energies into writing for the press, in the hope that he would be paid quickly for his work. Among the periodicals that helped to alleviate his financial burden was *L'Artiste*, which published his short story *The Unknown Masterpiece* in two parts, on 31 July and 7 August.

The Unknown Masterpiece begins on a cold December morning in 1612, as the young painter Nicolas Poussin waits anxiously for an audience with the venerable artist Porbus. Accompanied by the Old Master Frenhofer, Poussin enters the studio in the Rue des Grands Augustins, where he notices that Porbus is working on a portrait of Mary of Egypt. When Porbus asks the two men for their opinion of the painting, Frenhofer laments the coldness of the image, which he proceeds to bring to life with a single, well-placed brushstroke. As Poussin and Porbus look on in stunned admiration, Frenhofer claims that the painting pales by comparison with his own portrait of the courtesan Catherine Lescault, whose death has prevented him from completing the canvas despite his having worked on it for ten years. Like Porbus, Poussin is curious to see Frenhofer's painting, and offers his own lover Gillette as a model. After protesting that only he should be allowed to contemplate the beautiful Catherine, Frenhofer eventually agrees to the proposal, and finishes the painting in a burst of inspiration soon afterwards. However, when Poussin and Porbus arrive to view the portrait, they find it covered in a mass of lines and colors, with only a delicately painted foot still visible in the corner of the canvas. Seeing the disappointed reaction of his fellow artists, Frenhofer burns all of his paintings in a fit of madness, and dies the same night.

That Balzac chose to write a story about art at this point in his career was by no means surprising given the prominence of this theme in his fiction before 1831. In 1830, artists had featured as characters in two of his works: *At the Sign of the Cat and Racket*, which recounted the tale of a failed marriage between a portrait artist and a shopkeeper's daughter, and *The Vendetta*, whose two young protagonists fall in love in an artist's studio. Moreover, between February and April 1830, Balzac had published three articles under the collective title "Artists", in which he defended the importance of artists to French culture and society, and called upon his compatriots to show greater appreciation for the works of art that hung in the galleries and museums of France.

As critics have long agreed, however, the most important source of inspiration behind *The Unknown Masterpiece* appears to have been "The Violin Lesson," a short story by E. T. A. Hoffmann published in *L'Artiste* in April 1831. Hoffmann's work proved enormously popular in France during the 1830s, captivating readers—including Balzac—with its blend of fantasy and realism. In "The Violin Lesson," Hoffmann deals with the world of music rather than painting. At the level of plot, however, the story reveals striking similarities with *The Unknown Masterpiece*. Like Balzac's text, "The Violin Lesson" features three male protagonists. Foreshadowing the master-student relationship between Porbus and Poussin in *The Unknown Masterpiece*, Hoffmann's Carl is a young violinist who has learned his art under the guidance of a more experienced musician, Haak. In order to develop his skills further, Carl asks Haak to introduce him to the violin virtuoso Baron von B., who agrees to take on Carl as his student. Like Balzac's Frenhofer, the Baron is supremely confident in his artistic abilities. However, just as Frenhofer covers his treasured canvas in a blur of paint, the Baron's obsession with perfecting his work ends in failure when he takes up his violin and produces only a series of grating, scratching sounds. Balzac clearly read *The Violin Lesson*, and having reworked key elements of the story in *The Unknown Masterpiece*, acknowledged his artistic debt to Hoffmann by publishing the original version of his own text with the subtitle *Fantastical Tale*.

Balzac's ability to adapt Hoffmann appears to have made little impression on the first readers of *The Unknown Masterpiece*, with contemporary responses to the story tending to focus instead on its representation of love and romantic relationships. Critics in the 1830s were particularly sensitive to the plight of Gillette. Writing in the *Revue des Deux Mondes* in November 1831, Émile

Deschamps, for example, empathized with the anger that Gillette feels towards Poussin after he suggests that she pose nude for another man. Such appraisals would almost certainly have pleased Balzac, who had taken care to emphasize the emotional aspects of the narrative through his depiction of the relationships between Poussin and Gillette and Frenhofer and Catherine. Most notably, when he added new material to the text in 1837, the author discarded the title of the first chapter, "Master Frenhofer," and renamed the chapter "Gillette." In so doing, he underscored the importance of Gillette's personal narrative, and the anguish she suffers upon realizing both that Poussin wishes her to pose naked for another man, and that her lover's passion for art will always be stronger than his feelings for her. The title of the second chapter, "Catherine Lescault," functions as a similar indicator of the character's key role in the narrative. Whilst the deceased Catherine does not feature directly in the plot, Frenhofer remains obsessed with her image in the form of the portrait he has painted of her. The tormented artist guards the canvas as a jealous lover might watch over his mistress. To allow another man to gaze upon his cherished model would be akin to prostituting her, he claims, in terms which expose the themes of obsessive desire and sexual possession at the heart of the story.

Balzac scholars have spilled much ink over the character of Catherine Lescault, and it is tempting to speculate on whether this mysterious woman was modelled on a real person. Balzac's fiction abounds in references to historical figures, from Marie de Médicis to Louis XIV and Napoleon Bonaparte. *The Unknown Masterpiece* also boasts its own real-life protagonist in the form of Nicolas Poussin, who appears in the story as a young man, before he went on to make his career as one of the leading painters of the Baroque period. Catherine Lescault does not have any obvious counterpart in reality. However, the character can be seen to reflect aspects of several different women that Balzac knew during his lifetime. Among these women, the one who arguably mirrors Catherine most closely is Olympe Pélissier. Like the original subject of Frenhofer's portrait, Pélissier was a courtesan who also worked as an artist's model, posing nude for the painter Horace Vernet. Having begun her working life in the theatre, she became a well-known figure in Parisian society during the 1820s and '30s, and entertained the company of some of the leading artists and writers of the day. Balzac was a frequent visitor to her home, and enjoyed a brief, passionate affair with her in 1831, the very year in which he completed *The Unknown Masterpiece*. Whether the author had Olympe in mind as he recounted Frenhofer's obsession with Catherine we cannot be certain. The similarities between the two women are nevertheless intriguing, and add further interest to a story that continues to provoke debate almost two hundred years after it was written.

If the possible connections between *The Unknown Masterpiece* and Balzac's own life story have been clouded by the passage of time, the text itself remains well known today for its reflections on art. The reasons for this are largely self-evident. In his depiction of Frenhofer, Balzac captured two of the fundamental concerns that have preoccupied artists for centuries: the danger of overworking and consequently spoiling their own artistic creations, and the fear of being misunderstood or simply unappreciated. However, the fact that *The Unknown Masterpiece* is so often remembered as a study of artistic endeavour is also due to the successive generations of artists – writers, painters, and filmmakers – who since the nineteenth century have continued to recreate and reimagine Balzac's text in their own media.

One of the first artists to cite *The Unknown Masterpiece* as a key influence on his own career was Paul Cézanne. The Impressionist painter identified strongly with Frenhofer, and in particular with the character's struggle to realize his creative vision on canvas. In the 1860s, Cézanne produced at least two drawings of Balzac's fictional artist, whom he described as his favorite literary character. As Jon Kear argues compellingly, *The Unknown Masterpiece* also influenced Cézanne on a deeper level by informing his approach to painting nudes. From the mid-1890s until his death in 1906, Cézanne worked on a series of paintings in which he depicted women bathing. Painted in the Impressionist style more often associated with his landscapes, *The Bathers* reflect Cézanne's fascination with the theories of art espoused by Frenhofer, most notably the character's assertion that art should seek to express rather than imitate nature. During a visit to Cézanne's studio in the 1890s, fellow artist Émile Bernard commented that one of the versions of *The Bathers* reminded him of the painting described at the end of *The Unknown Masterpiece*, to which Cézanne replied simply: "I am Frenhofer."

Balzac's story continued to enthrall painters in the twentieth century, most famously Pablo Picasso. In contrast to Cézanne, who viewed Frenhofer as a mostly tragic figure, Picasso saw the character as an artist whose work was, much like his own, ahead of its time. The Spanish painter knew *The Unknown Masterpiece* well, and in 1926-27 produced thirteen illustrations for a centennial edition of the story published by Ambroise Vollard in 1931. The majority of these images show Frenhofer contemplating his models Catherine and Gillette, and thus reflect the importance of the artist-model relationship both to the source text and Picasso's own work. During his long career, Picasso completed numerous drawings and paintings inspired by this traditional theme. In many of these works, he gently mocks his reputation as an iconic artist, but also offers precious insights into the creative process by showing art in the act of being produced. In a manner highly reminiscent of Balzac, Picasso situated the relationship between artist and model at the heart of his own thematic concerns. Moreover, the illustrations that he completed for the 1931 edition of *The Unknown Masterpiece* appear to have fueled his enthusiasm for the story. In 1936, the painter took up residence in the Hôtel de Savoie in the Rue des Grands Augustins, in which Balzac had located the studio of the fictional Porbus. The move clearly inspired Picasso, who painted his own masterpiece, *Guernica*, there in 1937.

As well as exerting a profound influence on Cézanne and Picasso, *The Unknown Masterpiece* has captured the imagination of filmmakers. In 1949, American cinematographer Sidney Peterson directed *Mr Frenhofer and the Minotaur*, a short avant-garde film inspired directly by Picasso's fascination with the text. Better known, however, is Jacques Rivette's 1991 adaptation *La Belle Noiseuse* (*The Beautiful Troublemaker*), which took its title from the name that Frenhofer confers upon his portrait of Catherine Lescault. Rivette had long been an enthusiastic reader of Balzac, having first been introduced to the novelist's work by fellow New Wave filmmaker Eric Rohmer during the 1950s. Aware of Picasso's earlier interest in *The Unknown Masterpiece*, and ambitious to explore the artist-model relationship in his own medium, Rivette decided on a liberal retelling of the source text, transposing the action from seventeenth-century Paris to modern-day Provence. With an original running time of almost four hours, *La Belle Noiseuse* focuses on the slow and sometimes painful nature of artistic creation as Frenhofer contorts the body of his subject Marianne–played in a career-defining performance by Emmanuelle Béart–into a series of ever more difficult poses. Through its extended close-ups of the artist's hand at work, the film also reflects the sensory experience of drawing and painting, as we hear the scratch of an ink pen on thick paper, progressing to charcoal, and then brushes as they glide across the canvas. *La Belle Noiseuse* garnered critical acclaim upon its release, winning the Grand Prix at the 1991 Cannes Film Festival. However, the challenge of recreating *The Unknown Masterpiece*, with its complex interplay of art, emotion, and philosophy, drained Rivette, who seemed never to want to adapt another Balzac text until he reworked *The Duchess of Langeais* for the screen in 2007, under the title *Don't Touch the Axe*.

If *The Unknown Masterpiece* has inspired some of the most celebrated exponents of the visual arts, it is especially fitting that Balzac's story also holds an enduring appeal for writers. Echoes of *The Unknown Masterpiece* can be found in numerous works of literature, providing further evidence of the ways in which this text has continued to resonate across time and space. In France, Émile Zola's 1886 novel *The Masterpiece*, based ostensibly on the author's friendship with Cézanne, presents inescapable parallels with Balzac's earlier work. Like his fictional predecessor Frenhofer, Zola's protagonist Claude Lantier is an artist consumed by his devotion to a single project, an enormous canvas depicting the Ile de la Cité in Paris. However, when he finds himself unable to complete the painting, Claude slides into depression and ultimately commits suicide. More surprisingly, perhaps, *The Unknown Masterpiece* has also penetrated the consciousness of writers outside of France. In his 1842 short story "The Oval Portrait," Edgar Allan Poe recounted the tale of an artist who persuades his young wife to pose for him. As he labors over the portrait for many weeks, the artist fails to realize that his wife is growing weaker. When finally he completes the painting, the artist looks up and finds that she is dead. Similarly, the work of Henry James, like Poe an enthusiastic reader of Balzac, bristles with allusions to *The Unknown Masterpiece*. Among James's vast literary output, his 1875 novel *Roderick Hudson* takes as its eponymous hero a part-time sculptor who moves to Italy to concentrate solely on his art. Once there, he falls in love with a radiantly beautiful woman, Christina Light, whose initials echo those of Balzac's Catherine Lescault. In a manner that recalls Frenhofer's obsession with *la belle noiseuse*, Roderick is gradually destroyed by his passion for Christina, and after falling heavily into debt, dies during a storm. In ways that are sometimes obvious, sometimes more subtle, all of these works reflect the themes of love, obsession, and the destructive power of art that are so integral to *The Unknown Masterpiece*.

Walter Idlewild's *Catherine Lescault* stands as the most recent literary work to have been inspired by Balzac's text. The story revolves around a mysterious statue, buried deep in the earth and encased in virtually impenetrable materials, that an architect discovers during excavations for his new home. This striking bronze soon captures the attention of scholars at the local academy, foremost among them the writer and professor Joseph Frenhofer. Aided by a beguiling student, Gillette, Frenhofer seeks to unlock the power of the statue in the hope that it will enable him to complete his greatest novel, but in so doing unleashes a relentlessly tragic sequence of events. With its emphasis on the relationship between art and obsessive passions, *Catherine Lescault* returns us to the core preoccupations of *The Unknown Masterpiece*. However, the novel is by no means an uncomplicated recreation, much less an adaptation, of Balzac's short story. "The house of fiction has many rooms," observes Idlewild's Frenhofer. *Catherine Lescault* may reintroduce us to the familiar inhabitants of *The Unknown Masterpiece*, yet in his wide-ranging reflections on art, philosophy, science, and religion, Idlewild also transports us through the intricate and profoundly original corridors of his own creative imagination. True to the legacy of *The Unknown Masterpiece*, *Catherine Lescault* reveals itself as an inherently Balzacian novel built upon layers of depth, meaning, and artistic beauty.

DR ANDREW WATTS
Senior Lecturer in French Studies
University of Birmingham, UK

PART 1:

Religion

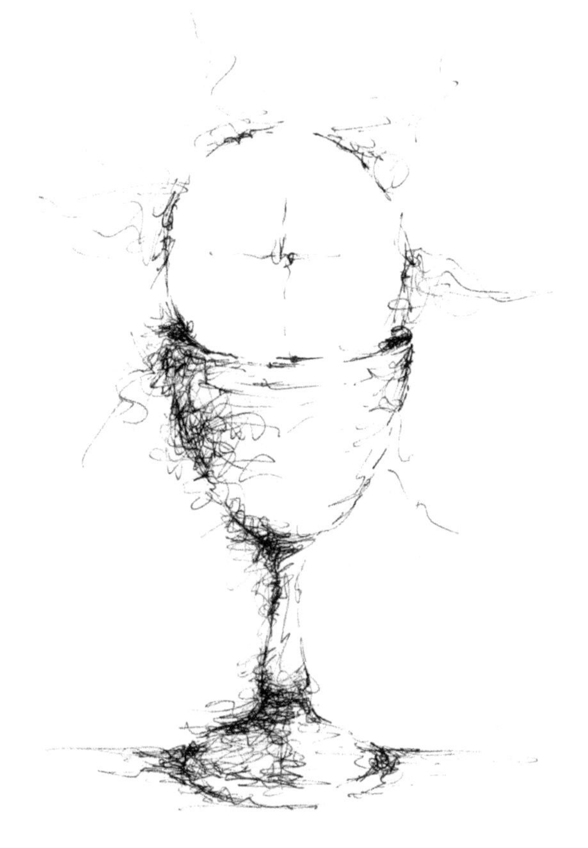

CHAPTER 1:

The Old House

Father,

That my response to your latest communication, having reached us just prior to our departure, has been delayed too long can only be justified by the compelling activities requisite to my husband's revised living arrangements. Please be assured your letter remained in my possession the entire time, its contents as delicate as they were illuminating, as always, and that I have destroyed the document without discovery.

You will not be surprised to hear that your expression of irritation, if not anger, at the secrecy of our relocation did not come absent anticipation. For the events of the past several days to remain unknown to you was to the success of Joseph's journey as necessary as its silence was regrettable. If you were to be privy to the report and the suggestion of my husband's physicians you would surely appreciate our decision in its method and manner. It is not without embarrassment that I admit, in the midst of unhappy events, I remembered from my earliest years, those in which you rendered to my education the deepest insight, your admonition against a stolid and unreasoning solitude, pronouncing to my young ears the wisdom of the philosopher of reason that to be fully human people must *look abroad beyond the smoke of their own chimneys.* And so we have. Glimpsing in the distance a rarified air, we have moved to an environment untainted by the injuries of our times and for that reason seeming in a moral position disinterested.

It is this house to which my own heart turns for a hoped-for healing effect on my husband. It is in a happy spot, surrounded by close hills covered with charming arrays of shrub oaks and pitch pines, the quietude of the forest and the invigoration of the air being to our souls a kind of sacred fount. We seem to be distant enough from the town and its prying eyes to pursue the healing process in peace, yet close enough to neighbors that Joseph may find stimulation requisite to recovery.

Morose during our journey and not prone to discourse, Joseph seemed to come alive a little upon our arrival. Architectural matters being ever of importance to his work, he immediately began to walk about the exterior of the house, placing his hands on the logs and their mortar, pronouncing judgment in a way favorable or unfavorable as the evidence, as he interpreted it, would support. Remaining at a discreet distance, I was nevertheless able to capture a few utterances, soft, muffled, characteristic of his mode of thinking, such as these: "The breath of the zephyr of centuries past," and then, "Built with the strength of Kratos." On occasion he turned thoughtful in his summary, musing as is his wont upon what falls into view, relating what is visible to the eye to what is felt in the soul. At such times he pondered aloud with words such as these: "How did the builder press into a form of wood a vision of mind?" And then, "To make that leap over the chasm, chilled and lightless. . . ." These expressions having occupied him for a time, he would allow his voice to trail away as he returned to his perusal of the house and its construction. Yet in that pondering, brief and pointed, you will easily see evidence of that monomania which for his colleagues had become anathema and in his mind had thrived so heartily on fertile soil.

And what of the house's interior? Is it of a nature conducive to recovery? Here the news is unsettling, for the house seems determined to charge us all with a resonance of its own, a suggestion more gloom of night than charm of day. At once upon throwing open the pine door and entering the foyer, Joseph clutched his coat tightly and began to walk with hesitation about the entranceway, glancing here and there into dark corners, each glimpse as quick and startled as it was seemingly understanding. At the point of ceasing his stray meander, glancing briefly at me with a lost look, and then again at the dark interior, he muttered a nearly incomprehensible dismissive for which I feigned miscomprehension: "I feel a dark spirit."

To this utterance Rachel and I strove to create a cheerful counterpoint, throwing open as well we could the house's creaking shutters, flooding the internal gloom with the late afternoon sun. To me, if not to Rachel, the interior did possess a certain chill, the breath of an invisible ghost musing upon its past, permeating walls, corners, chairs, tables, and other elements of the murky rooms.

Be these matters valid or imagined? Be they no more than tainted aromas natural to ancient rooms, consider, if my own sensitivity to these subtle chords seems acute, in what heightened forms they will manifest in the mind of your son-in-law, for whom the morbid is by nature less enervation to be avoided and more habituation to be nurtured. Indeed, Joseph seems to have embraced the consolidated gloom as an environment reflective and supportive of his state of mind. Refusing, as you might imagine, to consider an alteration in our course, any such suggestion from us was rendered by his obstinacy moot, and we have as a result done our best to scrub, rub, and polish the shadows with life-giving cheer.

We have tried to keep our cleaning tasks modest and little seen, so that Joseph does not become angry and insist on their cessation. In any case, he seems intrigued with the structure of the rooms, and has been closely examining the design of the hallways. He claims that the rear of the house, especially, seems to be somehow off-kilter, but he cannot isolate just how. And it is of course hardly surprising that he is taken with the library, and spending the great majority of his hours there rummaging through old shelves, the contents of which do not seem to have been touched for decades. We dare remove, save in the most discreet way, neither cobwebs from books nor scraps from corners.

Joseph has been inspecting the volumes and commenting on those he especially favors. Only yesterday my peek into the room, cloaked with the nervous shiver of discretion, observed the scholar unnoticed, removing from a shelf a dusty tome, turning it over and over, blowing away accumulated debris, and pronouncing in his way a validation, "The muse of the Greeks, the professor of us all. . . ," such pronouncement being not of the nature of an outlier. In this way he proceeds, day by day, night by night, the light of his acquaintances mitigating, we hope, the darkness of their dress.

If these matters seem more sobering than reassuring, I hasten to inform you of a happier matter: Joseph has turned his attention again, in a halting way, to that work for which the last decade of his life has been paramount. I realize you were displeased with the *donnée* of his novel, and yet I can hope that you understand that completion of this work, after the investment of so much effort, might well be for Joseph's return to full cognitive strength the deciding factor. Hence Rachel and I are doing what we can to encourage his efforts, providing solitude for thought, companionship for physical sustenance, and conversation, cheerful if occasional, for strengthening of resolve. To this time, I hasten to add, he has done little more than leaf through his accumulated pages, nodding here, shaking his head there, only to finally set the pages on the side of the library desk with his familiar complaint: "My powers are gone."

Companion to this utterance, however, is a glance to the abandoned work as wistful as was his penetration of the gloomy house distracted. If Rachel and I can adequately handle this cultivation of his proper interest I feel we can return him to his creative path. May our library, infused with the darkness of forgotten years, be a birthplace of new labor.

Mary

CHAPTER 2:

The Secret Past

Daughter,

Your letter, arriving as it does at a time of complex engagement in the affairs of our institution, nevertheless deserves the attention of a father and adviser. That the advantages native to these roles, as evident to me in their adequacy as they have appeared to you as the penultimate instance of the ineffective, were not among those to which you appealed in those critical days prior to your momentous decision, is regrettable. That the decision so reached, in consideration of the mental state of your husband, is beyond a doubt settled, is certain. That the ramifications of the decision are beyond your ken is a lack which this letter must fill; that the rendition of the matters is as unpleasant as the challenge to which your pell-mell rush will now engage your best efforts, is a matter to be proven as the course of this letter proceeds.

In brief, your letter confronts me with a duty which to the silent vault of history serves as a breaking of the lock. A propensity for due diligence being not among the most prominent notes of your nature, it falls upon me to fill in, with a chiaroscuro the shadings of which possess that robust nature nourished by a knowledge of past events and that feathered sensitivity which to the fragility of human nature it pays homage, that profile, in your mind yet faint and ill-formed, deliberately shy to the present day of observation by our family members, of the ancestor to whose favor you owe your current domestic extravagance.

You are perhaps not aware of the knowledge I possess concerning the letter which you received from a solicitor regarding a gift to your husband from a family member, the existence of whom remains unknown to the majority of her relations. It appears as if this lady, approaching the end of days, saw fit to dispense with a certain domicile, by way of explanation of such generosity offering her appreciation of work undertaken by your husband during the time of his position at our university. In this manner did this woman of mystery feed upon the vanity of a scholar whose achievements had not risen to the height mandate by ambition, that unhappy mismatch being not so distant from a similar disjointment which has arisen within yourself, if I may be forgiven for allowing my parental position to become for a more elevated array of manners master. If it is natural for any woman, more so for you, whose investment in your husband speaks to your moral goodness no less than to your dependence upon the fickle coquetries of the managed public profile, that one can conclude that in this case, as in so many others, including, if you will forgive my boldness, your selection of life partner, the complete or—if I dare so put it—partial understanding of whom I felt it my duty to nurture with the introduction of, and the support for, a *darling interpreter,* your clouded judgment has sacrificed prudence to the altar of what might be described, the virtue of good grace always ascendant over the harsh mandate of the crassly direct, as a romantic—if one might not quite force oneself to an endorsement of the more elevated plateau of the humanistic—*jeu d'espirit.*

This woman, to move at once to detail, is known to me as the last survivor of a long line of distinguished personages active in *belles-lettres*, from which inherited pedigree she enjoyed such opportunities as one might expect for the rendering unto the world what Caesar has provided—to perform, that is to say, those deeds if not of the height of formal achievement characteristic of the men of her distinguished line, then of the path natural to a human soul appreciative of the subsidiary channels available to invigorate for later generations the essence of the great works of the past. This woman had, in brief, every chance to leap the gap.

That it was not in the woman's nature to do so, that she was inclined more to let the bristles of her brush drop, is the reality. That she desired to pursue a life of a quite different nature, one in which the divine spark of human soul is extinguished by an impressive flood of animal spirits, is a fact which to her near cousins and entire family a filial interest brings a halt. Far be it from me, and far as well from my full family, to propagate hither and yon the details of her life and its tragic effects on her husband, save to acknowledge the event penultimate: the departure of the man by his own hand. Neither would the advertisement of these events for my career serve any service but a fall.

For these reasons, along with a consideration for the maintenance of your young mind's purity, has the story of your sudden benefactor been hitherto secreted as if written in a hidden diary. Not without good reason has the woman remained nameless to you—a discretion in recognition of which she has with a sensitivity—as commendable as it is unexpected to the observant finer mind—sent the announcement of your gift in the vehicle of letter penned by country solicitor.

Only now, only after your own heedless actions, arising perhaps from that same imprudent force which brought the unhappy lady of our discussion to a similar stretch of unsettled days, have I found it necessary to break the seal. Hence from out of the past comes a daemon for your future. To understand the nature of your path you must also know the nature of the individual who constructed the house to which you have brought your husband.

On matters relating to this person one need not hold back, and I feel free to render in this letter a name which you will surely hear again. I speak of Franklin Porbus, a painter known among the most refined individuals of his day for a remarkable ability to create striking portraits, to hold the mirror to nature, pictures that in their verisimilitude, I readily assent to his credit, avoided with commendable consistency that duplicity of soul which with natural replication becomes so easy consort. For his works, in the estimation of the cognoscenti of his time, did not so much render life as become for the condition of maximum sensibility the essence.

The extraordinary facility of this gentleman led to practical improvements in his living conditions: the well-to-do flocked to his studio; the press of the day lay on his crown a laurel; women and bankers pursued his fortune with equal diligence. It was that fortune which funded the construction of the house in which you now reside. While vacant for decades, from time immemorial the house was refuge for the refined lineage of its founding resident.

If fortune be the father of hubris, those of a nature in which the creativity of Orpheus has married the fortunes of Croesus have a propensity to imagine themselves as masters not only of their own lives but of the surrounding natural forces. By such proclivity did Porbus pretend to the throne aesthetic, taking it upon himself to construct an edifice of morality which by a magnification of spiritual greatness rendered a satisfaction of worldly desires. It did not take long for the man to commit indiscretions as unforgiveable to the people of his time as they are unfathomable to our own: imprudent liaisons; languors by individuals of ages old and young; laws ignored, broken; a virtual construction of a world of aesthetic prurience. Then came rumors of a young girl named Gillette, staying at the house. Was she compromised? No matter, the story decides the case. The law of the lower Earth showed its hand, arrived at the man's doorstep, only to discover . . . what? Nothing. The young lady had disappeared. A search of the nearby lake was fruitless. As for Porbus, he had fled to lands unknown.

So falls the flower of spring battered by winds autumnal. In the two centuries that have passed, the great man's descendants seemed to forget their founder's seminal impetus. To the recognition of the powers inherent in the written word, a heightened sensitivity to the matrix of natural forces released by engagement of creator and material, these people gave only the glance of the world traveler to the temple of Apollo. The children of Porbus floated easily on the shallows of life, allowing the grand rumble of the reflective realms to flow unbid below their feet. And they abandoned, and then forgot, the house of Porbus, the very existence of which was to the memory of the lost stern counsel. That the house has been put, in the common parlance, *out of mind*, rather than forgotten, is perhaps well said. Rumor after rumor, sighting after sighting, no other house has to the human mind been host to greater dread. All this does the house and its ghostly presence cry to those who hear.

Then came an exception. Will, at this point in our story, the identity surprise? The woman who has provided your gift of domestic escape possessed a devotion to her ancestral Porbus singular in its intensity and accompanied by that dual intention too often characteristic of those whose moral wagon rumbles over the road of life untethered to the reins of a prudent master. Her ambition was, to her credit, lofty. She and her husband would return to the world the victory of her ancestor: yes. Invigorate the materials on palette, wring from the refined body of earth the transcendent soul of heaven, spring from off framed canvas the soul of life: yes. Here was the ambition of Porbus, unhindered by fear of failure or mingy mockery, reborn in bride and groom and to their life a beacon.

The fabric of their fancy's robe so woven with a weakened thread, their efforts were in vain. One day, the husband, laboring long upon a portrait of his wife, when visiting the studio of a painter much admired came to recognize against a backdrop of greater canvas a cheaper cast. Shortly then he laid aside his brush, and then his life. His wife, as weak in her performance, turned her face full to the lower realm, a state to which my letter has referred.

If left this way the story would linger and fade, unremarking upon our present lives. A spark then struck and from its unexpected flame emboldened smoldering embers. Your husband's effort, that elucidation of the inner workings of the machine aesthetic, the treatise upon which his academic career was poised, an expansion of and beneficent of our own, came to the attention of your benefactor. Was not his very subject, arising to her consciousness by trick of fate, a random encounter with a gentleman connected with the very world abandoned by the *belle noiseuse*, a restatement of the internal encounter, that *intentional conflict* which to her life had been guide and destroyer?

Anew flames high the germinal fire. To support a work considered great: Could the woman thereby redeem herself, create if not on canvas then from earth itself an image which when seen in her own mirror became herself? To give the house to worthy recipient, to one who would redeem its rotted beams and tattered columns through a work of stature Praxitelean? Could not such restoration call to life a family lost? Could not Porbus himself be reborn? This way of thinking, extravagant in its premise and reasoning, led betimes to instructions to a solicitor, and further to that seemingly fortuitous correspondence concerning your husband.

This, to complete my letter, is the house to which you have brought your husband. Come live, dear scholar, in the house of the dead, pitched on a corner lost, on a crevice invisible, on one side nature, on the other the world ineffable. What environment, it will be perhaps to your reflection fruitful, could be less effective for the healing of his fractured mind than a house resting on a very crack in the natural world? Your position is delicate; fatherly concern, hence, must on the hearth of prudence cast a chill. It is my duty to inform you not of just the tale once told but of the story yet unheard: The strange details of your house's past are as pressed into the spirits of your bewildered neighbors as the implications are lost to their limited minds. So will the anecdote, the insight, the metaphor, the plot itself, all arrive unbidden to your door, delivered in bits and pieces by your neighbors, concerned, superstitious, helpful, challenging.

See that you steel yourself for a response founded upon knowledge, strengthened by the frame of reason, and infused with the vigor of commitment, withal constructive to engagement prideful to your father and productive in effect.

Your father

CHAPTER 3:

The Crooked Wall

Father,

Something strange and unsettling has occurred. A week after receipt of your last letter, the details of which have been of continuing reflection and interest, Joseph began a series of nocturnal ambulations, rising in the middle of the night and pacing the dark halls of the cottage for an hour or more. From our beds we, at first, heard a pacing, a *thump . . . thump . . . thump* proceeding in a halting way. Then, as time passed, the pacing grew more deliberate.

Awakened by the noise of his steps, Rachel and I opened our bedroom door ajar, peering as well we could through the darkness of the hall. We heard Joseph's voice, sounding as deliberately as his step a measure. "One . . . two . . . three. . . ." After some such counting he reached the end of the hallway and stood gazing at the corner turn. There followed a few minutes of concentration, then he proceeded further, rounding the corner, at which time only my hand kept Rachel from following him. I sensed that interrupting his work, for such I deemed it to be, would lead to the same outburst, grave and threatening, that accompanied any disturbance of his hours of library ruminations. In any event, scarcely a minute passed before Joseph returned, walking again down the hall toward us. Were his eyes closed? It was impossible to determine in the gloom. All we could see was a halt, another prolonged gaze at the wall, and a return to his room. That, then, was the unvarying nocturnal event. Each night since has this same sequence recurred, the mental measure of a world immingled with the roil of sea and rush of pine and wind.

This morning came a break. A sudden shaft of sun broke through our patterned days, our burdened leaden gloom, the welcome rays through forest branches shadowed on the table of the room. And in the sitting area, enjoying his tea, sat Joseph. To our delight he had risen before us. An early start and the hint of a cheerful smile: these, I surmised, were the result of a good night's sleep—for the previous night had been the first in which the scholar had ceased meanderings which to his spiritual peace must have been a disturbance.

Joseph pulled a sheaf of papers and a pencil from his robe and placed them on the table beside his tea. "Do you see these numbers?" he asked in a calm voice. He tapped the papers twice. "I have been making careful notes." I exchanged glances with Rachel. Upon Joseph's papers, wrinkled and torn, were digits penciled in tiny increments—page after page of numbers. Entered, added, repeated, again and again: Before us was the journal of a concentrated mind, the record of unending calculations.

"The numbers," he said, tapping at the pages and glancing at us, "do not add up." He leaned back, raised his cup of tea, and looked at us with the placid face of a man at peace with enlightened ambiguities. "There is something wrong."

I attempted to hide my disconcertment by preparing breakfast. "Something wrong?" I uttered in a weak voice, hoping as I did that my true state would not be revealed. "What could be wrong?"

If Joseph seemed to ignore my question, perhaps his thoughts were commanding his full attention. "Two ways we can view this cottage. One is of the carpenter: walls, ceilings, coves, overhangs—all shelters of the human mind. The architect manipulates the wood and beam, alters the brickwork, moves fashionings here and there, withal for the race. No associations, no aesthetic romance, no other presences. What is its usefulness? None? Tear it down and build it up, it is all the same.

"The other way is of the alchemist: What is the beauty of the creation, its harmonies? What is the shading of its shutters, weather beaten? To the memory of the past, what are its connotations, what are even its ghosts? Where do they live and what pathways do they walk?" He paused, raised his tea again to his lips, and gazed thoughtfully, his eyes following a nightingale which landed on the wooden railing of the deck, then flew away.

As I was about to break into his thoughts with an offer of juice and nourishment, he spoke again: "Destroy it not," he said slowly. "Wring from its ancient beam and brick the soul of a sorrowing dead. Squeeze from its shadow a hovel great in gable, built upon the angle of the sky, fed by the plankton of the sea, haunted in its hallways by the spirits always past, their wanderings meant to build upon the solid bulk of history a new cognition."

Here he paused, and seemingly deep in thought, gazed into the forest, the pines of which began to hiss with the rustlings of a morning breeze. I leaned toward my companion and whispered, "He is communicating with his daemon. We had best leave him be. Perhaps these musings will bring him to health."

As a few clouds drifted overhead, their shadows mingled with the scent of pine and cast over our forest enclave the ineffable languor of a dream. When Joseph again spoke his voice seemed distant, as if he were addressing those unseen. "This house has awkward windows—holes in a silent wall—yet piercing them jolts the world to life. Peer through this forest and what do you see? One darkness; another light. One death;

another life, lost paths or channels to the Divine. Each eye sees the image for which it prepares.

"Upon this forest we gaze, through *not one window but a million*. Reckon each, misshapen in its way, disconnected one from the other, each fashioned to a novel form. What brings these apertures to life? The vision of an author solitary, idiosyncratic, understood by neither host nor guest."

At these words Rachel and I exchanged glances, for they seemed to refer, for the first time in recent memory, to Joseph's neglected masterpiece. Could such speech be a sign of renewal? For this I hoped, yet his sullen countenance seemed to suggest, to my own awkward eye, a descent again into the shadowed world of spiritual malaise.

"The house of fiction has many rooms," he said after some time. He seemed to start at his own words, and he glanced over at us as if he had for the first time realized our presence. Then he opened his eyes a little wider. "But in this house a room is missing."

He peered first at me, then at Rachel, then again in my direction. "In the back of the house. Down the hallway. Something is wrong."

"Wrong. . .?"

He nodded slowly. "Have you seen the wall behind the library?" I responded in the negative, hoping that a revelation of what had troubled him during those nightly walks would bring relief to his troubled mind.

"Come with me. I shall show you." He pushed his cup away and stood, then led us past the entrance hall with its crumbling brick, the library with its aroma of ancient learning, down that corridor haunted by his nocturnal visions. We stood at last beyond that bend in the hallway which to his imagination had in his wanderings been so paramount a focus. Here he paused, retrieved from his pocket those pages to which he had previously referred.

"Behold." Again he paced, marking off the hall. "One . . . two . . . three. . . ." He paused at the opening of the small sitting room that had seemed so charming when we arrived at the cottage but which now seemed to hold a presentiment of doom. "See here?" He spread his arms and gestured to the wall. "There is a hidden room here." He paused again. "Cleverly disguised—look at the position of this little alcove." He gestured at an indentation in the wall, graced with a table, upon which was positioned an Istroclesian marble profile with a vase of poppies. "And see how the furniture in the sitting room is arranged just so. Small enough that no one will stop and stare, save he with sensitivity heightened to a full spectrum of natural forces."

I glanced at Rachel, for he had uttered a phrase characteristic of the work he had abandoned. I could not respond in any prudent way, for indeed it seemed to me that the stretch of hallway, when subjected to close inspection, did indeed present something of a gap. But what could the hidden room mean?

I steeled myself to speak evenly. “What could it be?”

Joseph pursed his lips as if musing for the first time upon the possibilities. He turned his gaze down the corridor we had traversed. “There must be an entrance to the room beyond that corner. Something in the library.” He pocketed his sheaf of papers. “Something not what it seems.”

He took on a settled air, gazing into the distance. I realized he had entered a private world, peering through a window not of this house but of his own. It was only when I determined to break the silence he suddenly declared: “I shall discover it.”

Here, then, is the disturbing development of the ambulations and their disquieting reflections. My fear is that far from a return to health and work, Joseph is determined to continue his architectural examination of this house and to right some kind of physical wrong. What this mania means for our future, I cannot say.

Your daughter

CHAPTER 4:

The Mysterious Beam

Daughter,

I shall discover it. Therein lies the power of our narrative entire. Uncommon prescience, and toothless to a larger purpose—Did I not indeed perceive in his first days with us your husband's intransigence, his monomania, his quest unceasing, his solitary resolve unsolicitudinous; indeed, did I not perceive his very nature's nut?

Forming anew, or attempting to form anew, from earth a monument—whose but his? *I shall discover it*, he says, and from the past again arrives an old remembrance. Was not his violence to make, his urge to fashion from the earth a dwelling for himself, *sans* interest or respect for those who came before, the very essence of his work in our domain? *I shall discover it.* Not spark of dialogue, not inquiry of acolyte, but the pronouncement from a great Olympic height: Now see his high battalion trample underfoot the horde.

Where have we seen your husband's like? Absent the unrelieved mental investiture, the whirl and grind of the generative machine, where else but the pack, pound, and agglomeration of that god of Zürich, from whose direction the lesser beast creates? Allow me now to trace the profile of that three-headed beast that feeds upon such hubris.

The first head is the battle of meaning and form. The former is to laugh at mysteries, toss genius to the winds, call out the pillars of the field of art. Knowledge, interpretation, understanding, bald statement: these initial tools of meaning's master are embraced, then rejected and replaced with insights nuanced. Not the earthen pillars of proposition, but the airy suggestions of dialogue, a quiet and uncertain peek at the world ineffable—this alone becomes the destination of the inquisitor. Where does this lead save to the moral depths, where any act can be defended, where the creator sits on a throne above the rabble? Was this not the first part of the journey of Porbus?

At last the seed corn is gone, the field is overworked, the intellect that feeds upon itself can only hunger for a deeper nourishment. The public accolades ring hollow. Poised at the edge of the garden, the adventurer turns to eye now not the poisoned apple of the tree of knowledge but the patterns of the ethereal garden, its charmed rows a penetration of the divine into material ideal. In the words of the priest of

Dublin: Not the *colors* of the language but *the poise and balance of the period itself.* Now the artist becomes master of the Eucharist, *transmuting the daily bread of experience into the radiant body of everlasting life.* Now mastery and mystery, not insight and meaning, become the artist's sole desire. Now *in the virgin womb of the imagination the word was made flesh.* To remake the world; to create a value cognitive through the manipulation of language with its intrinsic energies. No longer a conduit of meaning, a means of signification, language becomes a material of construction, an element of composition. What powers he discovers in words; how he wills their principles!

Hence did Porbus become a maker, a controller, an engineer of the natural forces in world as well as canvas. Now only the perfect image—not the outlines of the static investitures but the generation of the inner spirits; not representation but a generative engineering. *Beauty's very essence, form as divine thought,* the creative fire infused into *the medium of some corporeal being.* In this work our sojourner, intoxicated with his power, toils without end.

The mirror becomes the maker; the powers of the maker spin the moral compass; the human riven by the beast becomes the beast itself. No longer the weakness of moral relativism; now the power of moral certainty: In his heart arrives what the son of Goethe identified as *a tendency to equate the world and the human soul, and thus to strengthen the hold of the evil.* Rejected in the past, crimes that serve the master and his talent are granted favor. Did not we see the same with Porbus?

No less will satisfy a heart of artistry that beats beside the throne of God. What is the *science of beauty*, as Plato uses it, the single discipline to which our hero dedicates his mortal hours, but the discovery of the natural laws in the fusion of the ideal into the Earth's material? Where does this discovery lead but to the marshaling of these forces into arrogance and evil?

To this threshold then arrived the figure of your benefactor. Her mission out of nature with her skills, she sought another to perform her work. Even so, her ambition will be thwarted, for despite his power your husband toils in vain. As weak as are his earthen views as tarnished are his forms. How can the hand of earth contest the standard of the sky? *Not good enough!* Never good enough. He sees the truth that *language could but extol, not reproduce, the beauties of the sense.* Once more ring false the public accolades; arises now the monster's second head to feast upon the traveler. Years may pass in the *stern, stark service of form*, but the artist becomes more fastidious. No partial perfection will now do; the artist must bring forth from *the marble mass of language*, the stone, *the godlike work of art*, the living form of the living statue, stalking the corridors of earth, hand in hand with the god of the overdome.

This is impossible: What rises from the canvas is not normal being but monster. So will the very Porbus figure rise from fecund frame and walk the moldy hallways of your home. So will your husband, his pen a sword for the battle of the god, quicken the house you live in; beware the spirits which, released from beam and brick, come howling from their prisons into life and overwhelm their makers with their fury.

Can any artist fail but hear the rumble of these monsters; can any rumble fail but be the herald of his failure? Against the angels of the sky these spirits seem but shadow. What can follow, then, but the third head of the beast: *despair*. The ecstasy of youth is gone; the artist feels no more the *fiery place of fancy which is product of his joy*. No longer does the artist race to the studio, seize oils and brushes with the frenzy of the mad, call upon his frightening powers to compel the hidden sprites to mount their canvas, to dance upon heaven's dome. Ensnarled by the embrace of form, his soul expires; all becomes distasteful.

How can the author and the artist pass by the beast? The monster ties his victim in a knot; neither patient struggle nor rapid stroke will set ambition free. And so again the artist confronts that hesitation which for your husband is the topic paramount. How can the knot be untied? How can the artist exert a patient effort when the will to apply pen to paper is gone? How can he strike to swiftly break the ugly bonds when the sword itself is blunted?

By these means is your husband bound in his own tangle, intoxicated by his very binding, raging at the power of the bind, forgotten by the muses, having no friends save yourself and your assistant, dependent each and all upon what aid I can provide.

Your father

CHAPTER 5:

The Odd Neighbor

Father,

Today, catastrophe. Rachel and I had hoped for the arrival of some peaceful days during which Joseph could rest and heal, despite his preoccupation with his investigations into the structure of the house, his continuing search for his hidden room, his acute nervousness and single-mindedness, the import that your recent letters defined.

Our hopes were shattered in mid-morning.

"Dr Frenhofer!" These words, emanating unexpectedly from the pines, brought Rachel and I running to the deck. We peered into the trees. Who could be shouting for my husband? Who among our neighbors, as alien to our faces as to our cause, would be aware of his presence?

"Dr Frenhofer!" Again came the shout. Against the outline of the scraggling trees, partway up the hilled and wooded path, we perceived the slight figure of a gentleman, advancing toward our house as he supported his unsteady but determined walk with a cane. Time and again the man would make a few halting steps, progressing some part forward in his mission, then pause to stare piercingly toward the cottage. "Are you there?" His hoary head, pinched fast forward with piercing gaze, would return after his ejaculation as suddenly to its natural poise. "Dr Frenhofer!"

Perceiving us the deck, the man strode forward with livelier step. Before long we heard the *scrape, scrape, scrape* of his boots on gravel as the man closed in, wheezing, huffing, eyes agape, nodding to us in a stranger's apologetic deference. As he arrived at our steps he announced his presence with boldness: "Here I am!" Those words, in their attempt to vest upon his form the veneer of anticipated recognition, to our eye determined naught but a cipher.

"Poussin!" He stood bolt upright of a sudden, eyeing Rachel and me with the wide ovals of an owl, returning our gaze with what seemed to be a sharp but scant recognition of rude intrusion. "Nicolas Poussin. At your service!" Having educated us to his formal name, he provided to his signpost a cast of deeper intent, marking off, finger to finger, what appeared to be an array of the most salient of his natural characteristics. "Recorder of the stories of the local scene—" He paused here to point quickly to his forehead, only to return to his digital pantomime. "Of the tales and facts and filled-in fictions of these lands, whose work in the creation of the disparate elements a compendium of certain charms, has not made its way into the world absent a kind of recognition, begrudging, respectful, if less than—to the nature of its intensity—amazed." First to Rachel, then to me, he made a bow neither so slight as to offend with the appearance of the dismissive, nor so deep as to lend to his demeanor the cast of parody.

At last I came to myself. Engaging quickly with his words, their prolix convolution not so uncharacteristic of that scholarly dialogue to which Rachel and I had learned to be less bewildered strangers and more admiring compatriots, I nodded toward the chairs. "You are welcome here, Mr Poussin, if you know my husband."

The old man returned my nod, glancing with nervous eyes at Rachel, then back to me, before accepting my offer and reclining. "Know him." He paused. "By reputation, you see." He sighed and stretched his legs, then stared, as if transfixed, at the towering pines. "Who would have thought? Here! The great Dr Frenhofer." A pause. "Dr Frenhofer." This last was uttered with a sudden return to life, as his figure sat somewhat higher in his chair only to sink back again. "In this land of ours . . . in this town." At this last signification he hesitated, glancing about as if remembering a disturbing fact. It seemed indeed that he had forgotten us, or perhaps simply dismissed our presence, as he spoke his words seemingly to some unknown companion in the neighboring trees. "In this, of all places, this . . . *odd* house." He suddenly sat upright and turned his gaze to various places on the walls of the house, as if he had seen it for the first time.

As Rachel had gone to the kitchen to prepare tea, I sat on the edge of a seat near our visitor. I eyed him closely. "Do you live near here, Mr Poussin?"

He started, my words having disturbed his reverie. "Near here?" His eyes opened in what seemed to be incomprehension. He paused in place as if turning over some paradoxical thought, and then began to chuckle in earnest. One might call his emanation a giggle, his merriment launching on a high note and descending the scale, his body quivering in sympathetic delight. He raised an arm high and arched it skyward, then engaged with a downward arc. "Down the path." He raised the same arm, arching far to the left with such violence as to threaten his bodily projection from the chair. "And to the left, but a few yards."

He came to a heavily breathing rest. He glanced furtively behind us to the kitchen, then leaned forward and fixed his eyes to mine, his posture a conspiratorial invitation. "Do you know the history of this house, Mrs Frenhofer?"

His words, calling forth in my mind the cautions of your letters, chilled me. I could only stare at him dumbly, leaning slightly forward in surprise. He seemed to expect no response, and immediately began to narrate what his investigations had uncovered about our home.

"First made the seat of a mighty creative power, the fame of which traveled well beyond the boundaries of this quiet town, the house seemed to bring to the people a kind of pride. *Porbus*." Here the old man paused and seemed to search his memories for some thread. "I speak his name now and I shrink, as well might any man—Porbus had given to these people a gift of fame, a pride, a belief that one man in a million was capable of capturing with a skyful gesture the Promethean fire. Capturing it, yes—and from its flame conjuring the spirit of life.

"To this phantom of creation, what could his observers bring but a sense of wonder? Their eyes brighter, their walks quicker, their tone when speaking the name of their town to their neighbors of a higher flavor: This was the legacy left our town by the great painter.

"Then the fall. The narrative darkened. The fire of god became the flame of the damned. The very name Porbus became one which one generation could not mention to another. The house was closed, boarded shut, left to rot in the embrace of the surrounding pines, its cursed memories entrapped within each brick and beam.

"So it stayed. Generation after generation . . . before the *walking* began."

The old man leaned closer to me, resting heavily on his cane, peering intently into my eyes. "The *walking*... have you heard of it?"

I confessed that I had not, although his story to this point had only seemed to restate in shortened form the history of the house that your recent letter had already revealed.

He nodded quickly, as if approving of my ignorance. "Some being, some spirit come forth from this old house, creeping from imprisoning boards." The old man paused. Then with a steady, determined action he tapped his cane three times on the floor, chiming forth with linguistic cadence and peering into my eyes: "*Walking* . . . *walking* . . . *walking* . . . at night with a quiet solicitude that would raise the corpses from their earthen tombs. Down the wooded path, along the roads, strolling silently up to the very sills of the windows of the homes, staring with dead eyes into the rooms."

The old man's face darkened as he contemplated. "And other times—" Here the man pursed his lips and gave a slight nod, as if approving the validity but not the nature of the historic facts, and stared with deliberation. "He stood *within* those very rooms. Appearing suddenly, as if distilled from the troubled air, by the beds of the sleeping. A minute in one house; a second in another; in another still only a form of figure fleeting.

And in all of them an appearance that brought forth the cry of the hunted."

The speaker leaned back in his chair, his brow thoughtful, as Rachel arrived with tea. The speech had filled me with confusion and I could only utter a weak, unconvincing protestation: "Mr Poussin!" I turned my glance to Rachel and then to the floor.

Rachel placed the tea set on an adjacent table and poured for us. Some silence followed, during which our visitor breathed heavily and stared at the tea set as our cups were prepared. I had determined that he had reached the end of his tale.

I was about to speak when the old man suddenly broke his silence. "And then what happened?" he asked, assuming the position of his audience. I confess I rattled my tea cup in fright. He opened his eyes wide and answered his own inquiry. "Nothing." He raised his cup, only to pause its elevation as he glanced first at me, then at Rachel. "Nothing." He gave a slight shrug. "The *walking* stopped." He shook his head. "Just like that."

Our speaker again seemed to disappear into himself. He sipped his tea quietly. After exchanging troubled glances with Rachel, and having determined again that our visitor had concluded his tale, I was about to inquire further of his background when he broke his silence: "And then . . . began the *changes*."

The words brought me short. I leaned forward to hear well, for his voice had been tentative. “Changes. . . ?” I asked weakly.

The old man nodded, his eyes gazing vacantly at some apparition unseen. “Dormers. Crests. Cornices. Every element of the construction, shifting, shifting, shifting, as the days passed.” His eyes brimmed with wonder. “A terrace, once affording a view of the moon over the southern pond, suddenly appears on the house’s northern side, its view now a pinefull valley. A mansard roof—the one you see now—” He gestured briefly at the top of the house. “Turns into an ogee. The sloped turret of the tower—becomes a bell.” He shook his head slowly and sipped his tea.

This pause allowed me to intrude. “Mr Poussin, your tale is fabulous . . . I cannot believe that such a thing could happen. How can it be. . . ?”

“How?” The old man glanced up at me. His eyes widened. “By the power of the spirit of Porbus unrestrained.” He looked over at Rachel. “No longer stalking the pine forest at night, but now *captured* somehow.” Here the old man made a quick fist as if he had entrapped the demon. “Captured somehow, infused in form, just as he, in turn, infuses into beam and brick his soul.”

I could see that Rachel was becoming troubled, and determined as I was that the old man’s story was as damaging to our wellbeing as it was fantastic, I stood and glared directly at our visitor. "Mr Poussin, since we came here we have seen no changes whatsoever." I looked at Rachel, but was dismayed to see the troubled brow of a thoughtful person turning over difficult ideas.

The old man placed his tea cup in his saucer and looked up slowly at me, then at Rachel. "Since you have been here?" He turned in his chair, eyeing the near side of the house. His gaze came to rest on the bay window cornered farthest from the seating area, overlooking the garden. "That window?" he asked. "Is it not different from the one in the same position when you arrived?"

In exasperation at our guest and his odd story, but loathe to alienate a neighbor and a possible friend of my husband, I turned to examine the window closely. How could I recall its appearance from a time when my distress for my husband was my predominant concern? And if I could, to what extent could I certify the dependability of my memory? Before these reflections had an opportunity to mature, my thoughts were interrupted by a cry from Rachel. "Mrs Frenhofer!" My interpreter stepped forward toward the bay window, her eyes bulging, her hands in the air. "It was a *round* window!" She glanced again at the window. "It was round, Mrs Frenhofer. And its frame was . . . all different. Brown, indeed, brown . . . not this mossy green."

Our visitor stood. "A round window indeed!" he affirmed. "Just as you remember it! And an alteration in color!" He shoved his tea cup across the table, spoon rattling against saucer. He nodded vigorously and stood, an indwelling energy seeming to rise within him and agitate his features. "Round!" He faced me squarely and shook his finger as if concentrating on a critical point. "*Roouuund*! Do you see, Mrs Frenhofer?" I began to shake my head. The old man stepped away from the table, moving deliberately toward me, his face open with passion. "Mrs Frenhofer, you must *not* stay in this house."

I again shook my head, and tried to make my voice even and firm. "Mr Poussin, really! You will not drive us from this house with your words."

The old man scowled and extended his arm and thrust his index finger at me three times, just as his cane had earlier struck the floor of our portico. "You . . . *must* . . . *leave*!" He opened his mouth to speak again when his words were cut short by a cry and clatter from the hallway that led from the library to our deck. The three of us turned toward the door in alarm as the advancing tread of my husband's boots sounded on the stony floor.

At once appeared the figure of my husband, his form disheveled from investigations architectonic, his coat covered with the friated powder of shattered stone and mortar, his eyes wide, his muscles trembling with the energies of one to whom the gods have entrusted a message of power. He held forth an offering, a placation to fate, a gift to our odd visitor, the gold discovery of a searcher compelled in mission by force of mind. "Look! Look at it! Look and ponder." His eyes darted this way, that way, to me, to our visitor, to Rachel. "It was in the passageway. The passageway that leads to the hidden room. They tried to hide it. A painting. One they tried to destroy. But I found it."

In his hands was a square packet, bound in brown paper, secured firmly by a hand of seeming intent, wound round and round with a heavy twine, so no one would think to break its chainery. And written across the face of this paper, in bright red ink, were these words:

Do Not Open

My husband held his discovery high, turning and exhibiting his trophy to each of us. "See! It is this I foresaw in my mind. It is this for which the hidden chamber was constructed. It was for me to discover its passageway. And in that passageway I found what the house determined I was not to have. *This!* What can now be unveiled. And much more: *the secret to creation*; the key that will unlock *Catherine Lescault*." With these words he lowered his packet to the floor, held its top firmly with his left hand, and with his right began to tear away what surely was meant by its maker to retain upon the forces within an eternal hold.

Our visitor cried out and rushed forward. "Stop! Dr Frenhofer! You must *not* open that package." He was about to reach my husband when he suddenly fell to the floor, his feet having stumbled against his cane. Even this accident failed to stop his appeal, for as he rolled and jerked on the floor he reached out with one arm toward my husband.

The scene I have described happened so quickly, and my husband's intent was so determined, that Rachel and I had no time to intervene. In a flash, my husband had removed the protective shell. Then came his cry of triumph: "There!" His eyes wide in frenzy, he held his prize aloft in his right hand, the image stripped before our gaze. "There he is!" Joy seemed to flood over his face as he pointed at the portrait with his free hand. He slowly uttered the following three words, their resonance as deep and grand as the beats of a funeral drum: "Here . . . is . . . Porbus!"

The three of us stared: Rachel and I frozen in our steps by confusion and incomprehension, the old man, his white hair cascading over his forehead, only partially succeeding in righting himself from his fallen state. All of us peered at the figure glaring down from the painting. Dark, penetrating eyes, a demeanor natural to that of royalty or noble figure, and every line and shade of the man, empowered by the energies of the captured Promethean fire, seeming to overwhelm the scene and the people before him.

There we stood, bound by the spell of history. Only the fall of the titan brought us back to life. Joseph suddenly caught his breath, seemed to stare *sans* comprehension at the sky, then fell to his knees. His grasp on his prize loosened and the picture fell with a sharp report on the stone floor. It was only then that my husband seemed to separate from his mission. His eyes closed; he dropped backward; he fell heavily onto the portico.

As salvation from the gloom came the grace of unconsciousness.

Your daughter

CHAPTER 6:

The Unseen Creature

Daughter,

Of your husband's collapse and its causes, I shall render my opinion—more, if paternal prerogative be granted a measure of boldness, my complete analysis. What less but an embracing human sketch, its lines warmed by the chiaroscuro of human understanding, will to your frightening phantom serve as succor?

How little my previous letter served its purpose. Nothing therein, it would be less than prudent to insist, can for anything but the finer truth be testament. Yet, despite the boldness of my line, the cast of my work was pale. And here is why: My knowledge of those energies, which, invested in your husband, brought him to his current state—those timeless principles which for countless scholars have brought naught but sad impasse—gave to my missive more the fire of anger than the warmth of counsel.

What, to begin my assessment of his state and its instigation, is the nature of his discovery? From out of hiding he has brought his prize: a dead artist, mummified, boxed, now of a sudden rudely unpacked for public display. But why was it carefully wrapped, and wrapped, and wrapped, bound so thoroughly with twine? Why was it hidden in a passageway, a hall itself concealed? These questions seem difficult, but they can be answered if we consider the effect of the work upon your husband's mind, that being so little different from human makers of the past.

Tell me: By the time you receive this letter, has not Joseph invested the subject of the painting with himself? Has not he taken on his brow and eye the figure of the ancient painter? Has not your husband said in his dark night, *Porbus is I?*

And yet is not Porbus *dead,* to recall the words of the lady before her Bronzino? Should not your husband join the dying woman as he gazes into his own mirror? Should not he echo her misery and cry, *I shall never be better than this?* Should not he then abandon to the dead his trivial faming fancies? And if he does, will his wife understand? Or will the passage of years, the fine edge of a course ambitious, cut with its blade her judgment?

Recall from the days of your youth, educated as you were by my skills to a height of sensitivity, a height from which you have since determined to descend, the note of the legislator, that words give us *not truth, but only the semblance of truth*, and the result is *the show of wisdom without the reality?* Must your husband not in this sight in all modesty shade the glare of his labors from the world's view?

Your husband, then, once he sees the dead: Should he not see the image and story of Porbus as a lie? Should he then not gaze upon the oils which render the lie? Should he not poke them in a pocket of mistrust? And should he not see that in their falsehoods the oils do but that which his own words perform?

Shall your husband not see that the frame, for those of us who can see with vision unhampered by idle desire, to the false testimony of the oils give lie? And does its testament, valid, honest, praiseworthy, not match in form the task of the finished book which to story gives lie? Your husband, yet, insists on writing his novel: *why?* Does not your husband recoil from the ledge, cast himself back from the precipice, stop, cry, battle his better self, refuse, in short, to give up his drive? And is all this why, harsh against shell over shell of falsehood so revealed, does your husband say, *Porbus is I?*

Obstinate and furious will Dr Frenhofer make Porbus stride forth from the frame, for art, in its force and beauty, must, as the Master of Rye insists, make work *convulsed with life and brimming with blood.* Then let all hail the horrid assemblage: let life come forth and haunt the living; may Porbus infused in his oils and casting forth full showers of his blood stride forth.

How then shall Porbus stride forth? How can a spirit into matter make a living form? By what means does the bloom shoot forth from the stem? How, to put the matter in terms familiar to the modern day, can metaphor submit nature to fecund transformation? How else save by the shattering of matter by the force of spirit, and by its converse: the strain of matter on the soul?

This process, for your elucidation, I shall describe. Have you forgotten its details, I must ask, from the instructions of your youth? Then listen anew: allow my mind to set my thoughts upon their proper course; be a good student and charge me as the Athenian charged his minions: *Go and attack the argument like a man.*

To look at the painting, consider the house; to consider the house, look to the architect; to look at the architect, who shall instruct us? Who else but the philosopher, for is not the teacher of the king sufficient for his subjects? And the polymath tells us we can look upon a house, as a sensible substance, in three ways. First, the house can be matter, or the pile of bricks and stones from which it is constructed. Such is *potential.* Second, the house can be form—those natural principles or forces comprising the dynamic of covering, protection, shelter: *actuality.* Third, the house can be a composite thing made up of the material and the form: what the common people mean when uttering the word *house.*

Nothing has so far entertained design idiosyncratic. With a view of doing so, and simultaneously relating our analysis to the peculiar interaction of your husband and your current house, allow me to extend the philosopher's thoughts, for extension of thought is the role of the mature mind. Consider, again, the architect. Dissatisfied with the generic concept of *house*, with the dictates of science, with the imprisoning rules of *static form*, the *genius* insists on infusing into the work composite his soul, charging the material on palette with a force specific to individual cognition. The result is *dynamic form*, what you were taught to be the fruit of the individual voice, an example of *fine art*.

To this finished work comes the resident, the viewer, the reader, the co-creator, who from the foundation of our genius builds a *home*. Here live people who shape the world, give to the concept of house the cognitive value of *substantial meaning*.

As the house so the painting, poem, and novel. For the latter, consider the word. Shoved into a formal bottle, language is subjected to the rules of art, its meaning mandated by common usage, a compelled form or actuality. Upon the resulting composite acts the genius, shattering language into dynamic form, metaphoric shapes as unfamiliar as they are inspiring to the reader who, armed thereby with the instrument of the gods, wreaks human will upon the earth with the heavenly hammer of substantial meaning.

Hereby we arrive at our painting. The matter consists of oils on palette, the potential of the work. The form, the actuality, is the vision mandated for impression. Upon the composite works again the mind of the genius, creating a work as idiosyncratic in its appearance as it is attractive to the skilled viewer. And again comes the audience, the viewer, the co-creator, working as does the artist to harmonize a beautiful soul with a beautiful form in a substantial meaning which works on the world.

Here our analysis is at an end. Is it not clear that the writer performs the same task as the architect? And is it not clear that architect, poet, painter, novelist all create life? And that the final work of the co-creator is to bring that life into fruition, in the process subjecting nature to a transmogrification? Is it not clear, finally, that *Porbus shall stride forth from the frame*?

If it is not yet clear, can your father be condemned for charging you with neglect of your childhood studies? If the reasoning here presented does not recall to your mind those happy hours of reflection in the garden of youth, what else can the concerned instructor do to harness the wagon of reason to the master rein of will?

Finally, perhaps, all that can remain is a reminder of the insistence of the universal doctor, that the living human being is composed of soul and body, the composite of which makes *human nature*. Here, then, is the template fantastic, matter and form in their state primeval, from which composite the divine engineering transmogrifies the substantial meaning of the individual idiosyncratic. It is of this template which the earthly creator, in a fit of hubris, does revere, covet, embrace, engineer, and withal so obstinately obey. What emanates from this unwelcome imitation but suffering and failure? None but the foolish fail to pause their brush before the canvas.

Now is it not clear why Porbus must stride forth from the frame? From the task of breathing life into the painted form, Dr Frenhofer shall not shirk. And once Porbus the man walks the Earth, that phantom shall not rest until *Catherine Lescault* follows in the monster's wake, living, breathing, walking, mocking the dead and haunting the living. Who can doubt that Dr Frenhofer will prevail, that these dead creatures shall distill the ideas of their creator into an imitation of life?

By the laws of composition here described, their dynamic ripped from the roiling veneer of earth, shall your days be haunted by the creatures of a fallen world. Beware them rising; beware the rage of the beast when from the painting Porbus ventures forth.

Your father

CHAPTER 7:

The Human God

Father,

At first a shadow in the corner of a wall, revealed to the eye with the flicker of a flame fluttered by a moth; a rush but dimly heard when sudden air embraced the kitchen; a dash between pine and oak and thistle at edge of wood. Preludes all, emissaries sent to quicken our senses to the pitch of awareness, to the advent of the sacrament of the *deus artifex*.

Days passed. If terrible lucidity, casting its harsh shadow on the edges of the real, beckons too eagerly our mind, what can nourish more than the substrate of the sacred rage? Night after night we heard it: *Step. Step. Step.* Marking off the distance in the hall from the corner of the library to the secret room.

At last, in the stillness of a morning's early hours, Rachel arose from her bed. "I hear it," she whispered to me as she moved to the door of our bedroom. I saw her open the door a crack, then stare, her face having ever more the countenance of wonder, into the hall beyond. Her mouth opened to speak, then she halted, and at once she stepped backwards into the room, closing the door behind her. "It is *he*!" She stood with her back to the door and the twisted features of her face, enlivened with the energies of the image observed, was of such a moment that I could no longer remain abed in peace. I rushed to her side and peered into the darkness.

It was then that I first saw the shadow of a man, standing in the dim light at the end of the hallway, beckoning to me with an extended, craggy arm. *Come here*, he seemed to say, though no sound emanated from his moving lips. It was the image of a figure bending forward from the wall, then gesturing with his entire body to a certain place there. *Come here. Look.* All I could see from my distant vantage was a blank space, covered with paintings hung long ago.

The ghostly figure then stepped toward me, eyes widening, mouth opening, lips quivering, as someone passing through the gate of the moon whispering to a vanishing light. I bent forward, squinting to see him clearly. Of a sudden my heart stopped: The man lunged toward me. I screamed and turned back into the room, slamming the door behind me. As the creature threw himself against the door Rachel and I held it fast. I could only think of waking my husband to come to our aid. "Joseph!" I screamed.

At once the pounding stopped. We stood, holding our breaths. We heard more movements on the other side of the door, and then a tapering away. And finally, after what seemed like many long minutes, I heard my husband's voice. "I am here. Open the door."

With cries of relief Rachel and I complied.

"Did you see him?" he asked.

Rachel and I both assented. "Where did he come from?" I asked. "Where did he go?"

"He has gone into town." Joseph stared at me, then at Rachel, his eyes wide and—I was gratified and mortified to see—filled with a certain peace. "Later tonight he will return and go back into the painting. But he has done me a great favor."

"A favor!"

"He has shown me the way. Come."

Joseph pulled at my arm and led us back down the hallway with its painterly portals to that spot where the specter had pointed minutes before. There I saw a painting and its pendant. Joseph reached up and moved one painting slightly on its nail, then reached over and did the same with its mate. The movement of the second painting exposed a small knob, secured so close to the wall that it was scarcely visible.

As Joseph twisted the knob we heard a faint cracking sound. Then, amid a steady creaking, a section of the old wall rolled slowly away. Before us appeared a small room, vacant save for a single piece of furniture: a wooden cabinet standing against the far wall, tall enough to fill the space from floor to the ceiling, its hoary wood painted with fantastic designs in colors faded by time.

The room! At the appearance of this hitherto unknown space I felt a great unease and could not but stare at the lonely item of furniture. "What is in the cabinet?"

Joseph stepped forward and opened the cabinet's door, the iron hinges creaking, the old air from its antique interior pervading the forgotten room. And inside: nothing. "Empty," spoke Joseph. He turned to me, his eyes narrowing. "Save for one thing."

At a gesture from my husband, Rachel and I looked down at the base of the cabinet, where we saw a drawer with a bronze handle in the form of a lion's face. Along the edges of the drawer was an intricate pattern of nails and screws, many bent over, sealing the drawer from access. At a number of spots around the nail heads I could see a series of round impressions sunk into the wood, as if whoever had pounded the hardware into the cabinet had, perhaps from haste, occasionally missed the mark.

"Fastened with nails and screws," said Joseph. "It's as though someone were frantic to keep the drawer from being opened. But why? What can be inside?"

I glanced uneasily at Rachel, then turned to my husband. "Joseph. You won't open it."

Startled, Joseph glanced at me. "Do you not see? Look more closely."

"See what?" Before me was nothing but a drawer's old handle and faded colors.

Rachel, whose eyes were transfixed on the drawer, moved closer to the cabinet, bent down, and then looked up at Joseph and me. "Something is written on it. In faded ink." She peered at what I had thought to be an intricate horizontal design but which I could now perceive as some kind of script.

"What does it say, Rachel?"

She mouthed the words: "*Ille qui vivit intus vivit in aeternum*."

"What does it mean?" I asked.

"He who lives within lives forever."

Joseph nodded slowly, his eyes on the nails and screws. "The secret is in the drawer."

The silence in the room seemed to bear down and oppress our spoken words. I asked: "The secret to what?"

Joseph turned to me, and I could see his eyes were full of energy. "The secret of *Catherine Lescault*." He looked back at the cabinet. "It is that secret for which Porbus has led me here. The painter has become myself; he shall give me what I need and I he."

I frowned, crossing my arms and looking to Rachel. But I found no help there. I was about to speak when I heard a sudden noise, what sounded like a heavy step, from the far end of the hallway by the kitchen. My heart seemed to stop as I appealed to Joseph.

My husband nodded in sympathy. He, too, had heard.

Then Rachel confirmed our hearing: "A step."

Joseph spoke quietly. "It is he." He extended an arm, as if in protection, motioning for Rachel and me to step away from the door, further into the room. My mind was racing with thoughts, a comingling of fear and anticipation and wonder.

I heard a second step, and then a more deliberate pattern. The house was silent save for that mordant pedestrian drumbeat. *Step . . . step . . . step. . . .* Each tread, firm and determined, came ever closer to our little room. As the steps continued, each seemed not only closer but more certain, as if the creature which produced them had convinced himself that his course was predetermined, that what he sought was ever more near. Joseph, keeping his arm extended before us, raised his free hand to his mouth and placed a finger against his lips. "He is almost here."

I fixed my gaze on the open door. Again came a step, then two more. And then a shadow fell across the threshold: It was the arrival of the being, a muffled thunderclap.

He appeared. The thing was not ugly, nor frightening, nor threatening, nor torn with the disease of evil. Upon his visage was the cast of earth, shattered into the inconsequent, laughing at death yet living, withal the base equivalent of the human god, the *alter deus*.

The face of this being was marked by the features from the painting Joseph had discovered and revealed to the world: Here, it seemed certain, Porbus himself stood before us. The apparition opened his mouth as if to speak, but we only heard a long influx of air, as though the creature, arising from long death, were struggling to ingest life. A voice finally issued forth: "Dr Frenhofer. . . ." The beast turned his eyes to my husband and raised a hand as if in remonstrance. My husband kept his arm extended before Rachel and me, and peered intently at the apparition. The beast spoke again: "Dr Frenhofer. . . ." His voice was throttled as gasps of air rushed through his moldery body. "You . . . must . . . open . . . the drawer."

With that the apparition ceased. He continued to sway in the doorway, stepped back, nearly stumbled, and lurched against the far wall. Then there arose a low, ceaseless moaning as the old creature staggered step by step down the hallway, in the direction from whence he came. Joseph whispered, "He is returning to the painting."

There was a final racket in the hallway and the beast's departing words echoed through the halls as the afterthought of a dream: "Dr Frenhofer . . . inside the drawer . . . is . . . everything." This was followed by a low, drawn-out howl that trailed slowly away.

After that, as we heard nothing but silence, we stepped cautiously out of our room and peered through the darkened hallway. At the far end, in the dim light, we could just make out the object of our attention. The painting of Porbus had reclaimed its Lord.

Your daughter

CHAPTER 8:

Echoes from the Crypt

Mary,

"*You must open the drawer.*" So commands our risen creature: See now where your husband's unwise labor has to fortune led, and with it you? This monster—is it helpmate or villain? Shall your husband obey its word? Who can doubt that, mastered by his own mastery, your husband shall to the edge of night give crack? And from the gaping wound what shadow shall emerge? A face of the past returned to haunt the living, a creature partner of the fallen Porbus, an evil blossom with a will to grow, *to push into the light and air and flower there.*

You have seen yourself the walking specter: Proof anew that artists make not life but walking corpses. What good can come from their automata, their engines of springs and wheels self-moving and embraced by rotting flesh, which, as the author of *Leviathan* has written, but mimic those souls by which God made and governs earth? The art of the human maker, faint echo of the creative principle, has to these monsters granted the awkward grace of machination, employing for every heart a spring, for every nerve *ficelle*, for every joint a wheel. All substitutes ungainly, giving to their shells a kind of motion, walking forth upon the land as the Hephaistosian tripods stalked their hill to Heaven, but all such motion giving to authentic life a lie.

Even so, time after time, have not through history humans set upon the world such monstrous things? Is there not a constant fervor for the form organic, a refusal obstinate to recognize the wall that stands so solid between art and life? Each manly maker to his workshop goes, intent with fire and tong to forge anew from earth the shape and form and substance of the wondrous shield, a living work upon which all gaze and wonder. Behold them in their fervor fire a furnace to their task. Behold again their Promethean ambition, see their flames stolen from the skies to create the real, to shape their clay into the figures of the living. Then see what follows: Does not every loving artist become paramour of a machine? Is not each and every one Pygmalion, lips pressed against a workshop stone? What artist has quenched a passion to surpass nature, to make *a second nature out of the material supplied to it by actual nature*? By such ambition through the bedroom of the human maker flows an airy death.

Let your husband beware: all the world was made by God; the human maker seeks in hubris the diary of the Lord, the journal of Heaven. Be his work the extension of inner light, as half the world says, or a child of the artist married to nature, as believes the other half, the human, in fashioning an imitation life from earthen substance, admits the shadow of the soil of the land. That dark insignia shall to every creative soul serve testament condemnatory: Let God's ape breathe soul through stone and with his fiery fume singe the face of the First, then shall a sorry monkey live imprisoned by his hubris until the squeak of the jailor's key and the march to the scaffold.

Remember the words of the dictator, taught you in your youth, forgotten with the passage of years but as true today, as valid tomorrow, as the day they were first uttered. Divine creation makes the fair and perfect world after a pattern unchangeable; human creation makes from an imagined pattern work imperfect.

This difference was well elucidated by the son of our work:

> *You did not work as a human craftsman does, making one thing out of something else as his mind directs. His mind can impose upon its material whatever form it perceives within itself by its inner eye. But how could his mind do this unless it was because you had made it. It imposes this form upon a substance which already exists and already has being, such as clay or stone, wood or gold, or any other material of*

> *this sort. But it was God who made the craftsman's mind, constructive material, and the intelligence by which the craftsman masters his craft.*

None but emptiness is a guarantee of purity: Because God *created* heaven and earth from a nothingness that was without form, and void, only creations of the *first principle* stand in our clear sight absent shade. In contrast, the work of nature and of the artist is but a reflection dim of the lucent source; the wax of the earth is deaf to respond to the rays emanating from the sacred heart. Life becomes an awkward machination for the hand that trembles.

Yet, who really lacks the knowledge of this first mover and the requisite source of the inspired? Is not its universal acknowledgement spring for the universal appeal to the universal form? *There is a god in us, he stirs and we grow warm*, wrote Ovid. Each artist seeks that warmth, cradle as it is to special sight, to broad view of the cosmos, to infusion of idea into substance that for the child of earth becomes the playmate of the soul. For the poet, *there is no invention in him until he has been inspired and is out of his senses, and the mind is no longer in him*.

Ignore these facts as you will; you and your cohort will pay the price. Steal the flame of the divine fire, infuse into word and oil the radiant halo of the universal vibration, and you shall release into evil the soul of your model, torn sharp from without her limbs, so that she turns on her lover and abandons her place on the Earth. Time after time the model is drained of her blood: *You say, even to your friend,* "Behold her whom I love," *and there is an end of love.* Even so, the artist laughs and moves on, even past the boundaries of the understanding, into a dim, formless fog, a chaos of color, a baffle of fantastic lines, half tints, vague shadows. And so on and on until art falls from its easel, rattles to the floor, and a ghost rises from the ruins. Now it is revealed that the clear reality previously rendered was a fable, was for art its story, was but a cover over the truth that lay hidden beneath. The curtains of the past fell away and before the eye lay the very spirit of the living line, *the very form of the living girl.*

Hence the passion of the artist and hence the rage of Porbus. He who destroyed his life must find a restoration, must free his soul from the remains of his deed, must still the energies that stab the quiet slumber of the dead. This alone becomes the goal of Porbus: Restore the girl to life, pull from the hidden chamber the soul of his model, the spirit of the young girl now locked in her pictured prison. To pull it from its chamber, to set it on its feet, to let her walk the earth anew; even to love with a human love, that love lost when a human first put paint to canvas. But at what cost to the young lady: What kind of life can she have, pulled from her casket and set upon an alien soil?

Such a question shall never be asked by Porbus. Blinded by his panic, pondering but his image, assuaging but his guilt, paying his price whatever the cost to humans live and dead, even to subject his client anew to the artist's taunt. All of these count for nothing. For so many years has the house of Porbus been baffled, his vision powerless. Now a glimmer of light shines through the old and gloomy halls. The beast rages.

For now to the domicile of the damned arrives your husband, blinded by the light of genius. Porbus, he believes, possesses the secret to life, the key to the lock of intention baffled, the spark to infuse the flame divine—possesses, in brief, the form requisite to his subject: the *womanly ideal* which when embraced by the author's mind will for model be magnificent. Far from this salvation lies the path of the walking dead. Just as God spoke the world into being, giving form to every creature with the divine Word, so shall the intelligible word of Frenhofer give birth to the fecund monster desired by Porbus.

Then see his weedy garden rise from over a moldering crypt and see his flower glow with tarnished color. The garlands of these mocking petals, the words of *Catherine Lescault*, shall harness the raging forces left by the crime of Porbus, embrace in a vicious grasp the spirit of Frenhofer, and channel all—spirit, passion, condemnation each and every one—into embrace grotesque, reshaping nature, enlivening the dead and mocking the living. Gillette shall live; Porbus shall sleep; Frenhofer shall die.

Your father

CHAPTER 9:

The Hidden Diary

Father,

So much has happened since my last letter, and since my receipt of your response, premonitory in its demeanor, chastising in its form, hopeless in its implications, withal filling me with that old familiar filial fear, that I seem to have entered what I can but deem a new world.

Joseph has had a fantastic dream. Or rather, it may be more to the point to write that he seems to have experienced a physical vision of another world, as strange in its details as my own. How are we to understand it? Rachel, to whom Joseph has confided the details, has rendered them in a document which I enclose with this letter and which I can only hope you can interpret.

As for the events which led to Joseph's dream, it will, I am sure, come as no surprise to you that my husband had, for the opening of the locked drawer of his cabinet, quickly fallen into a state of obsession.

Indeed, he began to devote what seemed like every waking hour to manipulation of the securing hardware which, interlocked as it was with intricate patterns, concealed from our reasoning every alternative corridor of passage. Our concerned neighbor, who had failed in convincing Joseph to retain the protective cover of the old portrait, renewed his prohibitory cautions as the general counsel of what he described as a disturbed, frightened, one might almost say angry town, attempting on their behalf to convince Joseph to abandon his new effort. Our entreaties failed. Joseph puzzled for hours at his charge, manipulating the screws and nails and chains first one way then another, applying to their baffling matrix the sundry commands of tools retrieved from a rusty box discovered in the house's basement. All such efforts brought to my husband's visage the darkened furrow of the martyr, the anxious reddening of the hero who shall for the love of the final effort sacrifice life and happiness.

Who will fail to understand that my own emotions, bewildered by events rapidly growing beyond the borders of reason, followed my husband's in a growing sense of unease and panic? It was only the passage of a few days, during which Joseph pursued his private interest to the neglect of his health, to the abandonment of his wife and friend, that kept me from a desperate tack: I determined to contact the woman who had given us our promised entry into salvation, that woman whose history you had provided me months before. Her knowledge and insight must be brought to bear on the will of my husband with an earnestness equivalent to Joseph's but with a result more positive to our wellbeing.

And so, against what I would take to be your will, I forced myself to call the woman, to appeal to her larger wisdom, her background, her knowledge of history, even her sense of moral rightness. Time after time I approached the device, and each time I stepped away, fearful not only of the response of our benefactor but of your own. Even so, another turn to the face of Joseph, twisted as it was with the furrows of the soul abandoned, brought me at last to a retreat from prudence.

I placed the call. How could I know that the woman herself was endangered to a degree greater than that of ourselves? For the person who answered my call was a helpmate for the spirit at the edge of life, a translator between the lands of the sun and the moon.

So, then, to my entreaty, passed on to my intended listener by means of a morbid translation, did I receive only the following response in the voice of her nurse: "Mrs Porbus says, 'Do not open the drawer.'" What could such a statement, bald on its surface and chilling in its implication, have upon me but a further sinking into a kind of despair? To this directive I responded in growing fear, asking the nurse if the words of the dying woman were as certain as that, and could there be some mistake, given the fragile nature of her patient, and, finally, could I speak with my benefactor directly? The nurse demurred, and who could blame her? Her dying charge was weak, perhaps pain-filled, passing in and out of consciousness.

It was only by an unforgivable personal entreaty, by an insistence that my matter was one of life and death, that the nurse relented. Bless her, she placed the receiver close to the dying woman and bid her speak. And then I heard the words, their meaning distinct, rising as they did from the roiling froth and fever of a fallen form, through the guttural hiss, the rasp, of human flesh struggling against the grip of death. The five words so spoken—sounding in their soft and hesitant manner like hammer blows—have since that day been imprinted on my mind: "Do . . . not . . . open . . . the . . . drawer." Those are the words I heard, as I say, distinctly, their disjointed presentation to my ear sounding as the cry of the condemned before the fall of the axe. When I opened my mouth to answer my benefactor, nothing came forth. Even then, in the back room I could hear the continuing wheeze and gasp of Joseph as he hacked away at his fatal lock, as he cursed one and all—even Rachel—and bid everyone to leave him in peace.

An amalgam, a cascade of contradictory thoughts baffled my consciousness. What could I do with Joseph now? Then, again, the voice of the nurse came from the phone: "Mrs Frenhofer, I am sorry." I returned to the present matter, asking the nurse forgiveness for my intrusion. At the other end of the line was a pause. "Mrs Porbus has died."

Then too let angry angels render forth. At that very moment, from the house's back room, came a cry of triumph from my husband. "It is done! The drawer! I am victorious! The drawer is open!"

Rachel and I hurried to the room. Joseph had collapsed backward onto the floor, the force requisite to the final retrieval of his object having forced him off his knees. In his hands was the object of his desire: the wooden drawer, a few inches deep, not as wide as a placemat, trimmed with carvings of beast and man and stars and flora, all protected with what looked like a thin wooden cover.

We removed at once to the library. Joseph walked quickly to his desk, turned on his lamp, and set his prize below the light. "Now we shall see, finally, what is *true*," he stated, glancing sharply at Rachel, at me, and finally again at his prize. He began to pull gingerly at the contraption's cover, attempting to slide the wooden lid through the retaining grooves. While it seemed that the passage of years had worked its will on cementing the cover, making its removal difficult, with a final effort Joseph pulled it free.

The three of us leaned forward in a hush, peering down into the wooden drawer.

Inside was a book. Its cover seemed to my eye a kind of dark leather, and upon the artifact and the surrounding vacancy the years had deposited a thin layer of grey dust. Beyond this–there was nothing.

We stood speechless, gazing at what evidently no living person had seen since the book's owner had condemned it to a living death. Joseph nodded slowly, as much to himself perhaps as to us. His voice broke the silence, his tone a suggestion of ideas distant and hidden: "Now we shall see." He nodded to himself. "Now we shall see."

Then Joseph, gently and hesitantly, fearful by all evidence of damaging the ancient material, began to lift the book's cover. We three peered intently at the page that was gradually revealed–a page of writing, only faintly observable, produced in what seemed to be an elegant and crafted female cursive.

Were the fragile lines even readable? Joseph shook his head in some impatience, sat down and peered closely at the writing. Retrieving a glass from his desk, he brightened his desk lamp and adjusted its angle so that the rays of light cast revealing shadows across the ridges of script. He narrowed his eyes, drew still closer to the page, and then spoke in an even voice: "Rachel. Take a pad and pencil, please. I shall dictate." As Rachel did his bidding, he lifted the book and turned it one way and another, seeking the most revealing angle.

As Joseph eyed the text closely, his hands began to shake with what I took to be not only nervous exhaustion, but the struggle to restrain the force of a fervent desire's discovering energies in acknowledgement of a fragile material that seemed ready to crumble at one unconsidered move. And finally, after yet one more piercing pause, Joseph recited these four lines:

"I am a bronze maiden, but I lie upon the tomb of Midas.

For as long as water flows and great trees thrive,

I, abiding here at this much-lamented tomb,

Shall announce to passers-by that Midas is buried here."

The recitation hung heavy in the air. Joseph glanced up at Rachel, then back down at the page. He frowned and furrowed his brow, angled the book, and peered anew at what he had read. That stanza of poetry, arresting in images, suggestive in implications, seemed to be all the author had entered on the book's opening page.

The silence was broken by Joseph's voice: "What say you, Rachel? Interpret for my wife."

Rachel nodded, then spoke these words: "An audience is presented with the voice of the daughter of a king, her form transmuted by royal decree into a statue of bronze, such material in those times the strongest available, to guard her father's tomb. Resting on a protective platform above her charge, the woman recites a poem of love."

Joseph nodded slowly and glanced at me. Then Rachel continued: "The daughter's words have been dictated by the king's scribe in a productive form: They can be recited in any order and retain their effective meaning while engineering the surrounding natural forces. By this precaution, taken at the order of the king, the young woman can continue to recite her work through the centuries without fear of the text losing its transformative power. As the girl recites the lines first in one order, then another, then another, the variation renders to the passage's constructive material a transmogrification. The otherwise impotent significations of words and phrases are woven by this process into a canvas supportive of the woman's resonant meaning: a combination of the timeless greatness of her father and the production of a set of principles, or natural forces, engineered by the very recitation to protect her father's tomb from intrusion."

Joseph nodded. "That will do." He turned back to the text, nodding quickly at the page. "Now, who is this daughter of a king?" He squinted again. "Look closer still. One can see a signature below the four lines." He bid me help tilt his lamp to a slightly different angle. "Look," he continued. "Under the first line of the young lady's poem: Something has been scratched away, and then what was removed has been written over. What was put here originally?" He peered closer and then motioned with irritation that we bring him the lamp. He nodded, squinted, tilted the page to the side, all of which was evidently meant to manipulate the light so that the slightly elevated ridges of writing would be cast into high relief.

"I see some letters . . . a 'G' certainly here . . . but is this an 'I' or an 'e' . . .?" Joseph continued his examination, then of a sudden became animated. He started in his seat, and held the page closer to the lamp—so close I feared the heat would damage the paper. Finally he shouted in triumph: "Gillette! The woman's name was Gillette!"

Rachel interpreted again, in thoughtful tones: "The name of Gillette was eradicated. This young woman—or someone who came after her—did not want her name known. She was to be perceived by the world only in her bronze form." She paused. "This book was not to be read—not, even, to exist."

Joseph glanced at Rachel, then pulled his book close in a protective manner, looking at us as if we were thieves. "This book is a diary," he said. "It is the diary of the paramour of Porbus." He pursed his lips and looked directly at me. "Did Porbus not turn his paramour into a form immortal?"

I knew such form, such bulwark, was for my husband the goal paramount, and this book, he was convinced, would be his guide. Joseph's eyes began to fill with that roiling revel of monomania I had come to dread. "This diary contains what Porbus wanted *me* to have." His eyes widened as he again stared at us as if we were threatening to steal his prized discovery. "It contains everything. Its author scratched it out, and over the stricken words wrote still others—there was so much to say." He smiled broadly, his eyes filled with a wild enthusiasm that made me shudder. He let the cover of the book fall shut. "Porbus wanted me to open the drawer of the cabinet and. . . decipher . . . this . . . diary." In conjunction with the final enunciations he tapped the cover of the diary with his forefinger three times. Then, suddenly, his countenance became one of sobriety as he sat up stiffly in his chair, adjusting his glasses with an efficient gesture. He turned his attention to the book, at once becoming the scholar. "Porbus is assisting me in my work. In return I shall redeem him in his." He stared at the book, his words seeming to address a being far away. "As Gillette, so *Catherine Lescault*."

Thus began Joseph's many days of labor in his library, as, with the assistance of Rachel, he attempted to interpret the knowledge Gillette had entered into her secret diary. His first day of work revealed two primary challenges which were to bedevil him over the coming weeks. "It is all written in some kind of code," he announced. "Numbers. Names. Little teasing phrases. . . ."

And more: Joseph discovered that the entire volume was a palimpsest. He sought an interpretation from Rachel: "It appears as though some writing was erased, or scratched out, or something was applied to it to eradicate it, and then another layer of writing was entered over the old." He had established on his desk a microscope, abandoned years ago atop of one of the library's moldering bookcases, with which he could examine with finer eye the faint text.

"But why was the original story defaced so?" he asked Rachel.

Why the codes? I wondered to myself. Why was she attempting to conceal her thoughts? Indeed, what did the existence of the diary mean? That Gillette was paramour of Porbus we all know—you know, you have said so. That she died at the will of Porbus, the townspeople know—we know. But what did Gillette know of the death of the subject? By what force did she know, and why did she record what she knew? Was she compelled by loneliness? Or by a desire to redeem herself, even to come back to life? To tell her story, perhaps, to those coming after her?

Such questions, I wondered: Were they acknowledged in Joseph's mind? They must have been, at least implicitly, as he pursued his solitary goal: to extract from the record of Gillette what he considered her innate forces, the first principles of her nature, the amalgamation of which, so he believed, by injection into the nascent form of *Catherine Lescault*, would achieve a living transmogrification, the creation of life itself.

To this task Joseph devoted all of his waking hours, laboring at his desk long into the night, neglecting his sleep, eating only what I set before him, responding curtly when addressed, living, in brief, the life of a scholar set upon a duty frenzied in its energy and unreasoning in its devotion. And these labors, for the most part, involved attempting to decode the diary with the help of related arcane texts. Time and again he would turn over in his mind the diary's riddling passages, demanding Rachel assist him in retrieving from the library shelves one old dusty volume or another, the writings in which were to aid him, so he believed, in his interpretation of a text that seemed to mock the limits of human reasoning.

Is it any wonder that the pursuit of this effort, ambitious beyond reason and impossible in its nature, would in time condemn its generator to a kind of insanity? And thus it was to be for Joseph: one night he cried out at his desk, raging, screaming of his task: "It is impossible!" I ran to the library to see Joseph standing at the desk, his eyes wide open, his face red, his fists raised to heaven. Rachel rushed into the room and attempted to calm him. He shoved her aside, then moved a few steps toward me. I reached out to him, but too late: He issued one more cry of frustration and fell to the floor.

It was there, then, that he had his dream, the details of which I cannot but believe are themselves beyond interpretation. The next day, when he awoke, and we brought him to a condition of peace with coffee and sustenance, he narrated his dream to Rachel, who, at my wish, has recorded it in a document which you will find enclosed herewith.

Your daughter

CHAPTER 10:
The Fantastic Dream

As dictated by Dr Frenhofer to Rachel

Exhausted by my labors, the cursed diary having baffled my cognition with such codes, metaphors, indeterminate referents, as make in their collective the driving gear of the linguistic mechanism supreme, and irritating as all of this machination be to mind and soul, I finally fell to the floor beside my desk. My mind whirling, my eyes wide open but seeing little more than cloud and color, my thoughts turned to a fury and futility. And then there came a stranger. *Has here arrived, at last*, I thought. *The distinguished one?*

Not darkness, but light, it seemed, was the intention of my visitor. As I lay on the floor, my mind unable to motivate my arms and legs, I saw a corner of the library bookcase open, its motion as gradual as the rise of the moon. And then I saw, through a cave-like darkness, a room beyond, from which, to my amazed eye, came floating through the air three ladies, each with a hand on her companion's shoulder, viewing me with compassion, as they floated to where I lay. "Arise, Dr Frenhofer," spoke one woman who, I imagined, devoted her spirit to the grace of favor. "Arise from your place of death and view the land beyond."

The three ladies lifted me from the floor and floated with me, Daedalus-like, back through the portal into a cave of glove-like darkness. Stare as I might into my new environs I could discern nothing but a light, a flame, shimmering at some distance. My companions set me on the ground and before I could question their efforts, they flew away, one turning and addressing me with these words: "Dr Frenhofer, walk to the light." As I righted myself and stood trembling in the darkness and tried to accustom my sight to what lay ahead, I heard the great bookcase roll shut behind me.

My eyes gradually becoming accustomed to the darkness, I began to discern the outlines of some familiar forms. My library bookcases, still angry in their fullness, stood watch, it seemed, in the night, breathing with a vigor I had not in the first world noticed. There, my desk, covered in a dust of greater thickness than I had left it, my microscope still in its old position, my papers scattered in their places awaiting my perusal. But where was the diary? Had it disappeared? My attention was diverted from its discovery by a vision of myself, my body, lying supine on the floor, skeletal, motionless, seemingly absent cognitive soul. Surrounding this phantom scene was the slow ticking of a grandfather clock—the presence of which in my days of labor I did not recall.

I was startled by a voice from one of my three saviors. "Dr Frenhofer!" she again called out. "Move toward the light." Peering into the distance, I saw that what had seemed like a flame was in reality a lighthouse which was emanating a beam, short and hardly visible, round and round in rotation. I moved toward it, unsteady, lifting my legs as deliberately as a laborer hauls up his cement bags for practical tasks, my own mission equally practical and productive, I hoped.

Approaching the lighthouse after what seemed like hours of walking but which could have been only a matter of a few minutes, and turning for the means of such measure to the old clock—which had in the interim disappeared—I found myself at the edge of the room. To my surprise, the lighthouse extended further to the horizon, and, still more surprising, I encountered a young woman painting at an easel. Delighted to meet another human being living, or at least, in this murky environment, operating, I requested some information. Who was she and where was I?

"I am the painter who hesitates," the woman told me. She turned her eyes to me, then back again to her work. "I paint that distant lighthouse that has brought you to my side. And yet, what keeps me from its truthful representation? As I have said so many times to so many people, at the critical moment my hand trembles, the brush falters. Where to begin? Where to make the first mark? There is the gulf between the mind's image and the mark of the work."

These words were familiar to me. "Are you then the friend of Mrs Ramsay, Lily Briscoe, born, it seems, to contemplate for all the ages that moment's flight between picture and canvas?"

The woman nodded. "I am she. Behold here my life, both failure and triumph: Forever I pause before my canvas and yet my trial lives forever. At the end of the day, I have my vision; a new day dawns and the vision is gone and I pause anew. And then I begin again."

At these words I nearly shouted with excitement, for here was the germ, the living portal to my work. "It is you who inspired me," I told her. "Like you, I have studied for years the hesitation. And yet I pause still. What is its nature? What is the gear and turn of the machine that, for 'the still space that lies about the heart,' operates such relentless machination?"

The painter smiled at me and nodded into the distance. "Go to the gallery ahead. There you will see three paintings, each of which has a lesson. Ask the guide for help."

Much as I longed to remain with this living human, and little as I could discern, favorable or otherwise, in the forward room of inky darkness, I could not but obey the woman's will, promise as it did of a discovery essential to my life and work. I bid a goodbye to the painter, who returned at once to her never-ending labor.

And so I passed into the second room. Still more books, dusty and forlorn in their isolation, lined the walls. I resisted the urge to embrace them, to pull them to my heart and read them in a quiet corner. The words of the painter stiffened me to a moral pitch, and as I stepped forward into the interior, as my vision adjusted to the oppressive absence of light, I came upon another surprise: an old man, deep in thought, sitting at a desk.

Supposing this man to be the guide promised by the woman, I called out to him: "You have been promised me by the artist. Are you a dead soul or a living man? You can see I am lost in these strange rooms."

The man looked up from his desk without alarm, as if he had expected me, or perhaps it was only that he had grown accustomed to many such as I disturbing his thoughts. He eyed me with neither rancor nor study. "I live in your heart," he said. "Your determinate laws, the principles infused in your materials, your skills of dialogue, have from my heart been energized and from my mind been passed down through the centuries, and will be passed again to generations yet unborn."

I looked closer at the old man who, if his words were to be believed, was the founder. "Are you, then, the legislator? By what right have I to address you as I do, face to face? And you must surely have an answer for me, if I may be so bold as to ask a question: What is the place? Why am I here?"

The old man nodded affirmation, sighed, and closed his book, the name of which I discerned as the final testament of Pythagoras. He stood and took my arm in a loving manner, leading me toward a wall upon which was mounted a painting of a bird. "You have been brought to these rooms because you are compelled by fear, despite the support of a young woman who, bending as she does to the will of the Three Graces, and, if truth be told, encouraged by that trio sent to her by the patron of artists and writers, bid me leave the beloved confines of my infinite contemplation, break off the complexities of my inner dialogue, and come to you, knowledgeable as I am in this lonely place, and guide you safely through the three levels of creation. What I wonder is this: Why do you fear when the lady protects you?"

While the question, apparently to him, was clear and unmistakable, for me it added mystery to mystery. "What lady protects me? And why is all of this being done with me? What work can I do to repay the interest shown in me by those who are superior?"

Rather than answer my questions, my guide bid me gaze at the painting of the bird. "Consider this painting of a mockingbird." My guide paused and glanced at me with what I imagined was a smile.

"You are so concerned with meaning. Then, here is what the painting means: The first level of making is a representation of what has been observed but not seen, an echo, a structure of falsehoods thrust upon the world, accepted by the unwary seduced by the pleasant attractions of the unexamined. Look closely in the darkness. Look near the picture. See a man of stolid appearance? Speak with him."

Indeed, as my eyes continued to adjust to the darkness, I suddenly made out the figure of a man, apparently so lost in thought that he did not acknowledge our presence. Inspired by the will of my companion, I approached the stranger in a bold way that I would never have done before. "Sir, pardon me for disturbing you, but do tell me who you are, for this man who accompanies me is the region's guide and asked me to speak with you."

The man looked up from his musings. "So commands your guide many. He brings his charges here to plague me. And why should he not? He uses words in strange ways; abuses them, I should say, in strange ways. What do his words mean, I ask you? Are they simple and concrete? No. They are general, they are vague, they are meant to mislead, and they do so, I must admit, with a grace that testifies to his generous, truthful, and misleading—I dare say, evil—mission."

I felt a tremor as I heard these words. I turned to my guide in fear, expecting him to strike out at the man who had so forcefully committed the legislator to folly. To my surprise, my guide maintained his grace. "You hear how he speaks?" the old man posed. "So he has spoken since his days on Earth."

The stranger continued. "Under the guise of discussion he commits humanity to the worst absurdities. Under the mask of dialogue he promotes disputes. Alien to him and his cohorts are the specifications of clear, distinct, simple ideas, in words that are precise and well understood. In their stead he creates in his followers, from the promotion of general terms, and the confusion of a rainbow of differing names, a condition of perplexity which his school thereby employs to generate life."

The man's words, of a sudden, struck as a familiar mark in a scholar's notebook. "Are you, stranger, the sage of Puritan sympathies, that companion of the Earl of Shaftesbury, that man whose work on toleration in civil government, on human understanding has through the ages provided a solid foundation for the palace of reason? Or are you an imposter?"

The man looked darkly at me. "I am he. Many hear, but how many listen? Spare me your condemnation, your defense of this old man and his Peripatetic tot. They have wasted my youth; they shall not destroy my age." The man turned away from us and began to gaze anew at the painting of the bird. Perplexed, I turned as well back to my own target of observation, surprised to find him secure in the embrace of equanimity.

My guide, nodding in a universal gesture of secret understanding, secured me by my arm and led me from the scene. "Do you see how the man gazes at the mockingbird, thinking it a peacock? So proceed his followers through the ages, making as they do works of good intent, keeping their misapplied faith in the power of what is perceived most readily to their eye and mind, rendering the surface of reality by the materials of rude prose, works that entertain but do not enlighten."

A dark furrow appeared on the brow of my companion. "This kind of writing is like painting. The creations of the painter have the attitude of life, and yet if you ask them a question they preserve a solemn silence. And the same may be said of speeches."

My companion fell into silence, and, seeing I was about to speak, pulled me again by the arm toward another doorway. As we passed into a third room I saw on the wall another painting, this one of an owl. Pacing back and forth before the picture was a shrouded gentleman accompanied by six others of sundry ages.

The legislator nodded in the direction of the strangers, and brought me to them. "You who pace here so deliberately," he said. "Tell us what you see in the painting over your head."

At once the stranger paused his group and peered at us. "You know as well as I, old man. Why have you come before me yet again? Have you a new recruit?" Not pausing for a response, the stranger looked directly at me. "Before you, over our heads, is the symbol of the work that itself with symbol attempts to work the nature of the real into a formula. There can be no result in that desperate trial but a false wisdom, a hopeless set of wrong notes."

I addressed the stranger with some boldness, for his visage seemed as eager to teach as I was to learn. "What is this work of which you speak? And you and your companions, why do you walk here in this gloom?"

The man addressed my questions in turn. "Allegories. Machines driven not by the spontaneity of the living spirit but by the machinations of cobbled gears and pulleys, vain, misconceived symbolic art made only for the demonstration of some moral truth. Hence, you see that owl always before me—an ironic symbol of the art I hate. Beware the bird wise only in his feather: Start not from a concept and from that base foundation create for yourself an image."

As these words seemed so familiar to me, I sought in my memories the seeds of their wise branching. And it came to me, as the man was about to speak again: "Can it be you, the poet and the playwright of Sicily who brought your native land such renown, whose father ventured forth with the founder of your land to form an Italy of unification, and the author whose works so illuminate the margin between reality and appearance?"

The man nodded. "I am he, here with my six companions. We are dedicated to remain the interpreters of this painting, for all of the living who follow us we tell the truth of what is hidden behind the image."

"Now I understand you and your position," I answered. "And I can guess the work you champion, for you have told the world in another time."

The man raised one hand as his companions resumed their pacing. "Seek in the image—which must remain alive and free throughout—a meaning to give it value." I began to speak, but the man suddenly looked disturbed and turned to join his charges. "Now leave me, and allow your guide to take you to the adjoining room where the philosophical work rules as valid dictator. For I have my work to do: I must tend to these my companions, always chasing me, always compelling me, to make them live, *to live, to live.*"

My guide pulled me away from this impatient man toward yet another portal. "You see, Dr Frenhofer, again it is the different face of the same coin: the treachery of the printed word which gives not truth, but the semblance of truth, and to its users lends a torn cloak, the show of wisdom without the reality. For words have this contradictory nature: They can be used to discuss philosophy, but they cannot be used to state philosophy itself."

These words were familiar to me—but was this not a strange thing, to hear them from their creator, and in these rooms to meet the authors of ages past, addressing me in the present? By no means could I explain this, for that it was but a dream was to my consciousness neither valid explanation nor moment's contemplation. Such is the nature of the world of sleep.

As my mind whirled with the strangeness of this environment, my guide led me into the third room with this remark: "Now you will meet someone of a much different nature." And so we came upon a large man busy writing at a huge desk. Behind him was a cabinet, upon which boiled a mighty pot; the aroma of coffee permeated the darkness. On the wall over the man's desk hung a painting of a jackal. My guide turned to me: "Here is the great man of genius to whom you owe much."

Intrigued by this introduction, I peered intently at the stranger. Who was this man and why would I owe him anything? I was about to speak when he suddenly stood at his desk and stared down at us from his immense height, as a god might peer at humanity from the top of Olympus.

"*Genius*! Did you say *genius*?" Despite the interlocution, he seemed to be addressing neither of us.

He stood at his desk staring into the darkness, then pointed at his forehead. "The intellectual paradigm." He tapped his head several times. "I possess the intellectual maternal power of life." He raised his forefinger high to make his key point: "*And I shall wield it.* Genius informs material. Word, oil, drapery, armor. *Inspiration*"—here he pointed again at his forehead—"is the opportunity that genius may seize. It is the *frenzy* that leads to intellectual procreation.

"Absent genius," continued the speaker, "the artist fails. One can copy a model and the work is done." Here he stared straight at me. "But to impart a soul to it, to represent a man or woman, to create a type, is to snatch fire from heaven like Prometheus."

My guide nodded quickly at me, as if to encourage me to step forth with a question, now that the great man had acknowledged my presence. I asked: "Is genius, then, enough? Is that what I must bring to my work?" For it was clear that the need for quickness got the better of my judgment.

The man shook his great head slowly. "Genius is not enough. The exhilaration of conception must marry the travail of execution. *Constant labor!* Untiring, unremitting! It is the law of art and life. And the hand must be disciplined, ready, and obedient. The sculptor must know how to hold the chisel."

The great man paused, looked at me askance, or so it seemed, and became thoughtful. "Combine these tools of the intellectual titan and your work will possess *brio*, a splendor which every eye can see, even the eyes of the ignorant. Those with *brio* enter our hearts spontaneously through our eyes' double gateway and make their own place there. We are enchanted to receive them so, without effort—it is not art's highest achievement that they have revealed to us, it is art's sweet pleasure. For the laborer with faith in art there comes an indefinable quality, a mysterious element—a chaos of color, half tints, vague shadows, a dim, formless fog. These works do not instantly command attention but demand from even the most expert critic a certain effort of concentrated attention and close study, if they are to be fully grasped."

My guide stepped forward. "You have spoken well." He nodded toward me. "My acolyte has a woman who protects him. What say you?"

The writer seemed to deflate. He sat again at his desk. "A woman's caresses make the muse languid, and melt the fierce, the brutal resolution of the worker." He raised his hand and waved it at us in a dismissive gesture, then returned to his work.

My companion and guide interpreted this interlude for me as we moved to yet another room. "Now you have seen the result of a clear view of writing, for the maker becomes a maker of value, creating life, infused into works which can only be understood by readers equally as dedicated, as skilled, and in their cooperative work make power. All of this comes to be through the work of the dialectician, by the help of science."

My thoughts returned to the painting, which the great writer had not mentioned. "The jackal!" I blurted out. "Why a jackal? And why did the writer not mention it?" My companion turned to me and held up the instructive and moderating hand of the legislator. "He knows but will not speak; you must find the answer yourself. Now look, see the young lady whose entreaties have brought me to your side."

He gestured to the room ahead of us, and there I saw the image of a young girl, floating before me and gesturing for me to advance. *She!* I recognized her at once: Here was the one with the secrets requisite to my creation. Here was my chance to speak with her, to discover her knowledge. I struggled to move my heavy legs toward her, for it seemed to me she was the most valuable of everything I had seen in the dark caverns. Yet the more I fought, the greater the effort not only to move ahead but to remain standing.

The girl floated in my direction, eventually appearing directly before me, staring into my eyes. She opened her mouth and paused, then seemed to fight the bonds of her own flesh. With what seemed like a considerable effort she mouthed the following plea in a deliberate cadence: "Return me to life."

What was the meaning of those words? What was the meaning of the young lady herself? In despair

I felt myself sinking, and I could only think of the silent body, the bulk of myself, that I had left behind on the library floor and to which it seemed I was now returning. As I fought against my demise, against my falling, the Three Graces flew to me and lifted me skyward, then flew down with me into what seemed to be a deep pit, down and down and down and down, and laid me on a cold floor.

"Look up!" one of the Graces bid me. When I did so, I saw Gillette far above me, pointing with one hand to an elevated blue dome. Then with horror I observed the girl turn gradually from her natural color to a shade of bronze, then her body transform into what appeared to be the metal's very substance. She became cloaked with what appeared to be some kind of robe. Her form froze. She spoke no more.

Something of value had been gained and lost. I tried with all of my might to call out to Gillette. I opened my mouth wide to shout for aid, but could emit no sound. It was then that I found myself shaking my head and clearing my eyes that had filled with tears in the sudden bright light. My vision sharpened. Before me appeared the figures of my wife and her assistant, the latter to whom I have dictated my dream.

PART 2:

Science

CHAPTER 11:

Morning Song

No more than a quarter of an hour had passed since the rise of the sun over the rooftops of the town when there also arose in sympathy with the dawn, over waters shedding their fog shirt, a lyric. This verse came in the form of a gentleman's falsetto voice, and so pleasing it was—and so near at hand—that a woman, throwing open the shutters of her loft to get a look at the singer, was delighted to see the voice emanating from a young man reclining in thought upon a stone wall.

Discovering that he had become the object of attention by an attractive lady, the gentleman began to sing the following lyrics, accompanying his words with the strumming of his guitar:

"I'm bound to my sweetheart in Heaven above,
In Heaven above,
In Heaven above.
I'm bound to my sweetheart in Heaven above.
May mercy be cast on me now.

No penny, no token, no dollar for all,
No dollar for all,
No dollar for all.
What care I for pennies or purses at all
When my darling is pretty and kind?"

In response to this serenade, the woman narrowed her eyes and addressed the gentleman in a tone of suspicion. "Do you stir and grow warm, Nicolas? Or have you come this morning to mock me again?"

The gentleman did not respond, at least in direct terms, but returned to his melodic pattern:

"When my darling is pretty and kind,
When my darling is pretty and kind,
What care I for purses or money at all,
Or money at all. . . ."

Here the gentleman smiled and glanced slyly at his audience:

"When Catherine is pretty and kind?
What does she think of my rhyme?"

The gentleman ceased his singing but continued to strum his guitar in a tuneless rhythm, apparently—or so it seemed to the lady—attempting to weave his notes into the whispering laps of the waters.

Catherine addressed him again: "You break the rules of art and extend yourself not along a worthy line, but as a means to an end. Are you a born poet who is aided by art? Or are you a gentleman who by art alone would become a poet?"

The man did not respond at first, but continued to strum. After a while he looked up from his guitar. "My consort is harsh this morning." He smiled and glanced behind the woman into her chambers. "And your shrouds? They arise from your heart? They arise from a spirit growing warm within? How can a mistress of shrouds make life or question the life-giving powers of a fellow artist?"

Catherine narrowed her eyes and moved a bit aside on the portico as if to protect her art from her interlocutor. She shifted her eyes toward her room, then back to the gentleman. "My shrouds are filled with life. You are determined to make yourself disagreeable on this pleasant morning."

"There is no pleasantry in morning," Nicolas corrected her. "Your shrouds are in mourning, and in mourning there is no pleasantry." He thought again. "You choose to create shrouds because the colors of your soul are harsh; your lines are too boldly drawn."

With that the man returned to his strumming, seeming to lose himself in his thoughts, then nodded as if reaching an important decision. "Listen to this and see if there is life in it." He broke at once into a quick tune, tapping his foot dramatically and singing the following verses in a loud voice:

"While waters flow and tall trees grow,
As long as Midas sleeps below,
And that's forever—don't you know?—

She'll sing her song, in many ways,
She'll sing so many nights and days.
How o'er his tomb his daughter prays!"

This doggerel completed, Nicolas returned to his more reflective music. He glanced slyly at his audience. "Beautiful arachnid, did you weave a shroud today? Did you"—here he leaned a bit to the side and gave his companion an exaggerated conspiratorial look—"*hesitate*?" A shy smile flitted about his mouth.

During this performance the woman had stood erect, her eyes flashing toward the singular house not so far off over the waters. She maintained that posture as she turned her eyes back to the singer. "You disturb the air on this pleasant morning," she stated evenly. "You allow yourself too much leisure, and that prompts you to take chances unnecessary, unwise, and unproductive. Maintain your gambling in your house. Leave out mine." She nodded back at the singular house. "Don't bring them here."

Nicolas assumed an expression of exaggerated reflection. "Are you afraid? Solemnity, then, is in order throughout the city." He tilted his head to one side and altered his strumming to create a somber mood as he sang the following words in a lower voice and at a slower pace:

"All passers-by stop here and see the ashes of a king,
Open your eyes and see a mighty Midas and a shroud.
So long as trees grow tall, so long as grasses grow,
So long as waters flow: I sing to every passer-by."

The woman relaxed her posture but kept a wary eye on the singer, who returned to his directionless strumming. He asked again: "Did you *hesitate*?" Grinning quickly and returning to his theme, he glanced up with another conspiratorial look. "In the mind, the image rules; in the hand, the brush falters. Is that why you have come to your porch?"

The gentleman continued: "Have you grappled with contradictions, contrapositions, negations, antitheses? Have you compared the weight of the purse with that of the philosopher's stone? Have you balanced story with metaphor? The lie with truth? The simple with the metaphoric? Reason with emotion? But beware thinking too much: 'Painters have no business to think, save brush in hand. When theories and poetical ideas begin to quarrel with brushes, the end is in doubt.'"

Nicolas lowered his eyebrows and peered up at the woman, then began to vibrate his strings in an exaggerated mood of menace. "Yet those matters are just the beginning. Have you come to terms with 'the infusion of spirit into constructive material'?" Nicolas paused and glared. "Have you come to terms with 'the great machine and its masks'? History, symbol, or philosophy?" Nicolas frowned deeply and narrowed his eyes soberly. "Are you art in the making, or art in the thinking, or art in the image? Have you fit your form to shuttle, woven your material to ideal, made your procedure proud to your city?"

The woman continued to peer carefully at her interlocutor. "Why, in the midst of exposition, comes all this dialogue? You speak in riddles because you have nothing to say."

"What I have to say cannot be said."

"Then how shall we converse?"

"By your serious, academic, sustained attention to the music from my guitar. Is it not an instrument of our science? Do its notes not unlock the gears and pulleys of the aesthetic machine?"

"You are all reason and no emotion."

"On the contrary. My emotions launch from me as natural forces—recall that the professors speak of the heart in such terms. My feelings are wee rockets, they emanate from my soul and bounce off of you. In this, I rather agree with the academy. Notice, for your part, how they pierce your heart as well-aimed arrows, not, as is the case with words, striking *inches too low*. Feel them not?"

Catherine frowned. She saw the eyes of her musician consume her form. "You know everything, it seems. More than the professors do, say you. Know you not if I know not?"

Nicolas smiled. "Now you talk as I do, nodding to the Gordian knot. 'What power, what force, what mighty spell, if not your learned hands, can loosen it?'"

"So says the ancient poet, but when you see me see your form, you know my meaning, and the knot need be untied not."

Nicolas returned to his ungallant assessment. "You are as the actors spoken of by Aristotle. You want to be more than a hanger-on of Dionysus, but rather a fine artist, but as the Frenchman said, '*You have halted between two manners.*' You are like a child after larks, always on the point of catching the art, which is always getting away from you. Your shrouds: Are they useful, as mere works of the practical hand in sheltering death—or do they make life?"

"You have no right to ask, as you know you have no right," said the woman. She looked back over the water at the singular house. "Our city's girl will answer your questions—and mine as well—when she has been thoroughly educated."

"Educated, she will be, in the word. The city arises from the *natural laws of language*. Start with a letter, say our professors, and you end with the universe." Nicolas raised an eyebrow. "Yet a letter has gone missing."

"The city is growing and will be finished."

"The girl–" posed Nicolas. "Is she safe in the hands of the academists?" He turned again to his instrument, strumming a simple and elusive tune, only to return his gaze to his companion. "The girl is painting a portrait of her lover; her professors are displeased. The fox wants the meaning; the hart wants the form." He gave a tight smile.

"I don't like your images," said the woman. "Tell me a story."

The gentleman continued to strum his guitar in his absent-minded way. Then, just as it seemed he had forgotten the young lady's request, he began to tell the following story.

CHAPTER 12:
The Story of a Lost Girl

Here is the story that Nicolas told Catherine:

"One day, deep in the woods, a man and a woman abandoned a baby girl. By chance the infant was discovered by a wandering jackal who sniffed at the crying child, then took her to his den where he protected her and treated her as his own offspring. On the walls of her little home, the child began to scribble mysterious patterns and vague shadows—they can still be seen by people who know the location of the den and care to look.

"The little girl remained in the jackal's den until a monk from a nearby monastery wandered by and—poking his nose into the cave—discovered the hidden treasure. He took the girl back to his community where she was adopted and raised. The brethren fed and clothed the girl and started her education in order to break her wild ways. She learned to read and write and cultivate the grapes in the monastery's garden.

"All this time, the girl continued to paint the same kind of images she created in the cave of the jackal: forms that no one could understand. The monks would puzzle over the images for hours, consulting their books, but they could make nothing of what they saw.

"To the consternation of the brethren, every few days the jackal who had saved the girl would pass near the monastery and sit on a rock some distance away, staring at the girl's window. When this happened, the young lady would break away from her studies and gaze for hours at the animal who had saved her life.

"One afternoon, after communing with the jackal in her usual manner, the girl ran from her room down the stone steps of the monastery and up the hill toward the rock where the animal sat. A number of monks ran after her, but she had gotten such a head start that they soon lost her.

"The distraught monks hurried to the jackal's den, only to find it abandoned. They combed through the forest trying to find their little ward, but always returned downhearted. In their despair, they asked the priest from the Chapel of Joseph and Mary, in the nearby town of Newmarch, to give special masses for the girl.

"The monks had nearly given up hope when one of the brothers came running to the monastery. He had discovered the girl's bonnet in the forest a few miles away. The excited monks returned to the spot where the clothing had been found and began to look closely in the surrounding forest, seeking out isolated nooks in which some kind of living quarters—or even another jackal's den—might be hidden. Despite their best efforts, they returned to the monastery disheartened.

"Then one morning, the monks' prayers were answered as the girl appeared at their gate. The monks threw open the doors and rejoiced. They brought her into the kitchen and sat her by the fire, giving her a meal and returning her bonnet. The girl was mute to the monks' worried questions about her time in the forest, but she resumed her studies and her labors.

"Although the young lady went through the outward motions of her previous life, it became apparent to the monks that her days in the forest had brought about a great change. She was quieter, and moodier, and would spend long hours by the fireside lost in thought. But the most dramatic change of all was in her creative talents. She began to paint works that were instantly understandable: pictures of the vineyards and of the monastery rooms. But the most arresting pictures were those of the animals of the forest, especially one jackal in particular. 'This is my savior,' she would say, and the monks understood the pictured beast to be the one who had taken her to his den.

"Amazed by the lifelike appearance of the girl's pictures, the monks again visited the priest and asked him to stop by and see them. Everyone agreed with his assessment: 'They appear to be more lifelike than the living beasts themselves.'

'Who,' the priest asked, 'had taught her to paint?'

The monks shook their heads, for there was no reasonable answer: The girl had picked up her talent naturally. 'She has told us that Nature, and not an Old Master, is alone worthy of imitation,' one monk reported.

"The monks led the priest to the vineyard where the girl, as was her habit, sat under the shade of a tree creating a new painting. The priest was amazed to see that the girl was concentrating her attention on an old tumble-down wall, but instead of painting an impression of the ivy-covered stones, she was creating a remarkable portrait of a jackal. The priest widened his eyes and nodded to the monks, speaking in a low tone: 'The girl is divinely inspired. She is a *wunderkind* who can render not just the surface appearance of her subjects but their *essence*. Her work does not simply render nature but perfects it, finding in the image, which is to say the form, a meaning to give it value. And indeed, it is apparent, looking at her work, that she is "inwardly filled with forms," as Dürer once described the soul of a natural born artist.'

"The priest pointed at the tumble-down wall. 'When you and I see that wall, all we see are old stones and strands of ivy. Perhaps we also call up memories of our childhood days, hours spent near a similar wall, blending with the forms of the wall our playful actions. The girl is seeing the universal forces that make up not only the wall, but also, oddly, the jackal. For her eye, everything contains life that gives it meaning. By communing with the wall—as indeed, she might commune with any object—she ends up not rendering the surface appearance of the jackal but rather recreates, through the medium of her art, a living jackal.'

"The priest's words were repeated everywhere, and before long the girl's reputation spread throughout the nearby towns. People began to tell stories of the girl's remarkable feats. One time she painted a group of butterflies so realistic that they flew forth from the frame and disappeared across the fields. Another time she painted a vineyard so believable that sparrows flew down from the trees and landed on her canvas, helping themselves to a meal of grapes.

"People clamored to see the girl in person, all the more so when the story got about that, after months of work, the girl had almost finished her greatest painting of all. The priest decided it was the right time to introduce the monks' remarkable ward to the public. A day was set aside for the girl to visit the church and present her creation. The monks wrapped up her painting carefully in brown paper and twine, making sure that no one would see it and blab about its magnificence before its official unveiling.

"The day arrived—the church was packed—and the priest brought the girl to the front of the congregation to a great wave of applause. The girl of the 'divine paintbrush' was introduced and over the crowd came a solemn hush. Then the great painting itself was wheeled onto the stage. The priest unwound the twine that had secured the brown paper. The entire congregation held its collective breath as he reached to the top of the painting and ripped off the brown paper, revealing the work with a great flourish.

"At once a cry arose from the crowd and everyone stood to see the scene before them. The girl had painted a pack of jackals in sharp perspective, rushing headlong out from a dense forest toward the front of the picture. The teeth of the animals were bared and in their savage sharpness seemed to threaten whatever unfortunate beings stood in their path.

"For one and all the painting was nature itself, nature surpassed, nature infused into paint, the living force of Nature driven by the master force of Genius, compelled to do the bidding of the human god, unleashed upon a world that before the specter of the sublime could only stand agape.

"It is little wonder that the audience broke into spontaneous applause, cheering the child who had appeared so unexpectedly in their midst and graced their lives with the presence of the Ideal. At the bidding of the priest, the progenitor of the remarkable work smiled demurely and modestly, made a simple bow, and then stepped forward to address the crowd. Every person in the church strained to hear the girl's speech. Her voice being of the softest, her audience became hushed so that nothing she said would be lost.

"The girl took another step forward, and, in an innocent gesture, held out the tool she had used to complete her work as another child might present a shell found on a beach. 'Look, it is a mere brush,' she stated in her modest tones. The crowd began to murmur and the girl repeated her words so all could hear. 'It is a mere brush. And look. . . .' She moved to the edge of the easel and turned the apparatus to the side. 'You can see that this is really a canvas on an easel, and on the canvas is nothing but paint. Even so, you see how the animals seem to be the living force of Nature herself.' From another person these words might sound as braggadocio. No one in the church, however, interpreted them as anything but the simple words of a poor girl who accepted her natural gifts as a matter of course.

"Then, just as the girl was turning toward the audience again, her speech was interrupted by something unexpected: A woman from the middle of the congregation screamed. The sound was so extraordinary in that hushed venue that everyone turned to see who had disturbed the peace. What they saw was a woman with a look of intense horror, her arms held in a protective gesture in front of her, her eyes wide in terror, staring at the girl's painting. She cried at the top of her voice: 'The beasts are escaping! The jackals are coming forth from the frame!' Then she started to shove frantically at the people standing near her as she attempted to escape. 'They will kill us all!'

"That fearful tremor was enough to send a river of powerful waves rolling through the room. From the crowd arose a universal cry of terror. Each person began to push his neighbor in an attempt to reach the doors. The stronger ones pushed weaker ones to the ground and tread upon them.

"The priest raised his arms in an effort to stop the pending carnage, shouting as best he could that no one should fear what was nothing but a gift from the other world, and that the departure of the jackals from their painterly frame was nothing but the illusion created by an artist with a remarkable power to engineer the principles contained in the constructive material of paint. Against the juggernaut of fear his words possessed nothing but the weakness of reason, and his audience would have none of them.

"'She has made a pact with the devil!' shouted one man, and his words sealed the fate of the child who was spirited away through a side door by her protective monks.

"By the time the panic had subsided, a large portion of the congregation—the old and the infirm—had been trampled underfoot. The girl had been transported to an undisclosed location for her safety. As for her painting, it was wrapped in paper and twine and secured in a secret chamber of the church; no one could predict what panic might ensue if it were ever brought again to light.

"And the girl's name was never spoken in the town, save in hushed whispers, again."

That was the conclusion of Nicolas's story.

Catherine considered. "Your tale is another twist of the knot." She glanced away from the man, toward the empty steps leading to her manor. Then she stepped forward, raising her skirt to show her lower leg. "What is the first step in untying it?"

Nicolas peered closely at her, his face a blank. He strummed a few notes. Then he stated: "A letter has been found."

Catherine frowned and relaxed her pose. "What letter? What do you mean? Are you making another puzzle?"

"Look." Nicolas nodded his head at the singular house across the waters, then back at the woman.

Catherine followed his gesture, and, squinting, made out the form of a figure striding across the garden before the house. She heard the distant snap of a latch as a door swung open and the figure disappeared into the building.

The woman interpreted what she saw: "They are opening for the day. You are bold to mention them, you and your guitar." She narrowed her eyes. "What are you talking about? What letter?"

Nicolas looked down at his guitar and strummed his melody.

Once more he glanced at his companion, then back at his guitar.

"Found."

CHAPTER 13:
Crack in the Earth

Father Cephalus's first question when entering the vestibule concerned the anticipated convergence of the other academists (especially Protogenes) for the morning dialogue—the scheduled topic of the future of the city's little girl being regarded by the participants as one of the highest importance. Only the closest observer of human nature would raise an eyebrow at the change in the professorial visage to the news of delayed arrivals, exhibiting as that visage did features characteristic of a mind more distracted than engaged.

Close observation being for a second gentleman in the room the driving gear of a productive career, it remained only for this younger man to bring Father Cephalus's secret to light as easily as the lifting of a latch. Yet this second gentleman—standing as he was immediately in the laboratory's *petit salon* before a window overlooking the city's walls—felt his current duty less to civic order than to rank, that feeling itself testament to a measure of heightened sensitivity which for the advance of his political career had been a kind of supporting beam.

It was for this reason—that is, the presence of a heightened state of political sensitivity—that Father Theodorous's first remark took on the quality of a fair opening, of a channel into which the elder leader might navigate with an ease commendable to his bearing.

"Our rhyming young man has returned."

Father Theodorous seasoned his news with a quick nod at the window's blind, which he had drawn aside just enough, so it seemed, to allow an urban penetration with a gaze unobserved.

"Nicolas," Father Cephalus responded in statement and question. Pursing his lips slightly in a characteristic manifestation of consideration, he smiled tightly and pierced his companion with a dry gaze. "Building strong walls, I assume?" His features assumed that skeptical if accommodating form allowable by the continuing engagement of a set of personal characteristics notable as: experience of the world for length; understanding of humanity for breadth.

Father Theodorous nodded in affirmation, turning his attention again toward the window and squinting his eyes as he stared thoughtfully through the crack in the blind. "He has a paramour. An artist of shrouds." His easy smile at once betraying an unseemly simpatico to the back-alley, it only remained for an instinctive recognition of the value of professional prudence to cause the man to purse his own lips slightly—in further sympathy with the habits of a superior to whom was granted a swift glance. And then, to extend this conversational parry: "They have been discussing us." At this revelation, the older gentleman assumed a blank expression and draped his jacket over his chair. To which action Theodorous provided a note: "Both of them noticed that you arrived early."

Father Cephalus maintained a detached air, although his settled state of distraction was for his companion no less a matter of note. The older man broke the silence with an assessment, the words of which were supplied in even cadence: "Nicolas is a smart young man. Filled with a common brio. It is not a characteristic necessarily damaging to the city." While he made no move to subject the cityscape to surveillance, he continued to assume the position of marshal to scout. "What think you, Theodorous? What make you of Nicolas and his moody guitar? Delineator? Aquarellist? Something stronger?"

Father Theodorus gave up the minor hint of a shrug. "If skill of mind in making march in common with an image in a mirror, it is evident to me that our young man—whose own reflection is as bright as any observer can bear—is nothing less to the upper artisans than the *intelligible paradigm*. Still, it has not yet been for me to see the ending craftsmanship, what life has arisen from brick, mortar, and infusion. Hence I gaze and on my subject ponder."

The older man nodded quickly, then gestured a silent note of departure to the secretarial presence, who had been recording names and preparing messages all the while. "Fair enough. But let us leave Nicolas to another day." His voice took on a serious tone as the registrar departed the room. "Leave off your observations, Father Theodorous, and consider the news at hand." Here Father Cephalus's expression adopted in full the cast of the urgent matter which, until this time, had been only a scrap resting at the far edge of a table, the mere shadow of which Father Theodorous had identified as likely evidence of a matter momentous.

The target of this order allowed the window blind to snap back as he turned to the center of the room and then took a chair. "News about our little girl?"

Father Cephalus shook his head. "Protogenes will be for our Gillette our master. I am awaiting eagerly any good news he can give us—any which may relieve the pressure the upper artisans and the legislators have been exerting on me. Even so, the more urgent question at hand is the matter of the discovery by our archaeologists of a fossilized letter, the one of recent note, the one that the librarians imagine might lend to the warp and woof of our urban fabric a kind of substratum—and to our vast construction a principle enlivening." To emphasize his points, Father Cephalus struck the table with his forefinger. "If the essence of this object were to be given some moniker at some level of verity, the indication might well be the *artifact germinal*." The final words were uttered at a somewhat higher pitch.

"Ah. The find is more than rumor, then. Are you sure? By what evidence?"

The older gentleman leaned back in his chair and crossed his hands over his chest. His deliberate air implied that he was about to launch into a story. "It was a week ago that a gentleman, badly injured and close to death, was delivered to our docks owing to the merciful intervention of a passing transport steamer. He was taken immediately for medical treatment, subjected to procedures which—given the nature of his injuries—sustained his life for no more than a few days. Due to the severity of a slash to his throat the man could not speak, but with tremendous urgency requested pencil and paper from his saviors. With those tools in hand he insisted, against the advice of his protectors, to offer a narration of the events that had brought him to his end."

Father Cephalus leaned forward and lowered his voice. "The unfortunate gentleman's diary was the story of an adventure, what might be called an intellectual odyssey, extraordinary in its details for any reader, and for us, in particular, in its more general implications unsettling. It was during his adventures, so recorded, that the gentleman claims to have observed the discovery of a letter—that document being the object which has for our city been of moment."

"I see. And the nature of the letter—the discovered one?"

"Our gentleman—let me note that in his urgency to tell his story he overlooked relating his name, regarding it perhaps as an item of lesser importance than the details of his adventure, his role to the latter, in his own estimation, being less participant than reporter—had been engaged as a laborer in the excavation of a domicile located in a region known equally for an importance in notes historic and an instability in support geologic. The excavation, in brief, held the potential for the revelation of information so supportive of the general run of life, so magnificent in implication, as to present to the wielders of axe and pick a reward of brightness as to be more than worth the risk to which the operatives were by the nature of the terrain exposed. Accepting the attendant risks, then, our sturdy worker labored away at the turn of the archeological wheel, his motivation empowered less by the promissory note of public legacy and more by a pocketable salary—the level of which had been elevated to a height sympathetic to the ambitions of the academists into whose hands the expedition had been entrusted.

"One day, our man heard a commotion emanating from a nearby section of the excavation. Succumbing to curiosity, he sauntered over the broken terrain to the area where a number of the managers and workers had gathered at the edge of a deep excavation. 'There has been a discovery,' one worker said. Indeed, at the bottom of the excavation—our man estimated the depth at around fifteen feet—an archaeologist was chipping carefully away at a rock embedded in the soil. This enterprise continued for some time. Shortly, the gathered workers were asked by the archaeologists to return to their duties, and our reporter, complying, soon forgot about the disruption.

"His labors being of necessity hard and constant, the earth which he attacked being compacted into a turgid stone over the course of eons, and the atmosphere of the surroundings well qualified by that close, moist, smothering, and overheated nature familiar to any who have meandered through the terrain of ancient humanity, our man felt at the end of the day a deep fatigue. It was natural, then, if perhaps imprudent, for him to wave on his compatriots, wish them well as they left the excavation for their residences, and allow himself to rest alone in the wilderness.

"Determining to nap for an hour or two, our reporter fell into a long sleep. He awakened with a start in the middle of the night. Frightened by his situation, he sat up quickly and gazed about him. The forest had sunk into darkness and quietude, a coolness had impregnated the pine and oak. Overhead, the moon had risen high, its glow still visible through the entangled limbs of the surrounding trees as its lantern face crept across the inky dome. Its visage, peeking down at the solitary man, was so frightening and so filled with natural wisdom that its object was filled with paralyzing emotions.

"The traveler was faced with a decision: Should he wait out the night, allowing sleep to put him at a dangerous disadvantage to any comer, or should he attempt to creep his way back through the dark woods to civilization, the requisite motion necessarily allowing his profile to rise to a high state of visibility along quite a stretch of land populated by hostile forces? He turned the idea over in his mind this way and that, and finally opted for the latter course, determining that continual motion would at the very least allow him the advantage of an alert mind.

"Having then begun his journey home, carefully attending to the surrounding foliage, our man had not traveled more than a half mile before he was startled by an unexpected sight. A light was glimmering from the window of an old utility shed a few yards off an adjoining access road. At once he considered the possibilities: Were the people there friends or foes? Another question followed quickly: How could it be that there was life here, not all that far from the excavation site, of which the archeologists had not been aware? Our man crept low and made his way up to the window. Peering inside, and beginning to make out the profiles of the half dozen individuals gathered in the dim light, he saw to his surprise that they were the very academists who had been in charge of the excavation. They had not returned to their homes and offices at all, but had formulated a kind of seminar here, and were now deeply engrossed in the study of some small item. It did not take much imagination for our man to suspect the source of the item under investigation: the strange rock retrieved by the workers during that afternoon's disruption.

"This suspicion was quickly supported by some statements made by the scientists. Our man could make out their conversation only in bits and pieces, occasional words wafting through the open window in a continuing audial battle with the chirps of crickets and the incessant cries of the nearby lake loons.

"Because what he did manage to overhear, however, was of such great import, he committed the words to memory and so he wrote them down at the bottom of his account provided us, underling the words with a fierce sagacity." Here Father Cephalus leaned forward at the desk, stared at his companion, and spoke the following words with the intensity of a priest laden with the burden of the sacrifice of the altar in the grand old Papal days:

". . . and so here is that knowledge that I give you not wisely, but only from my duty as a loving father.

The key to the hesitational lock is written below. Keep it to yourself. Commit it to your memory. Then give it to Joseph only in the case of extreme stress. Take care—provide it to him only as a final antidote to save him from self-immolation. If he insists on opening the cabinet, look inside. Watch him study the substratum of the diary. Then do what you have to do. Look carefully beneath the puzzles and codes: There is a woman beneath. Above all, be certain to destroy this letter. Burn . . . burn . . . burn!"

After this recital, Father Cephalus leaned back in his seat, somewhat limp, and stared at his audience.

For his part, Father Theodorous pursed his lips, emitted something of a noncommittal sigh, rested his elbows on the table, and tented his fingers in a universal gesture of cognitive muddlement. "I see." He considered further. "The first indication of the *interpretive palimpsest*." He paused again. "And, it seems, the dear old recipient did *not* destroy the letter." He stared rather pointedly at Father Cephalus and adopted a knowing visage, which—coming from another and less-connected individual—would be condemned as the height of impudence. "Well. Item retrieved?"

Father Cephalus nodded slowly at his interlocutor, who finally asked, "Has Midas heard of this?"

Father Cephalus opened his eyes a little wider. "Exactly what I was about to ask you, your ear offering to the babble of the city unfailing allegiance."

The younger man, ignoring the implicatory pierce, looked askance at his companion. “Mother Rachel.”

“Indeed.”

CHAPTER 14:
Across the Moors

The driving gear of the conversational machine having arrived at last—the instructor of the city's little girl appearing at the door of the vestibule shortly after the advent of the other academists—Father Cephalus brought his conversation with Father Theodorous to a halt and turned immediately to the subject which had consumed the interests of the city for the previous months.

"Professor Protogenes!" Father Cephalus spread his arms wide and looked directly at the newcomer. "Professor Protogenes!" He hesitated as this second command brought the room to order. "What shall be done about our little girl? Everyone in this room appeals to you—" Here the speaker glanced about the assemblage in open query. "What can be done to bring round, to the requisite level of making, the days and hours of our Gillette, brought here as she was with such anticipation, saved with our regard for the balance of the wild heart with the reason of the intellectual principle, only to have before our eyes the evidence of more than a small retraction—indeed of a reversal—of a failure to go behind the surface of her work, and more: to sink beneath the lower pool of the human order?"

Protogenes stood humbly and raised a didactic finger in preparation of a response. He was cut off by a wave of the hand from his interlocutor, who began to pace a bit to and fro before the assembly, his head bowed in thought, his thoughts knotted to the pull of a greater line. "Brought as she was from a world of principles detached, secured here for her safety in a world of forces infused, for our city both ward and maker, our light giver, our girl was promised by us her development in the full strength of her native powers. 'Where goes Gillette,' said we all, 'there goes Platonopolis.' We deemed her powers not miraculous, but rising from the good spring of *lex naturalis*, sure of hand in the making of walls to extend our city, a native skill for her bold infusion absent halt, the engineer of the secrets of creation. And yet in the wake of our transport does now come this *terrible lucidity*."

Father Cephalus had given his final words a particular emphasis, and now he repeated them with still finer enunciation. "*Terrible lucidity.* Why has our little girl embraced clarity? And furthermore, why has she placed such boldness on such a subject—an ignoble beast that rises from her canvas, a human animal not with us but against us, as low to the ground as those jackals from whence the girl as babe escaped? What think you that Midas thinks? What else feels he but anger? What else from he who desires, deeply, that this girl paint *her greatest painting of all* and be such picture for our city bulwark—that this girl reveal to her saviors, whether by nurture of studied reason or by nature of native habit, the secret of her lack of the fatal hesitation, and hence, by that very revelation desired, lead our people through their living dream? Why has all this devastation come about on your watch? And what steps can you take to bring her back to us?"

Protogenes stood, silent and bowed, and, pursing his lips in reflection, began to enter upon a statement as detached from the preceding line as it was remarkable in its subject matter.

"Father Cephalus." Speaking softly, Protogenes nodded in deference to his interlocutor, then three times more to the assembled academists. "Charm. Beauty. Creativity. May they enlighten my words; may they carry me on their shoulders through darkness.

"In line with the general interest of this morning's inquiry, and proposing as I do to illuminate those who—to put the matter in its complete triumvirate form—honor the sphere of truth with a submissive mind, a welcoming embrace, and an engineering intent, I will now provide important news about the young girl whose education and development have been to my care entrusted."

In response to these words, Father Cephalus retreated to a chair by the side of the room, sat heavily, folded his arms, and stared at the speaker with a look not in the least forgiving, forgetting, or forbearing.

"Before answering directly the questions of Father Cephalus, I must position my response in the context of an event which has just transpired," began Protogenes. "As you know, Gillette has been painting at my atelier in a room overlooking the marshlands. Two days ago, very early in the morning, Gillette had been sitting by her window when a mockingbird suddenly landed on her sill. The bird engaged the girl's attention by fluttering its wings and singing a happy song. From time to time the bird would flutter off the sill and fly briefly toward the marshland, only to return in a great loop and once again hop about the sill, chirping away.

"Gillette soon understood that the bird intended a following. At once the girl decided to abandon her chair and easel, the demands of which had in any case become onerous, and left her room in pursuit of the bird, which began to fly in great arcs, first up, then down, gradually pulling its human friend across the moor.

"The bird led the way across the grasses that filled the marshy field and began to relate stories of individuals who, although now lost to history, had in their time been involved in deeds which for the residents of their time were of note. Pronounced the bird at one place: 'Here stood a cottage where a man and his wife murdered their two sons and a daughter.' At another: 'Here, in this fallen-in barn, a young man committed suicide by hanging himself.' At another place near the edge of the wood: 'A young lady from the town wandered into the forest here and was never seen again.'

"All of these stories, and more, were told to Gillette, and it was to her credit that—far from being filled with fear at such dreadful tales—she continued on with that strength of will and fortitude with which over the past few months her painterly labors have been engaged.

"The mockingbird took the girl to the edge of a cliff that overlooked still more plains and forests beyond. 'Out there no one has ever gone,' said the mocking-bird. 'Do you fear the land?'

"On the contrary, our young lady was delighted by the broad vistas. She stood high over the valley and let the wind blow her hair. She closed her eyes and felt the sun and wind, the nutritive breath of nature, buoy her spirit. 'Confident grows the grass,' she sang over the prairie, 'for the young sun will not harm it.'

"So went the travels of the girl and her guide, which, seemingly a bird of great ambition, flew perhaps a little further than anticipated. After a few hours, Gillette found herself by a gurgling brook that passed alongside what appeared to be a kind of excavation. The young girl walked to the edge of a pit expecting to find some laborers, or perhaps some evidence of archaeological adventures. She found the area entirely abandoned.

"Gillette looked into the tree limbs to inquire about the abandoned enterprise, but the bird had disappeared. To her momentary distress, Gillette had forgotten the way back home. Confronted with a wilderness which might be alarming to others but to her was only the echo of her natural childhood, the girl at once determined to sleep where she was, the weather being warm, the hour being late, and the surrounding terrain reminiscent of the forest where she had been raised as a baby. And so to sleep she went.

"It was only a matter of a short while before our girl awoke to the sharply cooling breeze of the night air. Looking once more into the tree limbs, she saw an owl eyeing her with a steady gaze. When the girl asked her new companion about her missing guide, the owl only maintained a silence.

"Disturbed that the owl had nothing to say, the girl was nonetheless delighted to see that the moon had begun to rise overhead. Over the next hour or so, as Gillette sat absorbing the spirit of the forest, the moon paced across the sky like a friendly lantern, its light blinking slowly now and then between the dense branches of the tall trees, sending its cheerful beams down to the floor of the forest. As she watched the moon, the girl found herself considering which course to take: to remain in her current spot throughout the night, or—an alternative which made her smile—to find her way out of the woods and creep over the moonlit moors. Suddenly, though, she was arrested by a slight shadow glancing along an open area just beyond her place of rest.

"'Who is there?' she asked. Immediately she knew the answer to her own question: The shadow belonged to that category of beast to which she owed her life. 'Come out,' she invited. And it was naught but the breath of a moth before there appeared from out of the bushes a jackal.

"The little beast eyed our girl briefly, turned and walked a few steps, then stopped and looked back. Realizing that the wolf desired her to follow, the girl did so. The jackal led her through a few groves, across a field or two, down a trail here and there, and eventually over to the edge of the forest. A few more steps and the girl found herself on a moonlit plain, upon which was situated an imposing stone structure with three broad towers, each facing a different direction.

"The jackal walked a few steps more in front of the girl, then halted. When he turned back to face his ward, Gillette saw that his eyes had begun to glow as red coals. He seemed to grin at Gillette, and then he spoke these words: 'Find in the image a meaning to give it value.'

"The jackal bounded back into the woods, abandoning the girl on the plain. Startled by the beast's departing words, and then turning to stare more closely at the structure looming before her, Gillette was intrigued to discover that all of its windows had been blocked in with stone."

Here it would be productive to pause, and to note that the instructor's story had been received in its entirety with commendable respect on the part of the assembled academists, the attentive looks on their faces testament to the patience with which they intended to entertain their guest's efforts. It would be equally accurate to insist, however, that one could invest full meaning in a word such as "entirety," without expecting a complete return of one's cognitive dividends. Reality being ineffable, the terms of common discourse being inadequate, and the course of human intent being more than a little a cipher, the prudent individual would subject to diminishment the level of expectations entertained for the success achieved by the launch of any term of common parlance upon the great and murky river of communication.

All of such reflection leading with certain step to understanding the response on the part of Father Cephalus to the concluding portion of the narrative of Protogenes. It was just at the point where the instructor had uttered the words "imposing stone structure with three broad towers," at which Father

Cephalus unfolded his arms, sat bolt up in his chair, frowned, and turned around to glance with disapproval at Father Theodorous and a few others in the audience. And then, as the instructor continued his narrative with the words "all of its windows had been blocked in with stone," Father Cephalus rose in one swift motion to his feet, his motion serving to slam his chair back against the wall.

Father Cephalus stood stiffly, stared wide-eyed at the instructor, pointed his finger at the man, and—ignoring the startled looks on the faces of the gathered academists—shouted these evenly paced words: "Why was I not informed, Protogenes? Her discovery happened yesterday and I was not told until now, and only with a communication made in common with the others. Why have you kept this from me? You and Mother Rachel were given control of Gillette. Where is she now? What has happened to our little girl?"

CHAPTER 15: *Mother Rachel*

"Allow me to relate some events that have transpired in recent months—events known only to a few of us and which have been kept from general circulation out of prudence."

The above words were uttered by a woman who had been invited to replace Protogenes, banished as he was to the back of the room by Father Cephalus. Mother Rachel—that was the woman's name—had been urgently summoned by the academists to interpret the troubling narrative given by Protogenes, its scandalous reaction on the part of Father Cephalus, and the implications of both phenomena for the overriding concern of the legislators: the infusion of the city's girl into the common civic web.

Mother Rachel continued her address: "As for the nature of that prudence, I emphasize first the physical safety of the city. Second, I appeal to the general interest in the well-being of the young girl herself—Gillette, our ward—who, child as she is, must always to our careful watch be subject, her childish emotions and tender spirit being vulnerable to damage."

This statement created in the room a general low-level buzz, as the academists conferred in low voices.

Mother Rachel continued in this way: "Before moving on into an interpretation, let me take the opening story of Protogenes to its conclusion. I believe you will see that the instructor and I were not so loose and easy with the city's credibility as at first appeared." Here the speaker eyed Father Cephalus.

"You will recall that at the end of the story, Gillette was standing at the edge of a clearing, overlooking an odd stone structure. A thousand unuttered thoughts surrounded the girl as she surveyed the plain and the building before her. Why had the creature brought her to this place? She was confused about the structure, forbidding in its bulk, looming before her. Was this an abandoned building? Why was it built in this lonely spot on the moors? Did it hide some terrible secret?"

Mother Rachel raised an instructive hand to the audience. "Gillette, strong-willed as ever, was *determined* to find an entrance to the building, and it was only the matter of a few false forays before she discovered several loose boards in the ancient structure, the removal of which was to her purpose sufficient."

The speaker leaned forward slightly and lowered her voice as if to keep from the general run of humanity the indications of the arcane. "A candle. A match. That was all it took, gentlemen, for our young lady to infuse within the gloom of a practiced darkness the illumination which to her nature is productive part and parcel."

Mother Rachel spread her arms slightly in a sudden openness. "What did she find? She found emptiness—room after room making a maze of solidity. She found abandonment—an air filled with the vapors of tales told long ago and forgotten."

The speaker paused. "And she found something else."

Her audience leaned forward.

"She found misaligned walls."

Again there arose a murmuring in the room. Mother Rachel hushed the sound with a raised hand. "Such is the powerful mind of our girl that—in the second room from the back—she perceived immediately that a wall had been set too far off line."

Father Cephalus, who had been shaking his head silently as the tale continued, here could not restrain himself from emitting a protest: "Unconscionable."

Mother Rachel nodded quickly to Father Cephalus, then turned back to the professors, all of whom had adopted a visage of complete bewilderment. At last she let loose her volley: "A hidden room. A place of keeping." She paused. "Soon Gillette had removed the few necessary stones to uncover the small room Father Cephalus had created as a hiding place."

At these words the entire room erupted. The academists rose to their feet, and with expressions of shock universal, began to remonstrate against the full measure of the civic discourse having to their advantage been denied.

"This is an outrage!"—that assertion coming from one Father Theodorous, who became red in the face and advanced toward the group's leader. "Father Cephalus—what have you been keeping from us?"

For his part, Father Cephalus himself had risen to his feet, raising his hands in defiance and returning to his inquisitor the same degree of venom. "Only something that should have by all rights and duties remained in hiding. Be sorry that I have failed. This revelation is a disaster! Mind you! The city will pay!"

"The city will pay!" A general ironic cry rose throughout the room as everyone turned away from Father Cephalus and back to the woman who had torn the veil from his deceit. "Mother Rachel! What has this been all about? Interpret this for us." And there arose a general call from everyone for Mother Rachel to explain the unusual and troubling events.

The object of their requests had meanwhile remained stoically standing at the head of the room. She now motioned for everyone to return their seats, and when this venture had been accomplished she resumed her story.

"I am sure everyone wants to know what Gillette found in that room. Well, I shall not keep you in suspense. Leaning against the wall of the room was a package, about waist high and an equal length wide. It was firmly wrapped with brown paper, and around the paper had been wound, and wound, and wound a length of heavy twine. As if these preparations were not enough to dissuade the intrusions of the casually curious, across the paper had been scrawled these words in large letters: *Do Not Open Me*."

The woman's story, developing in its way a greater measure of mystery, created among the assembly a general amazement. Now thunderstruck beyond comment, the professors turned blankly to one another, some with mouths open in mute wonder and others with expressions that no one, save perhaps Mother Rachel herself, might construe.

"Can anyone fail to foresee what from this manufactured mystery must then transpire?" Mother Rachel stood more solidly in her place, looking first at one professor, then another. "The young girl must surely follow her will, her natural curiosity, be it one far from idle."

Several professors interrupted loudly to a general acclaim: "Not idle curiosity, not at all—but wisdom." Others nodded their heads enthusiastically and uttered their own proclamations: "She was wise to do so."

Mother Rachel continued: "And open the packet she did. Retrieving a sharp stone, Gillette cut at the cords binding the packet. They fell away, and she used that same stone to cut through the paper—two lines in the form of a cross. It was a matter of no longer than several minutes before the girl tore the paper completely off and the hidden object received again the light of the world."

The assembly leaned forward in their seats.

"Does anyone not understand that Gillette had realized, from the very first, the essence of the object before she removed its wrapping? For the item was, indeed, a painting."

A murmur arose from the professors.

"But a painting of an unusual sort. Not of a nature known to all, not indeed to be rendered at all for the dull and paltry, yet known, easily, to our little genius. How can the essence of painted images be to speech transmuted?" Mother Rachel raised her hands in a broad gesture of benediction, holding them over the assembly and calling up from within herself her full powers of description:

"Here is what Gillette saw: A chaos of color. Lines fantastic. Shapes swollen and angled and weird. But within all of them was the authentic breath of life. The light poured in like a flood, and blended with the objects on which it fell. Paint itself raised here, lowered there, the light catching the resulting ridges and shadows occupying the valleys so that the work itself had lost its appeal to line. Art itself had vanished. You could not distinguish the canvas from the surrounding air. The work lived and breathed, in its full pride. Who would not fail to fall to his knees before such perfection?"

The room remained quiet for a moment. Then Father Lysis broke the silence. He stood stiffly, and with slightly bent knees, one hand resting on the back of the chair in front of him, he addressed the speaker. "Mother Rachel, there is only one way for the surface of a painting to be of the nature you describe—that is, to glow with the living breath. The work must possess that particular nature which your professional skills have been honed to interpret." The man looked sidelong at his fellow professors as if to thread them into his cognitive weave. "The painting is a palimpsest."

At this pronouncement many of the professors began to nod. Father Lysis turned back to address the speaker. "Hence, you have been brought to bear on the matter." His face darkened. "Beneath the surface of the painting, Mother Rachel? What, in regard to the interpretive palimpsest, was its tenor?"

Mother Rachel stared directly into the heart of her audience. "You are correct in your assessment. Beneath the visible layer of paint was an extraordinary subject—something no one among us could have anticipated." Her tone became somber. "The subject was a bronze statue of Gillette."

This announcement caused another uproar in the crowd, which rose to its feet in a mixture of confusion and anger. The academists began to confer with one another about this extraordinary turn of events.

"Kept from us!" Father Lysis said bitterly, closing his eyes and clenching his fists. Then he began to turn from one colleague to another in a kind of shock, repeating in thin tones: "Some painter, somewhere, has found the key to the lock." He looked blankly from one attendee to another. "But who can it be?"

Several of the participants turned to Father Cephalus, who sat glumly nursing his wounds. "Tell us, Father Cephalus! Who has managed this?"

Again Mother Rachel called the group to order and reclaimed her hold. "Silence, everyone. I shall explain the source of the painting, and you will understand, perhaps, why Father Cephalus thought it wise for the work to remain in seclusion." The attendees returned to their seats obediently, turning their attention once again to the speaker.

"Everyone here will recall that shortly after Gillette came to live with us, we were visited by an artist who desired to view the girl's work. Having heard about our girl's fame from many sources, this man felt that her work might inspire him to a higher level of creation.

"The result, as you know, was tragic. An understanding of the futility of doing any work comparable with Gillette's led to a psychological fatality. The man took his own life. From that time forward we have been less than enthusiastic about allowing anyone—save those of professorial dignation at a level sufficiently proven—view the girl's work." A number of professors nodded at Mother Rachel's narrative, the tragedy being fresh in mind.

"This story had a succeeding chapter of which you are not aware. A few months ago we were visited by the artist's widow who made a remarkable offer. It seems the wife had been taking art lessons from her husband, and upon his death she had abandoned her own hopes for a second career as an artist. We were delighted to hear that the woman's initial unreasoning anger at Gillette—certainly an emotion we felt understandable—had been replaced by one of an ambitious desire to assist the advance of our young genius in some way. Indeed, the woman felt such assistance would be for her husband a worthy memorial.

"This train of thought had led the artist's widow to the following idea: Her husband had been working on an ambitious painting at his death. Why not donate the painting to our singular house, our venue being for the painting a worthy frame, and the painting being for the house perhaps, when sold some day, a source of revenue?

"We immediately agreed to the woman's plan—not for any idea of financial gain, for the painter was unknown, a fact that for his widow's tune had served but soft pedal—but rather as a way of showing our appreciation for her thought for us and our sorrow at the loss of her husband.

"While we were making arrangements for the delivery of the painting, the woman provided a little more background that we found intriguing. It seems that she had only been made aware of the existence of the painting by reading a diary that had been kept by her husband and which had been abandoned in his desk upon his death. Oddly, the diary had been written in some sort of code, the lines of which had been covering some additional entries that had been frantically scratched away.

"Such a phenomenon is to me, of course, rather of the moment, but I felt that to impose upon a matter of the heart the duty of the academy would in the present case be neither prudent nor politic. Suffice to say that the widow—attributing the mysteries of the diary to the eccentricities common to the artistic temperament—was able to decipher just enough of the wording to recover the painting from its hidden room and provide it for our safekeeping."

Mother Rachel concluded: "Beyond what I have provided here, the details of the transaction are of little consequence. Upon the painting's arrival it did not take long for me to decipher the underlying content, the making of which was, I find myself compelled to say, on the ladder of painterly skill not of the highest rung. For which reason I called upon Protogenes, recently appointed tutor of Gillette, to apply to the work his quick and sure technique.

"Protogenes glanced at the painting, then looked at it with a more critical eye, then peered at it closer still. Finally he turned to me with a rueful smile. 'The figure is correctly drawn—see you, Mother Rachel?—and everything is in its place according to the rules of anatomy. But I see here the grammar of the novelist, not the life of a poet.' He looked again at me. 'Our painter has halted between two manners.'

"I nodded in agreement and proceeded to hand Protogenes the brushes and paint that we had stored in our cabinet, bidding him transform the flat face of the work into the chiaroscuro of life. The instructor looked at us as though we had handed him a bucket of mud. 'These brushes and paints should be thrown out the window,' he said, his face twisted in a wretched grimace. 'Along with the man who made them.'

"'Then return to your quarters and retrieve your own tools,' I bid him.

"At this he only smirked and turned to the canvas at hand, stating: 'Let me show you how to put life into that figure.' Protogenes mixed the paints we had provided him into a creative stew, applied a few strokes at what seemed to be random places—'There . . . and there . . . and there! That is how you lay it on!'—and to our amazement there rose from the painting—no more than two minutes had passed—a bronze sculpture of Gillette, living and breathing in our room. Did I say a sculpture? The word is inadequate; no proposition can signify the tenor of this interpretive palimpsest. When you looked at that painting, gentlemen, you saw a woman before you. Not a creature, but a creation."

At this point the professors broke into a grateful applause, everyone turning to nod in appreciation at the otherwise forgotten Protogenes, seated at the back of the room. The object of their admiration closed his eyes, bowed in his seat with exaggerated modesty in the general direction of the assemblage, and returned to his position of thoughtful deliberation.

"Our instructor, in short, had provided for our edification a lesson of a measure considerably more than we had bargained for. Our question, at that point, became a moral one: What should we do with the painting? Our initial thought was to mount it in a place of common access, its remarkable ability to breathe life a testament both to our city's efforts and by proxy to the glory of Gillette.

"We thus set the painting aside, in the care of Father Cephalus, as we determined the most attractive way to present the painting to our young ward. Then, unfortunately, an event occurred that cast our plans, ambitious and generous as they were, into disarray. Something happened which made the presentation of the painting to Gillette, or to the public, a threat to the young girl's life."

The assembly, so soon inspired by the story of the painting, took on a somber air as wonder was seasoned with alarm.

"In order for you to understand the nature of this event, and the forces which made it such a mortal threat to the young girl, you must understand Gillette's mentality at the time. In turn, before you can understand her mentality, you must understand the course of instruction with which she had become so deeply engaged. The best person to illuminate that course is her instructor. Hence I ask Protogenes to again address you. I trust that you will accept him for the good force that he is in our midst, now that I have explained his role in these proceedings."

Protogenes arose from his seat and walked to the front of the room. All of the gathered professors leaned forward to hear his story.

CHAPTER 16:

Form and Its Minions

Of the many things that came into the mind of Protogenes as he walked to the front of the room, perhaps the most salient was a feeling that the overriding sympathy of his audience, if having lost that luster of the pointedly skeptical, nevertheless retained a certain fold of a larger fabric of the ruefully reflecting, or perhaps the mortally anxious, so that the speaker—returned as he had been by the saving hand of his predecessor—felt it incumbent upon himself to give to the swelling plea for veracity a certain formal attention.

Toward Gillette's instructor the academists, for their part, had adopted a tone of greater deference. Now from every row of the assemblage there arose an honorable and silent tribute, each eye following the path forward of this gentleman who, solid as was his reputation in both tribute and deed, was to the eager listener as the call of the landing bell to the wayward voyager.

"Gentlemen!" To this command the listeners sat a little higher in their seats, stared in more refined penetration at the speaker, and determined to hold each word emitted as a priceless stone.

"Gentlemen!" Protogenes repeated, and the room became silent. "As to our *darling interpreter* and her testament to my nature, so over-generous as she was, I can only offer my gratitude, and in appreciation of her sagacity and of her purity and dependability, I can only request from each person here an assessment from one and all absent any varnish, any prejudgment, neither shadowed by a figure dark in dismay, nor brightened, in an unseemly way, by a light—welcome at its dawn for illumination simple, but resented at the hours of its long shining for harsh rays eroding—of acceptance absent any edge critical and moral."

At this long elegancy there arose from the academists an appreciative murmur. A few turned to their neighbors and nodded their heads in an agreeable way; others simply reseated themselves in poses open and free, their heads held high and forward, upon their visages the cast of expectation.

"In order to communicate the full nature of the tragic event which caused us to alter our plans for the painting of Gillette—and indeed, for the girl herself—I must set the context by narrating how, up to that point, the education of our girl had proceeded, and the result of this education on her mentality."

Protogenes paused to collect his thoughts, then addressed the academists in tones earnest and reflective. "It once was said that *no one thanks us for what lies beneath*. But what did the Old Master, to whom we owe so much, mean? Nothing more than this: The refined engineering of natural forces sensed at the peak of awareness, the engagement of the greatest productivity of the principles inherent in brick and stone, indeed the settled process of science as it has been developed in our city and now practiced by the upper artisans, this process which with engagement of skilled viewer creates both stone and life—in brief the *principle paramount*—has for its reward its own making. Nod of draftsman and smile of citizen, rare as they be for our Old Masters and limners, hold for our practitioners of beaker, brush, and oil no portion save that of a general goodwill. By their inner forces stand our walls; only by interests peripheral do our master makers hear those appreciations, sweet in savor but small in nourishment, to our plans, to our figures, to our cognitive urban postulates.

"That form is triumph of town is well settled. Through the constant efforts of those in this room has the city grown, through the continuing refinements of aesthetic mechanics—that productive conflation of the laws of the legislator with the principles of nature. Everyone in this room can be proud of the civilization so built. For no one will say that the special task undertaken by the people in this room—I speak of that skilled interpretation of the works of the upper artisans, that engineering of convoluted formal constructs which distill from the forces of nature the building blocks of the city—provides to the perpetual increase of our city anything but the greatest power. For this reason do we happily address each of you as 'Father' or 'Mother.'

"Even so, none of us has been able to discover a resolution to the critical flaw in the machinery of the aesthetic: that intentional conflict which dissolves the potency of even the most skilled *artiste-peintre*, and that threatens, as it grows in strength, to destroy our city through a destructive insinuation between brush and canvas. For this reason did the upper artisans give us their instructions: complete at all costs a full restatement of the natural law: discover the secret machinations of the great hesitation, then facilitate its resolution. What will be saved is nothing less than the city; no other course of action will assure in the minds of the people the validity of those legislators who by their shaping and controlling of society assure the collective happiness.

"With such promise, then, did we receive our ward, a little girl who had from birth communed with that very genie whose bottle we must uncork. To touch a brush to canvas and from frame to rise a beast: Never had such power from a child been seen. All of us desired the same goal, and little wonder you so voted: prepare the girl to fulfill her destiny as master maker of the city; construct from her life-giving powers the driving gear of that mechanism to which our city dedicates its life, the *principle paramount*.

"So it was that I, assigned the task by those cited above, to whom the matter of her education was of most interest, set myself upon the task of the forming of the mind and hand of our Gillette. Let me reiterate, then, the course of education which I determined the wisest for our little girl, and for which you academists gave assent.

"First, certainly, came a mastery of those skills of the lower artisans for which we maintain the respect due simple, honest tasks. Who in this room will be surprised that our student quickly mastered the bold lines beloved by the *delineators*? A sketch of a workman; an outline of a building; a trace of trail leading to a faraway field: all such representations were to our scholar as the dropping of a leaf to the forest floor.

"We moved without delay, then, to labor's higher level: the emulation of the works of the *aquarellists*. What a great array of flowers, trees, and seascapes! Could it have been more than the matter of a moment before Gillette had mastered, for the amusement of the visitors today to our public buildings—see them yourselves in our civic halls and marvel—such lively and colorful accoutrements?

"In this manner did Gillette complete the labors of the lower artisans. Honored we are to have such people in our city; respectful we are of their graven duty. In their works we see the happy play of simple minds; in our hearts we sing the words preserved from ancient times: *Those who hawk at larks have no less sport, though lesser quarry, than those who fly at nobler game.* Equally did she enjoy their myriad flashes, yet relentlessly does the heart of genius lash the beast of greatness: 'Allow me to weave,' said Gillette, 'my brush my shuttle, and my will my master, my finer fabric.'"

While the academists had attended closely to Protogenes's words throughout his speech, at this point in his narrative they all leaned forward in unison in anticipation of a certain crossing of a line, of a transition in the education of Gillette into the realm of the upper artisans. Father Theodorous jotted a note on his pad which he planned to reference with a question at the conclusion of the instructor's presentation; several other academists were making similar notes. For the most part, however, the members of the assemblage sat still, some stroking their chins in reflection, warmed by a golden glow emanating from the essence of the Protogenesian atelier.

"The time had arrived, then, to introduce Gillette to that work that lies between a thought and thing, the silent poetry that for every bridge is marker: the portrait work of the limners and the challenging works of the highest ranking Old Masters to whom we owe the strong walls and buildings of our city.

"Yet, take care! How many instructors have misdirected their students by making bold the brush's touch! Rather the foundation of the house of art, the power that drives the touch, lies hidden. It must be rooted out, presented in this way, that way, another way, before it can be mastered. Everyone in this room knows my meaning, for I am speaking of the force that powers the pillars of our city. Gillette's instructions in the higher arts, then, began with an elucidation of the embrace of the *intellectual principle*."

Here there arose a wave of appreciation throughout the room. Many of the assembled looked sideways at their neighbors and nodded in affirmation of the wisdom of this course.

Pausing in response to the general acclaim, the speaker remounted his narration in a more rapid pace. "I began by telling Gillette the story of my contest with Apelles, for its moral is one that goes to the point at hand." Protogenes began to pace lightly back and forth, his legs seeming to energize his thoughts, and while he bowed his head and furrowed his brow, he considered closely his words. "Although Mother Rachel has told you a charming story about my facility, the truth is that, far from being a champion of rapid manner, I have always been very much a detailer, a laborer, one who would rather invest three years in a painting that sits in a corner than toss off a quick wonder for the pleasantry of the public. And so it happened that one day, after having exhausted myself in a bout of three months' labor upon a representation of the Three Graces, I left my school—the one I had established for a time in Rhodes—in the care of an old woman, and began a walk of a week's duration, determined to, for the sake of my creative powers, substitute for the hostile and close atmosphere of the studio the enlivening air of nature.

"While I was absent, a stranger came by my atelier and asked the old woman about my whereabouts. That I was not at home, that I was not in the area, that indeed it was not anticipated that I would return before a week was out, was to the stranger duly reported. Asked his name, the gentleman, to the old woman's surprise, simply walked up to a blank canvas that I had left on an easel, picked up one of my brushes, dabbed it into red paint, and drew a line. 'Here is my name,' said the man.

"Upon my return, the woman related the story. I looked at the canvas and immediately determined that the stranger had been Apelles, my rival for the civic hall of Rhodes. No one else could have drawn a line so fair. Determined not to be outdone by a man whom Pliny had signified the greatest painter, I retrieved a brush and proceeded to draw, in a blue color, a line of such fineness as to be the hair of an angel against the strand of a spider's web. I told the old woman that if the stranger were to return, he should be shown my work.

"After a few days, I found it necessary to leave my atelier again, this time to engage with the governors on the possibility of the creation of a panel for the council chambers. During my absence Apelles visited yet again. The old woman showed the visitor the contested canvas. Determined not to be outpainted, Apelles again grasped a brush, dabbed it now in soot, and proceeded to paint a third line over the first two, of such fineness as to leave no more room for a victorious challenge. Of course I was amazed at this performance upon my return. In response to my suggestion, Apelles agreed that we should donate the work to the public baths, where you can visit and see it today."

Here the academists broke into applause and emitted various approvals of the skill and the generosity of Protogenes.

"Why did I tell this story to Gillette? Because there were two moral lessons necessary for our young ward to learn before her talents were tested with the skills of the higher masters.

"The first moral lesson was conceptual: The power of cognition compels the creative endeavor. The brush of Apelles was moved not by his hand but by his mind. And what fills the mind with power is mastery of the *intellectual principle*, a purified mind of genius reflecting on the quality of—and taking possession of the essence of—the prior forms, and through reason's natural wisdom mastering the earth-sculpting hand. For it is true that *from the beginning to end all is gripped by the forms of the intellectual realm.* Hence does the aesthetic scientist, in sympathetic command of natural forces, say *I gaze and the figures of the material world take being as if they rise from my contemplation.*

"The second moral lesson was prescriptive: If from a loftiness of contemplation on the truth of nature comes a completeness of execution, as we have just affirmed, it follows that the expression of nature, not its mirror image, is for our aesthetic science requisite. Hence the upper artisans distill what to the human eye is shy, empowering those ideals that lie behind appearance, creating a truer drama, the apparent form of which can only exhibit lines and colors absent the common representation of a false material surface. For the Old Master said, *The human body is not contained within the limits of line.* And that statement is true for all subjects, for *there are no lines in nature; everything is solid.* The true representation of the essence of one's subject, which is to say the successful engineering of its inherent principles, occurs when the internal forces of one's clay fall into a right pattern, one in tune with the moral tone of the primal lyre, all such patterns dictated not by the rules of art but by the laws of composition, the characteristic patterns of forces inherent in constructive materials."

From time to time during these comments some of his listeners broke into murmurs of appreciation, for Protogenes was expressing the most vital tenets of the city. Familiar as were his concepts, never had the academists heard them expressed with such elegance.

Protogenes suddenly stopped and peered closely at his audience. "So important is this lesson that I drove the matter home to Gillette with a story about my own work, the *Temple of Peace*. You may recall my frustration when the viewing public continually commented on the small image of a quail which I had foolishly—and as I must admit falsely and lazily—painted in a lower corner. Visitors to the atrium kept saying that the image was so realistic that the painting, if exhibited outdoors, would surely attract a flock of real quail. It can scarcely be necessary to remind my present audience that those well-intentioned viewers were responding inappropriately to the sensation of surface. Yes, the image resembled a quail—to those who had never seen one. For those who understood the true nature of the subject—and that understanding can come only by harnessing the power of the intellect to a sensitivity to natural forces at a level that occurs only at the peak of awareness—the little image was a mockery of the real. It took me but a short time to rectify my foolishness by blotting out the troublesome image, emitting a series of comments, I am embarrassed to admit, concerning the intellectual capabilities, or lack thereof, possessed by my admiring public. Allow me to open a personal parenthesis to say that—while I am pleased that the public seems to have forgiven my misadventure in the realm of the barbarian—I continue to flatter myself that my all-too-public outburst cost me the prize that year to Apelles.

"And so it goes with every practitioner of our aesthetic physics. A writer, to venture into the realm of linguistic mechanics, may represent a staircase not in terms of its surface appearance or its most obvious practical function, but as an amalgam of all of its internal forces—those emanating from its early architect and its late users—and the representation of the interplay of all them really is similar to the limner who eschews an obvious and dead reproduction of facial features and items of clothing in favor of a representation of a complex of emotions.

"Too much of the public will praise only the part of a portrait that reproduces the false representational surface of one's subject, yet before those elements which by their apparent distortion challenge the eye but by their creative powers construct walls, buildings, bridges, and, in every other way possible, extend our city, stand bewildered. And all of my comments, to bring them to a productive conclusion, recall my early cautionary: *No one thanks us for what lies beneath.*"

Again Protogenes paused to acknowledge more whispers. Then he continued: "Having established this cognitive foundation, I now began the education of Gillette in the skills of the *portraitures*. It was at this time, when presented with the limners' techniques, that Gillette began to exhibit the behavior which began to elicit our alarm and which caused us to ask Mother Rachel to join our atelier.

"Because of her resulting closeness to Gillette, her labors devoted to interpreting the actions of our ward and her understanding of the girl's needs, I ask Mother Rachel to again take over from me and narrate what happened next."

CHAPTER 17:

Imitation of Life

What, indeed, *had* happened next? That question for the assembled academists, stricken as they were with the foreboding that the security of their city's future by the savior in whom they had invested such value was falling short, was elevated to the highest rung. That Protogenes had returned full to their favor was evident now in the air of the room; that Mother Rachel had never left it—secure as had her reputation remained in that walled fortress of her achievements, not any the more invadable for her willingness to sacrifice her lifelong investigation of the *interpretive palimpsest* on the altar of the girl Gillette—was by the entire assembly never under question. Only under question, now, was the extent of the damage to the city—for damage of a serious kind did seem the message due.

Mother Rachel nodded approvingly to Protogenes as she replaced him on the dais and—again raising her hands over the audience in honor of the familiar benediction —entered without delay the stream of her predecessor's narrative. "I thank Protogenes for his kind words, and no less for his equally kind service to the city. It is my duty now to describe the appalling change that came over our young ward, the principal topic today. Protogenes has prepared my way with his description of Gillette's education in the skills of the lower artisans and the principles motivating the skills of the upper. Allow me to provide some important details about what happened during the latter course of the girl's education.

"Because Protogenes desired to reach the ambitious goals of everyone in this room, he sought to inspire in his student an understanding and enthusiasm for the critical work she was to perform for the city once she had become a master maker.

"Here, then, is how Protogenes introduced the higher studies to Gillette:

"'Your skills in the labors of the upper artisans, the limners and the Old Masters, once you have honed them to a fine thread, will serve through the centuries, without losing their transformative power, to enlarge the walls of the city and to secure it from dangerous natural forces. You will make one kind of work, then another, then another, and the variations of them all shall through their transmogrification in the penumbra create a cognitive resonance. In what order shall you create? No matter! Indeed, change the order at will. So will your labors, as master maker, resolve our difficulties, place above our city a protective over-dome, and withal give to our upper artisans the grace of pleasure, honor, and strength.'

"This charge providing a fecund foundation, Gillette's higher education proceeded with an emulation of the work of the limners. And the work of the limners, their skill in grasping the essence of the human being and infusing it into materials, thus creating in league with the skilled viewer the very presence of life, has always been the step of transition from the lower works to the higher. Because it has always been dealt with as such by the city, it was appropriate that the elevated work of these painters be of the greatest interest for professor and student.

"For this reason, Protogenes built a program of limnerial education upon a solid foundation: the words of the early Egyptian from whose writings our city takes so much nourishment, who insisted on the axiom which for the master of the form is pivot: the work of that skilled practitioner who would represent the essence of the human being is *not a portrait but a creation in which the sculptor's art has concentrated all loveliness.* Allow me to pause here in the spirit of narrative completeness: A similar position must be maintained for any material the resistance of which is subject to reduction by a master maker who would pursue a duty—seemingly miraculous to the uninitiated but to the skilled viewer a matter of material engineering

—by reaching for the archaic penumbra, and, when grasping it, producing *something more to gaze upon than the mere work produced.*"

A collective gasp arose from the academists for here was a succinct narration of the annunciation of the will of the city to Gillette; how would the girl react?

"This was a challenging call, to be sure, for an artist at any level of competence, even for one as our Gillette to whom the reliant energy for the creation of lower level life seemed less artisanal skill and more natural instinct. Yet rise to the challenge she did, or seemed to, and suggested to Protogenes her initial work in these words:

"'May I begin with the portrait of a man about whom I dreamed last night?'"

A stillness, unheard by any save those in the possession of a sensitivity of the keenest edge, seemed to arise from the collective with these words. Several of the academists who had so recently anticipatorily leaned forward now reversed their postures; others narrowed their eyes a bit and stroked their chins. One or two looked to the side as if to consult another professor, but their eyes seemed to focus not on the face of a fellow but on a window or featureless portion of a wall.

Mother Rachel, who either remained uncooled by the sudden chill or determined to ignore it, continued her recital: "Protogenes smiled at this, and assured the child that she might start with whatever she liked. Gillette immediately snatched a brush from the hand of her instructor and made a quick sketch of the man she had seen in her dream. Protogenes was immediately struck by the child's sure touch, her mastery of movement, and the clarity of the resulting profile, which, at a refined point of accommodation, combined an outline of the general with the specificity of the individual.

"I must pause here for a parenthesis. It was about this time that the woman—I am referring to the widow of the artist who had committed suicide after seeing the work of Gillette—arrived at our city and offered us the painting that I spoke of before. You will recall that I mentioned that we decided to secrete the work for the time being until we had determined the best way to present it to our girl. Our decision to do so proved, as you will see, fortuitous.

"To return to my narrative, over the next few weeks, Protogenes worked with Gillette on the filling of the flat drawing of her portrait with the glow of a fecundating matrix, continually urging her that to achieve more than the semblance of life, one must call down from the penumbra the fire of Prometheus. And continually he cited the words of the master to whom we owe so much: *Color, feeling, and drawing are the three essentials in art, but they count as nothing without life*. The subsequent manner of beneficial compulsion was to be predicted: when Gillette balked at yet another fine touch of the brush, a second and third and fourth round of transmutation of color, a frustrated Protogenes would rail: 'For wolves you are fine; for men you are unworthy. Look closer at your subject, that image that is in your mind, and engineer its presence onto your canvas. You must learn to marshal the full force of the *intellectual principle.*' He tapped on the girl's work several times at various places: 'It is all there, and there, and there, and yet it is not there. What is lacking? A nothing, but that nothing is everything.' When Gillette expressed frustration, Protogenes urged her on: 'Continue! Do not give up. It is not the finished work itself but the attempt to work—that attempt fused to the work—which lives forever.'"

Mother Rachel paused, and glanced at Father Cephalus. "The nature of this work of Gillette is not unknown to you. It was at this point in her training that Father Cephalus inspected the girl's progress and determined that she had not yet mastered, in terms of the interpretive palimpsest, the creation of a tenor sufficiently nuanced. It was for this reason, paired with a continuing information since obtained from us as to the girl's slow pace of progression, that Father Cephalus addressed all of you earlier this morning, questioning as he did the potency of the instruction of Protogenes.

"And it was equally in response to this work, so close to success but still lacking the germinal fire, that Protogenes urged Gillette to higher performance. The training, while rigorous, was not so different from that given to many of the academists in this room, nor from the courses those academists have given their students. One day, the frustrated girl threw down her brush and strode away from her canvas, turning on her instructor with a challenge: 'How many will get out everything that we put in?'"

These words caused an outcry in the room. Here was something unexpected, for Gillette had just expressed one of the driving forces of the great hesitation. A cloud of fierce whispering arose throughout the assembled academists. Several frowned and shook their heads.

"Everyone here is familiar, I am sure, with the linguistic penumbra possessed by those words of our ward. That vicious matrix, that interplay of principles which to the creator serves as a kind of halt, is a disease from which no person, save our few upper artisans, is immune—even, as it happens, our Gillette. However, consider that evidence of this condition only arose when the artist was necessarily compelled to create at a level higher than that with which she had previously been engaged. To represent the human being, to condense into a meaningful matrix the colorful rainbow of emotions of which that subject is composed, is a matter far different from the representation of the lesser animals. It only remains to be seen at what point Gillette reaches a firm stop. Has she reached a border the crossing of which conflicts with her nature? Or is she merely faced with the task of achieving a greater degree of self-discipline—not only in terms of her personal goals and ambitions, but also in mastery of motion, command of hand, empowering of will? Is Gillette, then, an exemplar of that condition described by the Old Master Mabuse: *The brush is not recalcitrant but the heart is weak?*"

The assembled academists pondered this question as well as the drift of Mother Rachel's narrative. Many of them seemed to vanish into their own thoughts.

"That question remains unanswered. From this day forward, Gillette began to sulk, to spend more time by herself—that is, away from the presence of Protogenes—and to exhibit in general a great degree of discontent with her duties. Her moodiness was combined with another characteristic which troubled Protogenes more: Gillette began to spend hour after hour in proximity to her developing portrait, staring at her represented man for hours at a time, dabbing here and there with her brush in an effort perhaps at perfection and perhaps—who can deny the possibility?—from compulsive frenzy. It was at this time thought prudent by her instructor to appeal to the people in this room, who have the most to lose from a failure of Gillette to fulfill her assigned mission, and it was decided by you to gain my assistance at a greater level than before."

Many of the academists nodded their heads, the vote to enlist the assistance of Mother Rachel fresh in their minds. Others, however, retained a countenance of worried thought.

"Motivated as I am by a desire to strengthen the city of science, it was but the matter of a moment for me to agree to help interpret Gillette. It was not known to you that at the time of your summons I was engaged in the study of a certain artifact, a kind of communication that had been subjected to a state of fossilization, discovered in an excavation just north of Newmarch. Given the field in which I specialize, it will perhaps be of little surprise to know that this artifact had a potential for treatment by a skilled practitioner of the art requisite to the interpretation of those dynamics peculiar to the interpretive palimpsest. This object, which I feel now free to announce to the assembled academists, is believed by some of our archaeologists to be the *primal letter*, a keystone, or even the key, to the lock of the *fecund epistolary array. . . .*"

The academists suddenly rose from their seats in a spontaneous action that seemed to suggest the alarm of a wild beast. "This is extraordinary. . . !" Father Theodorous shouted over the din. "Can the letter be read?"

Father Lysis, who had also leapt to his feet, had a related question: "The other letters, can they be nearby?"

And from a third academist: "Does the object address the *intentional conflict*?" This question in particular elicited a sympathetic cry from the academists.

It should be noted that some of the academists sat still at this revelation, their forms relating a certain measure of stolidity. These individuals gazed at one another with faces a little troubled. One academist, seemingly lost in thought, stared off above the figure of Mother Rachel. Someone close to him, if possessed of the power to observe the inner life, would have heard this: "If the words of the epistolary array are found, what shall they say and who shall pay?"

"Gentlemen!" Mother Rachel again quieted her audience. "It is far too soon to know the ramifications of this finding. We are still examining the fossil, but have little hope of deciphering the bulk of its message. To this time we have been able to extract some hundred words of text. We know that it seems to have been written by a disciple who apparently possessed knowledge of the primal forms, or claimed to. Among the words we have extracted is the phrase *the key to the hesitational lock*." Here, as Mother Rachel nodded to the academist who had asked about the *intentional conflict*, the audience erupted in a cacophony of discussion.

"We do know the letter's author intended that it be destroyed by the recipient," continued Mother Rachel. "That it was not destroyed–who knows for what reason?–is now as certain as its mystery, for what the heat of fire did not destroy, the cold hand of time has frozen in its grip." Mother Rachel paused for her audience to absorb this information, then seemed to catch a certain remembrance. "As for the other intervals of the array, perhaps they are nearby, perhaps they are not. We are proceeding gradually in the excavation."

The academists had reseated themselves but a constant murmur of excitement continued to fill the room as they bent to the side to confer in low voices with one another.

"In any event, this work of mine was brought to a temporary halt so that I could live in close proximity to our girl and interpret her behavior. It was my acquired skill in this very art I have described above, as you know, which caused you to think of me and to enlist my aid in studying the work of Gillette for any potential to fulfill its destined role. And so I did. I made my way to the atelier of Protogenes for an extended visit, I introduced myself to our Gillette, and I flatter myself to say that the girl and I, in terms of feelings of relative simpatico, seemed, as the saying goes, to 'hit it off.'"

The academists had settled back into their chairs, and had returned a great portion of their attention to the morning's principal topic, although the unsettled expressions on many faces seemed to reflect a division of mind.

"As it happens, Protogenes had a room adjacent to that of Gillette, and it was here that I was quartered.

For the next few days, Gillette and I spent a great deal of time together. I requested from her instructor not a cessation of, but a reduction to the number of hours spent in training. This allowed time for the girl and me to bond. We discussed many things, from the girl's infancy with the jackals, to her life as a young girl in the monastery, to her deliverance to our city some months ago. She seemed to be hanging on to our daily conversations as a drowning man clutches to a lifeline. It was during these conversations that I became aware of a negative element in the personality of the girl. It seemed, to put the matter bluntly, that she had lost all interest in life.

"Now, I must interrupt my narration with yet another parenthesis, for it was at this time that an event occurred which made it impossible for us to consider ever showing the painting—I am speaking of the painting of the bronze sculpture of Gillette—to its subject. It was the third day of my stay at the atelier of Protogenes that there was delivered to me a note from Father Cephalus requesting my presence at the singular house at my earliest convenience, the subject to be dealt with being one of the most urgent nature. The next day, I made my excuses to Gillette and traveled to the city to see Father Cephalus. Upon my arrival, my host shook his head at my questions, raised a hand in a bid for silence, and nodded in the direction of a hallway which we traversed.

"In two minutes we arrived at a heavy door, outfitted with an iron lock that the legislator unlatched. Father Cephalus placed a finger against his lips, bid me enter, and then bolted the door behind us. He nodded over to a corner of the room where I perceived, resting on the floor and leaning against the wall, a package wrapped securely in brown paper and twine. Of this object Father Cephalus said: 'It is the painting of the bronze sculpture of Gillette.' At this news I could only raise my eyebrows and frown, for to secure the work in such a manner—a work which, after all, we had considered a joy and a wonderful gift to pass along to its living subject—was strange.

"Father Cephalus was about to enlighten my understanding. He walked over to the package, lifted it, and began to loosen the twine. After this had been removed, he began to pull at the paper, in the matter of a minute or two freeing the painting from its covering. Father Cephalus then raised the painting high in the air and turned its face in my direction."

The strange words of Mother Rachel had upon the assembled academists a profound effect. Throughout the room there was to be heard neither whisper nor breath. The professors, nearly to a man, sat forward in their seats, their eyes glued upon the speaker as those of the condemned upon their hangman.

Mother Rachel continued. "What I saw caused me to stagger, to reach back and clutch the handle of the door to support myself against a fall." She paused and stared at her audience. "The painting had been changed. The bronze figure of Gillette was covered with a shroud."

CHAPTER 18:
A Little Girl Found

The revelation from Mother Rachel caused the academists to rise as one to their feet, all turning to their neighbors open-mouthed, unable to put their feelings into words. Father Lysis began to shake, and, holding onto the back of the chair in front of him, turned his aging body slowly to the side to request of no one single colleague in particular an explanation of a phenomenon that—to his mind—seemed inexplicable. "How could this happen?" he asked, his face a blank canvas, his eyes open wide in incomprehension. "What has happened to our little girl?"

Mother Rachel again raised her arms over the assembled academists. "Gentlemen! Gentlemen! Be seated. I will conclude my story of Gillette's education and tell you what I now propose as the best course of action for our ward."

The academists slowly took their seats, their faces none- theless troubled by the course of events turning their dream into a nightmare.

Mother Rachel began with the decision concerning the donated portrait. "No one will now fail to understand why Father Cephalus decided to secure the painting in the house of its own making. The protection of our Gillette was our first concern. As the child was already exhibiting those troubling symptoms which I have described, any decision to expose her to her dreadful portrait, cloaked as the painted sculpture had become with a cover of death, would to any disinterested observer be criminal. Furthermore, everyone will agree with the decision, for the sake of public peace and private posture, to keep the news of the portrait from everyone in this room. Once it was exposed to the light of the public mind, it would be impossible to protect Gillette."

Here again arose a whispering from the crowd. Several of the academists turned in their seats to nod to their colleagues in approval. Others slumped forward in their chairs, their down-held heads a reflection of heavy hearts.

"The donated painting, then, was transferred away from our city to its hiding place. A delegation charged with determining the cause of the mystery was sent to interview the widow who had donated the work. What did they find? She had died, taking whatever secrets she possessed to her grave. Was she a deliberate agent in avenging the death of her husband? It seems likely. Perhaps her early and interrupted education in the fine arts had by some odd pathway led her to a command of oils idiosyncratic, allowing her to engineer their forces in a way which even for our Old Masters remains, one presumes, undiscovered. In any event, we shall never know. Any productive results from a search of her house were obviated by the fact that she, or someone, had burned all of her notes along with those of her husband. And so our search for the true story behind the painting came to an end.

"More important work was, of course, to be done. Less compelling to our city was an explanation of events of the past than a productive engineering of principles still in play. And so, my work having been completed with Father Cephalus, I returned to the atelier of Protogenes. To my distress I discovered that our poor girl had been expressing a devotion to her painting at an even deeper level than before. Hour after hour she would sit before her man's portrait. She would move only reluctantly from her room to work with Protogenes; her labors before the easel were lackluster; her engagement with her instructor was distracted. It took me but a day or two to see that a fundamental change for the worse had come over her. I was especially disturbed by the fact that she had difficulty rising early and during the day she seemed sleepy.

"Given the girl's continual expressions of sleeplessness, it occurred to me that she was spending the nights tending to her portrait. Consequently I asked Protogenes for the following service: The next day I would take Gillette onto the nearby moor for a refreshing break. During our absence he was to drill an observational hole in the wall connecting Gillette's room with my own. The potency of this channel would be facilitated by the happy presence of a large painting on the wall dividing our rooms, the well-known portrait of Catherine Lescault. The eyes of this painting had been so worn away by time that a watchful observer, facilitated by the darkness of a night-filled room, would be able to observe from their obverse what was happening in the room beyond.

"The deed was done. That evening we retired to our rooms. I slept for an hour or two, then awoke fresh to my mission. Creeping as quietly as I could to the adjoining wall, and making sure that no light came from my side of the observational channel, I pulled aside the cover to see what was transpiring in the adjacent room."

Mother Rachel paused to assess the state of her audience. It would come as little surprise that the academists sat transfixed, mouths agape, eyes wide, hands clutched to the sides of their seats, every mind dumbfounded at the tale they were being told.

Mother Rachel narrowed her eyes. "It was as I had supposed." A collective gasp came from the room. "Our Gillette was sitting in a chair that she had placed before her painting. She sat transfixed, a Pygmalion before her living Galatea, her eyes centered on those of the man she had made. The light of a nearby candle, dim enough to avoid casting beneath the occupant's closed and locked door a confessionary flicker, offered illumination sufficient for the young girl to adore her creation.

"Secreted in my dark observational spot, I watched the girl commune with her painting in this manner for nearly an hour. It was then that I heard it." Mother Rachel paused. She stared soberly around at the assembled academists, from whom could be heard, for those possessed of the greater sensitivity, a disturbed fluttering. "A low, almost imperceptible male voice began to be emanate from the painting. I saw Gillette respond by leaning in closer to her work. She asked the creature to repeat his words. A few seconds passed, and I leaned closer to the wall. Then I heard the voice again, mouthing the following words in a halting, exaggerated enunciation: '*Porbus . . . is . . . I.*'"

The academists at once emitted a collective gasp, then as quickly fell back into silence, their eyes fixed on the speaker.

"To this the girl nodded her head slowly, in an understanding way," continued Mother Rachel. "She leaned in as if to kiss the face of her beloved and then spoke her own words, in mimicry of the man's form of speaking clearly and distinctly: '*Darling . . . come . . .*

forth . . . from . . . the . . . frame.' Receiving no response from her audience, she quietly repeated her invitation two more times, pausing patiently for a minute or so between each iteration. I pressed my ear tightly against the wall to catch every word of the man's reply. When at last they came, they sounded weak and halting, as if each word were torn from a frozen page: '*I . . . did . . . you . . . wrong. I . . . did . . . you . . . wrong. I must . . . rectify.*' In response to these words, Gillette's eyes widened a little, and, after some time in which she seemed devoted to thought, she spoke again: '*Come to me . . . come forth from the frame . . . I forgive you . . . I will help you.*'

"Peering through the darkness as I was, it seemed to me as if the oils of the portrait were vibrating slightly from their canvas, or perhaps such movement was but an illusion cast by the flickering candle. I could not tell from watching Gillette whether she shared my perception. I began to hear what seemed to be the breath of struggle from the painting, a very gasping for the energy requisite to power the creature's will. At last I heard these words emanate from the painting: '*Come close, Gillette.*' I frowned as I watched our girl lean in close again to her creation and listen intently to what she was told—for I could not hear these words, so much quieter as they were than the previous ones. But I could see the girl nod slowly, as if in understanding.

"At last she responded. 'I will do so.'

"What was this, that the created being commanded? As much as I tried to hear, it remained a mystery—but one that, as you shall see, was only too soon to be resolved. Shortly I heard what was to be the final communication that night. From the painting came these faint words: '*Tomorrow . . . tomorrow . . . tomorrow . . .*'

"Then all was silence. Despite the girl's attempts to communicate again with her creation, the painting remained stubbornly quiet. Gillette sat before her painting for another half hour, leaned forward to give it a kiss, and then, snuffing out the flame of her candle, retired to bed."

The academists sat in wonder at this story. "All of this happening to our poor little girl," said Father Lysis, shaking his head and glancing around at no one no particular. "What have we done?" None of the others responded, each seemingly lost in private thoughts. On each face was the countenance of one who had been informed by a reputable scientist that the Moon would shortly crash into the Earth.

Mother Rachel paused to collect her thoughts. "And so retired us all. My first thought was to waken Protogenes, remove the girl at once from her room with its monstrous creation, and preserve her from what could only result in a tragic end. Then I thought better of the plan: Would this sudden shock of such a procedure push the girl over the edge? I thought it likely. Salvation could wait for the purifying light of day. With this thought I went to bed, tossed and turned with the genie of my conscience for an hour, and finally fell asleep.

"And so I arrive at the final chapter of my story. The next morning, after I had informed Protogenes of the transpirations of the night, we decided at once to pursue the course I had considered. We therefore went to the door of Gillette's bedroom and knocked quickly, demanding that she rise and unlock her door. And the response? Nothing.

"Alarmed, we continued knocking, louder and louder, and, still receiving no response, and hearing no noise from the other side of the door, determined to knock down the object which prohibited our mission. Protogenes threw himself against the door once, twice, three times. We heard a cracking, a larger cracking still, and then a final crash as the old wooden door fell before us.

"We rushed into the room and encountered . . . what? An emptiness. Gillette had vanished. We turned to look at the painting, which appeared to be unchanged. The eyes of the man in the portrait—an individual named Porbus, as he had identified himself—stared out at us as if nothing unusual had occurred the previous night. In the entire room there was only one living thing: Upon the sill of the window, which had been left open, a mockingbird sat and emitted for our edification his catalog of songs. As he performed this array, he hopped about on the sill, flew out the window, seemingly to flee our presence, only to return and continue his performance.

"Protogenes and I at first stood silent, absorbing this scene. At last the instructor spoke, walking to the window and peering out at the marsh lands, vocalizing his conclusion: 'She has fled across the moors.' I nodded in agreement, and the two of us took each other's counsel on the best response. We agreed upon three things: First, that a search party consisting of the entire staff of the atelier must be dispatched at once. Second, that the upper artisans must be informed of the event, and their counsel obtained. Third, that news of the flight—panic-inducing as it would be—must not travel beyond the atelier. It would be soon enough, we reasoned, for the news to be distributed to the academists after the search had completed."

With those words, Mother Rachel looked directly at Father Cephalus, who remained in his posture of defiance, seated at the back of the room. "Whether our decisions were correct, we leave it to others to assess. Our prudence, however, is a quality which, I believe, cannot be challenged.

"And so the staff of the atelier fanned out over the moors, seeking the lost girl. The entire day and the following night as well were spent combing the forest, in conjunction with representatives from the upper artisans. The next morning, Protogenes suddenly started, stared intently into the marsh behind the atelier, and motioned for me to join him at his vantage point. 'Look,' he said. 'Over there . . . look just there–' He pointed more vigorously. 'In the field very near the tall trees.'

"I performed my own reconnoiter and was myself startled to see a small figure, limping toward the atelier, falling suddenly to its knees, then rising and walking again toward us. 'Could it be–'

"Protogenes did not speak further. He leapt from the window and bounded across the field. Not a quarter of an hour had passed before he had returned to the atelier carrying in his arms our little girl, for whom we immediately sent for nurse and doctor. We set the girl to bed and treated her scratches and bruises. We listened to her broken words, as, through her delirium–she was half awake and half unconscious–she related the tale of how she had followed the mockingbird to the forest, how the jackal had taken her to the stone mansion, and how she had discovered the hidden painting: the very story Protogenes has related to everyone in this room."

The academists rose to their feet and all began speaking at once, nearly all frantic to express their indignation at what had transpired. "We were wrong, gentlemen," said Father Lysis, and the others around him nodded vigorously in agreement. "Little Gillette cannot only not help us, but we have done a terrible thing to her." He shook his head sadly and then turned to the speaker. "Mother Rachel! No more of this! Remove our girl from the atelier and take her to a quiet place, a place of sunshine, where a little girl should grow into a young woman." The other academists expressed their concordance in bold voices, and so the communication continued until Mother Rachel held up her hands to bring them all to silence.

"Gentlemen! Gentlemen! Please be seated. Everything has been taken care of. Protogenes and I anticipated your reaction, as sure of it, indeed, as we were unsure of the same prior to the full elucidation of the facts. Be seated."

The academists complied, their collective voice of alarm reducing gradually in intensity.

Mother Rachel spoke again. "Gentlemen, our city's experiment with Gillette has come to an end. Even as I speak, our ward is being escorted by guard to a place which is just as you say: one where a young girl can grow up absent the contrivances peculiar to our city's mechanics. Just as important, the dreadful painting of the man Porbus is also being removed from our city—it is being taken by our constable to a location unspecified, unmarked, where a monster that should never have been granted life shall be destroyed by fire."

Mother Rachel paused. "Let us hope for the best for our Gillette. Adjusting to a new life will be difficult for her. Imagine her feeling of loss, given that her portrait of Porbus has been taken from her. And how will the girl adjust to a quiet life absent all the attention she has received in her short years?"

Father Lysis interrupted: "A monastery, similar in nature to the one where she was living before—that would be all right." The academists began to emit a surprised murmur. "I never thought I would consider such an option. But we have to think of what is best for Gillette, not what is in the city's interests."

At this idea, Mother Rachel demurred. "It is best not to consider options in this room. It is important that the whereabouts of Gillette remain secret so she can mature without the warping whirl of the sacred rage." She paused and reset herself. "It remains, gentlemen, for us to consider the next step in the city's progress, our experiment with Gillette having failed. And for this I ask Father Cephalus to rise and come to the dais."

And Father Cephalus was about to do just that when he was interrupted by a crashing noise at the back of the room. The academists turned to the back door, through which rushed a messenger, wild in eye and countenance, shouting harshly with a hoarse voice: "Mother Rachel! Protogenes! You must come at once." The messenger stooped and breathed heavily to recover his strength. He finally gasped: "There was an attack."

Protogenes leapt to his feet. "The guard with Gillette?" The academists rose and howled with anguish.

"No." The messenger looked around at the assembled faces. "The constable with the painting. Someone has attacked him. He's dead."

CHAPTER 19:

Evening Song

Protogenes sat exhausted at the edge of the cliff overlooking the canyon, feeling the chill of a mist rising from the river below, and watched two men struggle toward him from the lower portion of the hill. Who were they? One of them, crowned by a trim shock of white hair, stopped on occasion, stood, and cupped his hands around his mouth. "Pro . . . to . . . gen . . . es!" he shouted, lending to each syllable the exaggerated enunciation of a man appealing to a distant ear. "Where . . . is . . . our . . . little . . . girl?"

The man's words echoed faintly against the shale of the canyon before their thin tones died into silence. As if expecting a response, the two men bowed their heads in concentration, cupped their ears and waited.

Protogenes was too tired to respond. His mind numbed by shock, his breath still heavy from recent exertions, he watched with dull eyes the men resume their climb upward. For older gentlemen, he reflected dumbly, they were exhibiting a commendable measure of spryness. As they closed in, their features sharpening into visibility, Protogenes recognized Fathers Lysis and Theodorous. In a few minutes they were upon him, staring wide-eyed, their faces red with exertion. Open mouthed, they shifted their gaze from Protogenes, to the canyon, to the surrounding barrenness.

Father Theodorous finally caught his breath. "Where is our little girl?" he asked in a whining voice.

Father Lysis followed up with his own query: "Protogenes, tell us, where is our Gillette?" Both men appeared a breath away from crying.

Their questions received a response only slightly shy of mute: Protogenes nodded soberly toward the canyon below. An expression of shock came over both faces of the new arrivals, as they looked back and forth from the canyon to Protogenes.

"Down *there*?" asked Father Lysis. He stared at the steep cliffs as if they were the outcroppings of another world.

As they absorbed this news, both men knelt on the rocky terrain, their heads held in their hands. And then this followed shortly from Father Lysis: "What happened?"

Protogenes, his own breath gradually subsiding into a normal rhythm, reached out and gently held the shoulder of Father Lysis, as if to calm him. The instructor paused to consider, then said finally: "It was the man from the painting. The portrait Gillette had painted, of a man who apparently called himself Porbus." He looked at Fathers Lysis and Theodorous, and slowly shook his head. "We had been too late in arranging for the burning of the painting. Somehow, it seems, midway in the journey to the field of destruction, Porbus came alive, stepped forth from the frame, and attacked the constable."

Fathers Lysis and Theodorous gasped.

"We found the constable near death, a firearm still in his hands. In the back of his wagon was the canvas of Gillette's painting—now absent its subject. We tried to get the wounded man back to the city for treatment, but he died on the way. Before he died, he was able to communicate what had transpired."

Father Theodorous looked away. "Firearms . . . violence . . . death. . . ." He shook his head in incomprehension. He looked back at Protogenes. "Where is the monster now? And Gillette?"

"I shall tell you. It did not take Porbus long to divine the location of the girl and her guards, hold his fire until the latter were asleep, then remove his prey from their hands. On the way out of the camp, Porbus was wounded, but was able to continue on with his captive. And so it was that he brought our girl to this isolated area, where he felt they could evade detection. It was here that I found them."

Protogenes paused to collect his thoughts. Then he continued in a more subdued voice. "Porbus was near death. He was lying beneath a limb not far from here, and when I found him I was disturbed to see that Gillette was not with him. When I asked her whereabouts, he gestured with his hand up to the rocky area where we are now. He could hardly speak, but he was able to provide this parting message for his paramour: 'Tell her I shall live as a memory on her palette; tell her that my doing so shall be life for me afterward.' Seeing that he was near death, but caring more for the safety of our girl, I was about to leave him to expire, when, to my alarm, he grabbed my arm with a strong grip. '*Protogenes!*' he said. '*Wait.* One thing more.' He paused to catch his breath, nearly the last of which he would ever have. 'Destroy the painting.' I thought his words referred to that empty canvas which had so recently been his home and cradle, and of that work's early destruction I was about to assure him, when he added a line that sent my thoughts in quite another direction. 'Do not allow the statue to step forth.' I frowned as I realized he was referring to that dreadful work, secured in its own stone mansion, of the shrouded bronze statue of Gillette. '*Protogenes!* Destroy the painting before the statue steps forth.'

"Then the monster expired."

Fathers Theodorous and Lysis, open-mouthed, seemed to be barely capable of speaking. The former finally uttered these few weak words: "And Gillette . . . what happened to her?"

Protogenes nodded in anticipation of the question. "I immediately abandoned the corpse of Porbus, making my way as quickly as I could up to this rocky spot. I easily divined that the girl, having lost her imagined lover, was in equal measure eager to lose her connection with those people who had torn him from her side and who were now responsible for his demise. Even so, I determined to come to this spot, to engage the girl in communication, and to assure her not only of our regard for her safety and happiness, but of our willingness to work with her to position her in a far different place where she could pursue the kind of life she wanted."

The two listeners nodded.

"And so I made my way to this rocky bluff. I looked behind one outcropping after another, and was about to cry out in despair of my mission, when I suddenly saw a movement here, at the spot where I am sitting. Peering closely, I could see the outline of Gillette. I moved at once toward this spot as quickly as I could, while tempering my movement to avoid causing alarm to the girl. And I was but twenty feet away, half hidden by the outcropping you see to your left, and just about to open my mouth in a gentle greeting, when I was interrupted by the speech of the girl.

"'*Protogenes!*' She said in a clear voice, looking suddenly in my direction. '*Stop!*' Of course I did so, not knowing what the girl intended. I could only raise my hand in a tribute and utter my far weaker words that I wanted to help her and that we would do whatever we could do. And I was about to provide her with the same sentiments I had just expressed to you when she interrupted me with these words: 'Everything is over. It is time for me to go.' Then, to my alarm, I saw her walk over to the small ledge you can see just before us, overlooking as it does the deep canyon below. I immediately surmised that she was determined to throw herself from the cliff and I moved, perhaps too quickly—how can we ever know?—toward her.

"'Wait, Gillette,' I implored, and I slipped forward to grasp hold of her when she raised her hands toward me and shouted: *'Stop, Protogenes! My life is over!'*

"It was then that Gillette flung herself from the ledge, and it was only by an equally quick movement that I was able to grasp her wrist as she fell away. I dropped to the ground and held her dangling over the edge, determined to do everything I could to pull her back up. 'Gillette,' I cried. 'Come to me.' As I pulled on her arm, I peered over the edge of the cliff and stared into her face, her eyes wide not with terror, as mine surely would have been, but with grey resignation.

"Then she said: 'Protogenes, let me go.' She stared into my eyes and her words came forth like a prayer: 'Return me to life.'

"I gritted my teeth and did my best, despite her entreaties, to pull the girl to safety, but she refused to assist in her own behalf. With growing horror, I felt her wrist gradually slipping through my hand. It was but a moment later that I cried out in despair—for now I felt only emptiness. I looked downward and watched Gillette fall to the canyon below."

At this news Fathers Lysis and Theodorous stood and raised their hands skyward, giving voice to their own despair with lamentations, with sounds that could not be rendered for any observer in any but the mysteries of the human heart, into the crude shapes of the spoken word untranslatable. And so the three mourners remained in their place of death, overlooking that terrain into which Gillette had disappeared, steeped in their sorrow as dusk fell over the canyon.

Anyone traveling down the road by that lonely spot as the shadow of evening crept over the sand and stone towers would have seen three figures, clustered together at the edge of the cliff, staring at the darkening waters below, silent in their thoughts as over their heads the stars began to announce their arrival with shy twinklings.

It so happened, however, that not everyone was sitting so quietly. Back in the city, only a short time had elapsed since the shroud of night had fallen when there arose in sympathy with the darkness, over waters subsiding into the stillness of a melancholy sleep, a lyric. The verse came in the form of a familiar man's voice, and so charming it was to hear, accompanied as it was by the melancholy tones of a guitar, that people in their homes stopped their activities to listen.

This evensong was interrupted, but only for those close enough to hear, by the staccato patterns of a woman's steps. A shrouded figure, pulling her cloak about her against the evening's cold breath, was walking beside the waters to our musician. At the arrival of his audience, the man stopped singing and resorted to strumming his instrument at a lower volume. He glanced over at the woman, and, greeting her with a smile of melancholy, uttered these words: "The *darling interpreter*. Have you come at last, the distinguished one?"

The woman adopted a stolid expression, peering sidelong at her interlocutor. Then she glanced at the nearby veranda. "Where is your paramour?"

"Engaged with her art."

The woman invested a pause. "My work is done. I am leaving the city."

But just as the woman turned to go, the man nodded quickly toward the sky. "Look," he said, smiling slyly. He repeated his gesture. "Look just there."

When the woman peered into the inky dome she saw exactly what everyone else in the city would have seen, had they looked in the same spot and had they possessed her level of perception. What else could it be but two twinkling stars?

The man returned to the strumming of his guitar as, far overhead, the two stars seemed to revolve merrily around each other, dancing to a symphony only they could hear. "Stop and listen," said the man. "Can you hear? They are whispering a love that lies hidden in the depths of their hearts. If only we could invest some meaning in what they say! Wouldn't that be valuable?"

PART 3:

Art

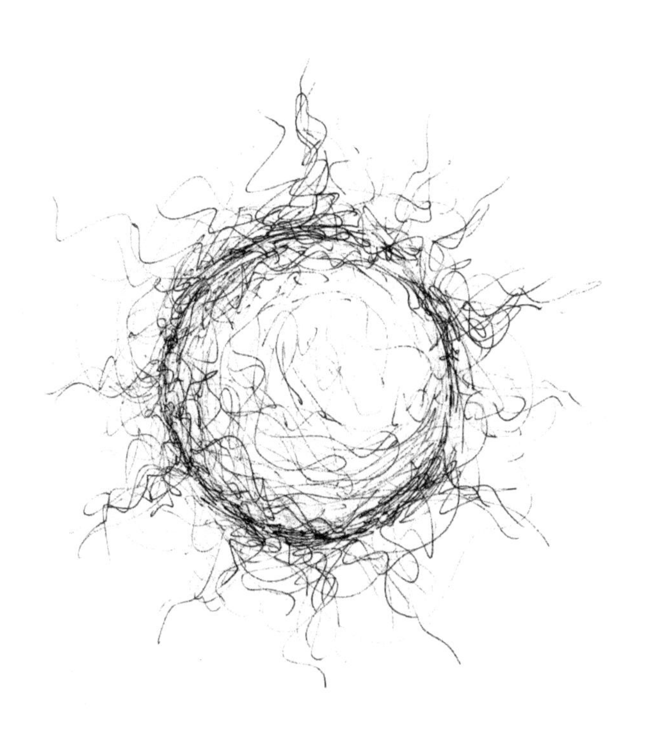

CHAPTER 20:

Christmas Eve

We had gathered round the fireside that Christmas Eve, the occasion being our academy's annual holiday fest; and it would be no large exaggeration to state that our preceding supper—its array of New England treats an echo triumphant of our pedagogical tradition—had established for our spirits an easy camaraderie. Suitable to the occasion as it was, our conviviality was enlivened by the many seasonal accoutrements: from the old stone fireplace flickered cheerful flames; from the worn brick hearth emanated a soothing warmth; from the mantelpiece height and its candles, settled in their magisterial bronze extravagances, flew forth into the room a chorus of fairy emissaries, touching lightly first upon the rug, hopping brightly then upon the chair, dancing here, there, upon the faded paper of the walls and the creaking frames of the windows, only to vanish without a trace into the crisp night air beyond, leaving behind the melancholy sighs of the windowpanes and a suggestion of distant worlds rising in faint aroma from the room's shadowed corners.

It was just this sentimental milieu that infused as a scent of winter pine each nook and cranny of our souls—and how generative it all was of our creative spirits! Little wonder we began to tell stories—and tales we told aplenty. Alexander, Newmarch born, uttered a frightening saga of a mansion haunted by the ghost of a painter who had—of a sudden and to the consternation of the old home's residents—walked straight out of his portrait and into the streets and homes of town. Beatrice, the winner of honors in physics and chemistry, had brought to the evening's fest a story of a young lady—someone not unlike the tale's author—who had into her diary written pages of bewildering runes, overwritten with mystic symbols, salted here and there with ancient hieroglyphs—a diary which for the many who attempted its decipher offered naught but senseless palimpsest. And before I forget—allow me to mention the offering of Nathan, a musician well regarded among his fellows, who, to the tune of his guitar, sang us the charming story of young lovers crossed by fateful vagaries, victims if you will of a saga all their own, worshippers of the stars who had in forgotten gods found celestial embrace.

Stories, then, and poems, too, and more: visions, drawings, dances, paintings—for creation triumphs when merrymaking fills the atelier. To reason and its sober visage no one made appeal: We welcomed the fruits of our creation as nature's own, accepted everything for its own sake, the necks of the artists saved by the spirit of the season from the critic's bloody axe.

After a time on that crisp New England night, as the frame of the country house creaked and yawned and settled in its moonlit slumber, the stories and tales and mimes and songs came to an end. Which event, it happened, was but the instigator for a new round of egg nog—and it was no longer than the time it takes for the eye to catch the tail of a mouse before we students turned our thoughts to a topic fresh—that of the relative merits of those forms of art which over the preceding year had been the focus of our studies.

"Which art then," Douglas asked, "is the finest?"

This question was greeted with an outburst of peculiar blend. A cognitive chef blessed with a higher sensibility might in the boldness of the general cry identify a dash of perverse merriment, a sprig of easy cynicism, a generous quantity of wary anticipation—a recipe, sweet as it is for youth, for age is but suggestion of a treat more easily baked than digested.

Answers, true, abounded. "The theater offers so much more than any other form," proffered Lily, who had devoted a year of work to rendering Lady Macbeth. "The stage enfolds and magnifies each element of the soul. No other form can transport the mind through time and space to distant lands, only to isolate and illuminate those universals which through the warp and woof of the human frame offer the finest weave."

To this elegance, however, was not granted universal assent. Giorgio, for one, began to wag his finger before the young lady had finished. "Not so! Not so!"

And more chimed in: Theater, said Michael, was fine for the entertainment of an evening but could not hold a candle to the novel, so revered for its flexibility; music, said another to the contrary, was simply of superior merit to every art—save, of course, the dance. So continued the discussion, fueled by holiday spirits into a state of furious scholarly intensity.

Failing to reach consensus on the topic of their dialogue, and sensitive to a general sympathy that the question was one that could not for the evening's success remain but cipher, the students appealed to their resident Socrates, the one individual at the academy who through the years had proven that in matters of the aesthetic it was possible to reveal truth, or at least to cast upon a close impression of the Ideal a bright beam. And the beam so cast was deep as well as broad, for the *commanding principle* in the present case arose, so the students believed, from proximity not to an isolated flame of the sacred fire but to its rage entire. The gentleman now called forth, by virtue of his years dedicated to the arts in full embrace, could for any scholar lay claim to a level of insight achieved by the refined engineering of the principles enlivening an impressive array of forms—those very insights inspired by an intense level of interest maintained by effort concentrated, tireless, and sure by steady hand.

This new Socrates, as Providence would have it, was none other than our evening's host—Dr Jean-Antoine Houdon. In their wise estimation of the professor, the students had relied on observation and reputation. As for the latter, perhaps it need not be overemphasized—indeed it is the counsel of respect both professional and humanistic that the topic need be mentioned only in passing for the benefit of those new to the field—that the professor having achieved for his veneration of a past far greater in extent than his mortal middle years a reputation as the *intelligible paradigm*, the members of the academy had by a common and unstated agreement excused what for all the world was a veneer of the antique that had settled upon the gentleman's views, the essence of that very penumbra recalling to the minds of his colleagues something akin to a velvety rub impressed by time upon the surface of an old clock, visible to the eye only when viewed at a delicate incline.

It was this revered timepiece, if I may put it, who because he was for the moment absent from the parlor became for the students the target of a general call. "Dr Houdon!" chimed Patricia, her peers offering appreciative echoes. "Dr Houdon! Where are you? Come forth!"

Come forth he did, but not before the passage of a bit of time characterized by a general confusion, throughout the course of which was conducted a hunt. The professor, it was discovered, had secured himself in his den to toil at a ragged rag of writing, an item of some cognitive subtlety having occurred to him in the course of the evening.

Blinking in the brighter light of the parlor, nodding a bit to one and all in a congenial manner which to those who knew him was characteristic and anticipated, the master appeared once more in the midst of our celebratory affair. He strode with some hesitation, his legs a bit unsteady from their master's extended time of sitting and pondering, his eyes opening a bit wider in response to the eagerness with which he was greeted, to that area before the fire where the scholars had engaged in their splendors creative and blunders critical.

At last he stood before us, lowering his visage a bit at our prostrate figures, adopting a professorial look solicitous, curious, and—if my own ingenuous eye at that time had achieved any degree at all of mature discernment—amused. The fellow's eyes darted to this student and that, the broadness of his visual address testament to his even-handed treatment of the nascent talents before him. "And what," he submitted, "is the question of the evening?"

It was not long in coming. "What," raised the general cry, "is of all art forms the greatest?"

Houdon pursed his lips, narrowed his eyes and elevated them a bit as he gave our artless question some thought. He rocked a bit on his heels, placed his hands behind his back, tilted his head to one side, nodded as if granting his approval to some early response—not one of us had uttered a peep—and then bowed his head. There followed a silence of some time, our professor frozen in his attitude of prayer, during which extent I believe no one could help but reflect on the display before us of a cognitive drama, its dialogue, its authorial intrusion, its very structure, masked by nature but revealed by a common sympathy, as the professor appeared to rifle through shelves of accumulated wisdom.

At last Houdon gave a quick nod. His gaze lifted from its supine reflection and darted a few times about the room, resting first on a student by the fire, then on another by the cozy couch, and then on yet another—perhaps dozed off—on the fluffy rug, as if he had noticed all of us for the first time. At last he stated: "It is a question worth asking. Indeed, it has been asked time and again through the ages. Who can forget the days of long ago when poetry, for example, was established on the highest mount while music—at least, that music that inspires in the hearts of its listeners anything less than loyal dedication to society and nation—was denigrated, even banished?"

Not anticipating a response, Houdon lowered his eyebrows and again pursed his lips, rocking quickly on his heels. "In my younger days, I would have answered your question by examining the nature of the principles inherent in the constructive materials native to each medium," he proffered. His visage darkened a bit, his thoughts perhaps torn between the forces of reason and illumination, and his eyeglasses glinted in a candle's reflected light. "I would have asked, for example, which constructive materials are most resistant to the infusion of energy from the human will? Which materials are most robust, hence responding to infusion with a vibrancy—a productive resonance rather than a shattering?"

Many of the students nodded in understanding. The professor shook his head slightly and raised a hand in a gesture dismissive of his previous thinking. "Ah! Constructive materials, restrictive hooks, formal components, and all of those techniques of exploitation utilized by the most talented among us—what were these but hints of the true dynamics that occur in the creative process? But examine these hints I did, and in my examination identified first one medium, then another, then another, as possibly the one that offered to maker and seeker from the aesthetic grail the strongest draught. Hence passed before my assessment poetry, drama, dance—all seemed to lay equal claims to the finer lay of the creative shuttle."

Here the professor paused and appeared to lose himself in thought as he turned to the implements beside the hearth. His brow furrowed, and it was impossible to tell if he was grappling with our common intellectual conundrum or with the practical challenge of the evening fire, the logs of which he began to prod with a poker, causing sparks to fly into the chimney. As the flames renewed their furious dance, the fire began to provide a new and welcome warmth. Houdon replaced the poker in its rack, and, turning again to our group, began to pace in small steps as he rejoined his topic.

"Painting." He stated the word as a dagger thrust, stopping in his tracks and fixing his eyes on a student as a scientist might pin an insect. "Its canvas authentic, its material robust, its patterns of exploitation a rainbow of colors, shades, designs. Who can deny that to the throne of Apollo the art of the easel possesses the mightiest claim?" An appreciative gasp arose from our group, and one or two students began to nod vigorously. Painting, being the discipline of greatest study, was the clear favorite.

"Of course," spoke one young man quietly to no one in particular, his bearded head nodding rapidly as he adjusted his glasses with a poke. "*Sans* question."

Houdon, however, seemed to ignore his audience's responses. He began to pace again and turned swiftly to peer at the young man who had uttered agreement, his eyes the thrust of an academic dagger. He then issued a demurral: "But it was not so." Another gasp arose from the crowd, and the young man who had spoken in such an imprudent fashion widened his eyes, staring at the professor as if he had practiced upon his scholastic flock a vulgar stage joke.

The professor placed his hands behind his back, nodded quickly in a gesture of certainty, and made a second pronouncement: "The novel." A sigh passed through the students as a breeze-borne melody from an Aeolian harp over flower-scented meadows. Here, then, was the truth, for Houdon had achieved a kind of reputation, in his early years at the academy, for his investigations into the cranks and pulleys of the narrative machine.

Houdon seemed to withdraw into himself as he recited the novelistic claim to the laurel of the muses. He spoke as if he were repeating the words of some teacher unseen: "A canvas which is time itself; a material of the toughest fiber and the finest weave; a continuing alternation, in the hands of its masters, of fertile picture and fecund scene: What other medium, to recall the assessment of the Master, offers to its minions' hands a substance so high along the incline of elasticity?"

Applause came from a good number of the students, the novel being a favorite of some. Just as several of us began to cheer in triumph—the optimism of the young breast being never for the real world meet, Houdon closed his eyes, tilted his head, and raised his hand in caution. Again came a disheartening assessment: "It was not to be." The crowd hushed. All eyes were on the legislator as he nodded again, this time, it was apparent, in recognition of a truth the certainty of which could not be denied: The time had arrived for a pronouncement true and appropriate. Houdon spread his feet a bit, planted himself firmly, and raised an index finger in the universal gesture of the teacher presenting to his followers the greatest of profundities. "I shall tell you now what I finally discovered."

The students hushed and leaned forward, all eyes on the scholar. He furrowed his brow and passed his gaze about the assembled group. Then from the Olympian height came forth his decision:

"The greatest form of art is the sculpture."

CHAPTER 21:

Smoldering Embers

Neither sigh nor cheer, nor applause nor groan, came forth at first from the assemblage, for indeed the respectable response to Professor Houdon's pronouncement—as disturbing as it was unexpected—was nothing short of a roaring silence. It would take no more than a minute to understand the reason for what for all intents and purposes seemed to be a kind of universal shock. For the fact was, not one of the students had pursued what the professor pronounced the medium of greatest vision.

After the shock had subsided, there arose a general cry of disbelief. The students looked about at one another open-mouthed, as if the professor had announced that he had determined to switch his focus from art to sports history. "Surely it is painting that is the greatest," said one student to no one in particular, and those words sparked an aura of common acceptance that the professor's pronouncement had failed to inspire.

An equilibrium of discontent having been gradually established about the assembled scholars, it remained for one student—Barbara was by general assent designate—to challenge the decision. "Dr Houdon," she began. "Surely the plastic art of figure and form, revered as it was for centuries by the ancient Greeks, copied in its physical majesty by the Romans, transformed into a virtual pathway of thought to the Divine in the Middle Ages, and in our present day transmogrified into charming assemblage and sparkling of the found, has in terms of its reputation achieved eminence undoubted. However, by what reasonable analysis can your favored form lay claim to the crown? Has it not arrived at a present state which is, as it were, a dead end, the reputation of its stone and clay fossilized in the antique pantheon but in the arena of our own day resigned, its wellspring dry, its power of procreation impotent, its command of the mechanism essential to the living art sacrificed to the eroding power of time?"

Throughout this speech many students had nodded their heads in silent agreement. For his part, Houdon listened closely to the scholarly challenge, lowered his eyebrows and pursed his lips in his characteristic mode of thought, and began to pace slowly back and forth as he considered the proffered ideas. At last the master turned, and having digested the challenge from the young malapert, defended his decision in terms both seasoned and lucid. "I have the sense, one not unanticipated, that the art of painting has, for the great majority of you, the favored position." The professor paused, lowered his head in a semblance of sobriety, and cast a sly gaze about the collected students. Indeed, a good many were sitting with hurt expressions, some with their arms folded. He continued: "Far be it from me to cast upon this evening's festivities, saving the greatest necessity, a sober shroud. And indeed, I readily admit that all of you have had, from my own lectures over the course of these years, support for your painterly position more than sufficient." Houdon paused. "Yet there is more to consider. The passage of time brings in its wake something more than the erosion of the powers of the sculptor of yore; it provides as well a unique, even idiosyncratic, perspective for anyone who takes due note."

Houdon paused. "And the fact of the matter is this: Earlier this evening as I was gazing into the fire and listening to your charming stories, I was struck at once by an unusual insight which, I believe, is the fruit of that very seasoned perspective to which I have referred. It was the power of this insight which compelled my departure from the evening's celebration, my duty to my conscience drawing me into my cloistered den where I could most conveniently access my work. As for the work so accessed, I shall here expound a little on it, instigator as it is of our current discussion.

"Most of you have heard a rumor that for the past ten years I have been working on a manuscript, a kind of diary or record or history, if you will—although I believe that, upon its release some may insist on its more appropriate residence in the haunted hall of fiction, which attempts to distill into the material of written text certain principles which, oddly, every human being perceives without in the least being able to render. And it was my evening's reminisces of that very manuscript—fired by—who knows?—perhaps some items of narration in one or more of your appealing stories—which seemed to proffer to my consciousness a sudden lucid image. It was this very lucid image, for its part, which compelled my conclusion regarding the question which by some unexpected quirk of fortune you posed to me upon my return to this parlor. All of which is to say that I would be less than honest if I were to make any such assessment other than this one—simple and bold and rude as it is in form and for its purpose, I confess, inadequate: The material resistance of stone holds an eidetic image more securely than oils."

At this pronouncement a general rush of disbelief could again be discerned emanating from the audience. Despite the assurances from their professor that his assessment came from the warp of age rather than the woof of outrage, the students nearly to a person insisted on an explanation of what had been provided only with the support of a substance Platonic and form unapproachable.

Houdon raised a Socratic finger and brought the disturbance to a hush by holding his other hand palm down in a gesture of seeming benediction. To the hushed gathering he offered this defense: "Consider nature—is its manner not curve within curve? In all of the world do you ever see a line? The answer is no; everything in the world is solid. Surely what we envision with the eye, indeed what from our eye's vision is impressed upon our mind as image, results not from the drawing of the hand of a master but rather from the peculiar effect of the cast of the light of day upon the material of earth. Hence the assertion from him to whom we owe so much: *Nature's way is a succession of curve within curve.* The distribution of light alone gives to a body the appearance by which we know it. Hence, what can the painter do when drawing but disengage the rendered object from its setting, and in so doing, rendering for the world a falsehood? And consider the converse: Who can better represent the valid forms than the sculptor with his rounded materials, their dimensions for the signification—even the elucidation—of truth most suited?"

At this the students turned to one another and began to murmur. Our professor, pausing in his speech at what seemed to be an acknowledgement of a general discontent, attempted to calm his acolytes. "Do not be disheartened by this, students," he said. "Strange as my speech may seem to you, you will understand the truth in it someday."

Was there truth, indeed, in Houdon's words? With the other students in the room, I turned his logic round and round, considered his reasoning this way and that, cast upon the solid platform of his policy the vibrant insights which, through the years, had for my own views compelling force, and attempted to grant our respected professor the benefit of my doubt. It seemed, however, that for my compatriots, involved as they were in discussions heated and contrary, that the case before them rested, in their lights, on principles of dubious validity. My impression was confirmed when Lily, who during these discussions had taken a lead in the defense of her favored form, stood and addressed Houdon with a challenge that had, it seemed, from the entire group endorsement.

"Professor Houdon," she began. "All among us possess for your wisdom the finest respect, for your years of instruction the fondest memories, and for your ethics pedagogical the greatest trust. None here, on the contrary, charge you with a will disingenuous. Your pronouncement on this serious matter of the aesthetic, however, has cast a shroud of trouble on our souls." Here there arose from the group renewed murmurs of assent. The young lady turned to acknowledge their support, then again faced Houdon. "All of us agree: With all respect, we request from you a defense more certain than your spindly props—gathered as they were from ages past, revered by all for their veneer of settled wisdom, but as support for the higher hurdles of the modern day too short. We students all, in brief, believe that in your manuscript, the one upon which you have labored for these ten years, you hold the key for the secret of our mysterious box. Surely then, in your role as our teacher, you should by all that is right offer us now the fruits of your labor, burnished as that fruit has been by the toil of your years, glowing in a power generated from that dedicated study, and revelatory from its harmony with the primal forms."

The speaker fell silent. She returned to her seat and gazed at Houdon with an expression of expectation—one that seemed to be reflected equally on the visage of every student present. Of a sudden the students broke out into applause—a sound which by its spontaneity awarded the woman's challenge a seal of common concordance.

Houdon, for his part, stood in silence, pursing his lips, nodding his head quickly time and again to the words of his youthful challenger, closing his eyes in thought—only to snap them open from time to time and peer first at one scholar, then another—as he digested the import of the claims that the assemblage, acting in chorus as aggrieved party, had laid upon him. At the conclusion of the student's speech, Houdon began to pace in his characteristic way, arranging his thoughts. He paused, retrieved the poker and jostled the logs—which by this late hour had diminished to a few smoking twigs—and turned to answer his rebellious acolytes.

Houdon eyed the woman who had possessed the temerity to challenge his pronouncement, then set his eye on a number of other students before turning his gaze to ponder an indeterminate spot on the wall. "Your request, I understand, is not out of line. Indeed, the possibility of finally giving my cloistered manuscript a public airing has, over the course of the past few days and especially over these few merry evening hours, acquired in my own mind a certain undeniable attraction. The years have eroded my confidence in my analysis and my hesitation to cast before the ravenous eye of the public my work, the principles of which have long sought a resolution for their sorry conflicts. Has such resolution been made?" With this rhetorical question, the professor paused and turned his back on the studentry. Again he retrieved his stick and poked, in what seemed to be an absent manner, at the smoldering logs.

Perceiving the professor so lost in thought, gazing so intently into the flames, gazing perhaps on the wisdom of the ages, the students sat transfixed. One bent over and whispered to a classmate, "He is communicating with his daemon." Smoke arose from the disturbed fire bed and a few lonely, brave sparks attended their shroud-like progenitor up the chimney.

Suddenly, it seemed to me, Houdon appeared to shake himself out of his trance. He shrugged, poked at a wayward log, and shifted his eyes quickly toward us in that manner he had of—who could say?—assessment or slyness. Was he weighing our gullibility—was he laughing at us? Or did he intend to communicate a kind of secret insight into the truth and wisdom of the story he was about to relate? Even now I can see the old scholar—impressed as it was upon my mind's eye—poking away at his fireplace and casting that sidelong glance—what was its meaning? The question haunts me to this day.

The fact remains that for what seemed like several minutes, nothing was heard from our host as behind him came the cracks and snaps of the dying fire. At last Houdon gave a deep sigh, returned the poker to its receptacle, and faced us. "The time has come." The crowd gave off a subdued hush which the professor seemed not to notice. He peered intently at the group, then nodded his head with a quick jerk. "Yes. The time has indeed come. Tomorrow I shall unlock the drawer in my den and release my manuscript from its long captivity. Here—before the hearth—shall I read to you all the story that—in its remarkable and fantastic detail—shall to your suspicious ears provide proof sufficient of my pronouncement."

And so the evening came to an end. The students, whose vigorous investment in the holiday festivities had been somewhat tempered by the sobriety of their professor's reflections, rose from their seats, and, as they made their way to the door, thanked their host for the evening. "You will all be here on the morrow, then?" Houdon asked, and we all professed our consent most eagerly. Who would fail to show on Christmas Day, our revered instructor having promised to reveal the manuscript which for years had been at our academy the subject of intense rumor?

We students, one and all, filed out from the warmth of the professor's parlor into the crisp winter air. As we passed along the walkway to our living quarters, our boots crunched loudly on the packed snow, pressed as it was by the severe night cold. The group broke into its components and I found myself at last in my bed overlooking the grounds of the academy. Exhausted by the evening festivities and by the accompanying cognitive disruptions—had they affected me more than my compatriots?—I prepared to enter my long winter's nap when I took one last glance out my window, peering across the great lawn, silent in its shroud of snow, to the professor's house where all of the windows had gone dark save one. A light shone from Houdon's den where the professor sat revising a work to be read to us on the morrow.

What is there left to say from a mind other than Houdon's? It was certain that we students, sure in our youthful frenzy, napped. It was equally certain that our progenitor, embattled with his fighting angels, pondered. Scratch, erase, scribble, and sigh.

The next morning, we rose to a bright sun and walked again across the crunching snow to our host's home. Houdon was ready for us, standing in silence before a freshened fire as we took our former seats. Did I perceive upon the professor's face that peace characteristic of an individual who has, after profound spiritual struggles, reached a momentous decision?

Manuscript in hand, Houdon bid us remain quiet and listen. There followed the most unusual story I have ever heard. Decades have come and gone and I have achieved an age even somewhat advanced over Houdon's at the time of his revelation. As most of the classmates from that evening have followed our professor into the higher world, and as Houdon's manuscript has, according to the academy librarian, been lost, I now feel both the freedom of the newly released prisoner and the compulsion of the conscientious elder to render for posterity the best recollection I can give of our professor's story, the entirety of which, even to this late day, seems firmly impressed upon my memory. Although I have felt it necessary from the nature of the medium to recast the perspective from narrator to observer, and although prudence has compelled me to omit some details, for the most part the chapters that follow recreate the story as best I can recall.

CHAPTER 22:

Christmas Day

As the day crept on into early afternoon, the gentleman before the fire was feeling that rootless discontent familiar to anyone who has exhausted the duties of the morning without fully acceding to the necessity of those that follow—who has stumbled, indeed, into a general enervation which can better be felt by the emotions than signified in the common parlance. Challenged by a gap between feeling and articulation—challenged, indeed, by an unaccustomed difficulty in general of fastening onto the tossing mane of language the clasp of the editorial harness—the gentleman resorted to something possibly of equal familiarity: surrender. Our man, in short, quite gave himself up to the spirit of the holiday, sinking into the softness of his chair, stuffed, fringed, and—although of all items in the room the most modern and hence for the devotee of the classical tradition the most vulnerable to the charge of vulgarity—by its very closeness to the cozy flames enjoying from he who would seem to have the greatest claim against the furniture's formal improbability a pardon.

Absolution, then, was in the air, and so in equal measure was the soothing realization of the pending arrival of a second gentleman, one sharing the profession of the first, but who had, from time to time, exhibited a distance, a variance in proclivities. Distance, to be sure, on this afternoon was less the matter of import than disruption, for it was a conversation with this friend which for the malaise of our main quarry seemed the most promising antidote.

The friend arrived; Christmas greetings were exchanged; aperitifs were poured. "The students were here last night, I take it?" posed the new arrival as he seated himself, easily preceding and following his query with quick gains on his Lillet. Casting about at the ruffled decorations, he then added: "Your celebration, I hope, was enjoyable?"

"As enjoyable as tradition permits," was the answer, the convention spoken of being the annual Christmas Eve festivities for which the professor served as host. There was more than a little in the tone which would give anyone pause; the visitor, however, decided to take the most obvious interpretation: Life with the studentry, after all, held in small doses the charm of a pleasant aperitif and in larger ones the bloat of a revelry lengthened to a stretch imprudent.

Hence a detour to a gentler path: "And this morning you have been engaged with your work?"

At this, the host pursed his lips and peered down into his glass with narrowed eyes. "And they returned this morning," he stated, as if unhearing of his guest's question.

This announcement having for the friend the effect of a mild shock, he paused before speaking, turning over in his mind the implications. He leaned a bit forward, resting his forearms on his knees as someone who desires to receive his signals more clearly. "Pardon me. The students?" He glanced up at his host and added, rather weakly: "Here this morning?"

"Yes." The man nodded and stared into the fire.

The guest glanced to the side. "Whatever for?" He turned again to his host and emitted a brief chuckle. "Did you hang their stockings on the mantelpiece?"

"There was a bit of a discussion in the evening about the relative merits of artistic forms. Positions were taken." He paused and looked askance at his companion. "I found it somewhat unpleasant."

"And?"

"I determined to settle the matter, or at least provide for my charges the benefit of the work I had done on that subject—the work for which they exhibited an intense interest. Hence I invited them back." He tossed his head quickly to the side in a gesture of dismissal. "And this morning I read them my work."

The visitor sat bolt upright. "You don't say!" A bit more emphasis than required was placed upon those words, and there followed a pause rich with reflection, then a thrust of new angle and greater surety. "Really, Porbus, I am astonished." The man exhibited this bewilderment in deed as well as word, widening his eyes a little and settling his gaze on a couple of unspecified objects one after another, quite at sea. "Whatever compelled you to do such a thing? All these years in which you denied any of us poor scholarly drudges access to your findings. Now you trot your conclusions out before a group of students who cannot have any but the slightest regard for your interests, or, for that matter, for those of the academy." The inquisitor allowed that to drift about, then shrugged at his own perception. "Ah, well. Your decision." He shook his head quickly and was about to draw from his glass when he paused and uttered: "How much egg nog did the students pack into you last night?" At which he issued a suppressed torrent of glee as he finished his drink.

His host remaining silent, the visitor continued: "I don't mind saying it would be a feather in my cap to be the conduit of your findings to Newmarch—both on the academic side and on that of the public who have learned to revel in your novels." He caught himself. "I wonder how much has been retained by your audience. Were your acolytes sober and attentive?" He chuckled again.

Porbus considered, stood, and moved to the fire to revive the flames. "I would say they were sober when they left."

"I dare say." The visitor gave his glass a few rotations and turned things over in his mind. He recalled a previous conversational investment that had gone unrewarded. "Well, that accounts for your paltry labors this morning—you were involved in something else."

His host frowned and furrowed his brow. "I had trouble concentrating. Somehow the words would not come."

His companion again sat upright and pierced his audience jauntily. Finally he said: "Another surprise! Just don't tell it to Frenhofer." His face was lit with a simple, companionable cheer. "You should hear him talk about you." Here the speaker compressed his features in mock seriousness and began to speak in low tones of intense sobriety, issuing his words in solid, widely spaced syllables, so that no one could fail to perceive the words to be but the echo of emanations from the old academist himself: "*Porbus possesses the key to the lock. The key!*" This was accompanied by profound gesturings and a still more intense facial compression. "*If only we could grasp it! If only we could unlock the . . . secret . . . cabinet.*" The final words were uttered slowly and mysteriously with gestures of mocking stagecraft, the performer rubbing his hands together greedily and staring with wild eyes at his audience.

Porbus laughed out loud, a long parade of guffaws descending in a deep musical tone, his dark moodiness apparently dispelled by his visitor's pantomime. He turned from the fire and grinned broadly at his guest. "Bravo, Houdon. You have captured him. Yes, 'the *master*'"—a little bit of extra emphasis there—"is always talking about a secret cabinet of some sort, or else he's babbling about a room he can't seem to get into." Porbus paused and rested a hand on the poker. "I wonder how much of his act is real and how much he is putting on. Do you think the old *lansquenet* is laughing at us?"

"Well, if he is, I say more power to him. His acting talents are at least as rich as his powers over language. He's certainly led the directors in a dance. They can't decide whether to put him in charge of the department or lock him in a cage." He paused and eyed his quarry. "Quite a dynamic has built up between you two. A rather odd relationship, marrying the collegiality of the symbiotic and the tension of the territorial. Don't you agree? That's how the board views it, anyhow."

"Ah," said Porbus. "Does the board view it that way?" In this formulaic there was an impressive sheen of the non-committal.

"Well, you must know what the consensus is—or perhaps I should tell you."

"And is there such a consensus? I had no idea I, for example, was a matter of great interest to the board."

Houdon allowed the bait to drift. “I don’t mind saying Frenhofer’s wife and family are distraught. They are worried that the old man is losing his mind.”

“I don’t doubt they are. And I don’t blame them. As though he hadn’t misplaced it long ago.”

“He is plagued by self-doubt, and can’t seem to put the finishing touches on that novel upon which he has labored a decade. Hmm—*Catherine Lescault*—I rather like the title. He has shown me some parts. He seems certain it will be his ‘greatest novel ever,’ as he puts it.”

With this, Porbus expressed a new interest. “You have seen more than I, then. Far be it from the great man to show his work to his biographer. I should love to steal a peek at his divine mess! What, if you feel free to tell me, has he written?”

“Nothing that I can relate in terms other than the original. Indeed, I wonder if anyone can explain what the fellow’s linguistic convolutions amount to. Ah. . . .” Here Houdon paused for a remembrance. “Yes, there was one paragraph I actually understood. A bit about the courtesan’s foot being worthy of the esteem of the King. And—would you believe it—when I next saw the author, he had done me the service of crossing out that sobriety!”

“Too lucid for his readers, I suppose. I never met a successful writer so determined to reduce his audience to the zero mark. It’s a good thing he has developed a reputation as an eccentric. Now the curious—or the elite who affect only to appreciate the resonant images of the *archaic penumbra*—will buy his novel."

"And there is more difficulty."

"More?"

"He has adopted the habit not only of constructing sentences of involved convolution, but of continual erasing, crossing out, writing over—making quite a mess of his document. The thing is a shapeshifting monster: one time it appears to me to be constructed in one way; the next time the whole thing is built differently. What a reviser the man is! And to add mystery to mayhem, he has accommodated to a diminishing expanse of paper by condensing his thoughts into what look like hieroglyphics, codes of some kind, which he squeezes into his margins. It's all rather impressive when viewed as a work of art."

"Exactly. If we can't read it we can frame it."

"And in explanation, he says that he is grappling with a paradox: The *meaning* of his novel, he says, comes before its *rendering*. This sets his propositions and their connotative shells into a kind of free-for-all. The result is that the work exists on more than one layer, as a kind of what he calls an '*interpretive palimpsest*—'"

"Ah! I knew that was coming. . . ."

"All the while, of course, he is presenting the thing to me as if I were some kind of interpreter. He keeps asking me if I can assist him in understanding what he calls the 'misaligned walls' of his manuscript. As if I had the foggiest idea what he was talking about! Talking with the man would be alarming if somehow he didn't come across as perfectly sane—which, come to think of it, possesses somehow a secret line of its own—"

"I like that word 'somehow,'" broke in Porbus. "I should like to know more of Frenhofer's secret line."

Houdon nodded quickly. "Which brings me to a rather delicate point. Concerning yourself."

"And the board."

"And their view of your relationship with Frenhofer. Well, they have grappled with the rumors. Not all of which they believe. . . ."

"Not all. That is heartening."

"And all of which they are digesting in the unpleasant environment of Frenhofer's subject matter—the career of his titular heroine—which for Newmarch, odd as it seems in this day, is a topic less of resonance and more of distaste."

"Well, they can't seem to get out of their minds that nonsense about the young lady, I take it. It is folly, of course, to go over that again."

At this juncture in the conversation, the two academists were interrupted, if only in a suggestive sense, by footsteps crunching through the snow toward the front door. It was no more than the matter of a few seconds when there followed a slight creaking metallic sound, then a *thunk*, and then the dying away of the footsteps as their owner retraced the walkway. Houdon paused and looked over his shoulder at the front door, his face reflecting mild surprise. "Someone has dropped a letter in your box, Porbus. On Christmas."

Porbus turned his own gaze in the same direction, squinting through the window at the departing individual. "Our neighbor. Most likely a letter was misdelivered yesterday. I'll get it later."

They returned to their conversation, Houdon rejoining the path: "Related as your history with the young lady is, in a less than rational way, to be sure—with Frenhofer's subject matter, the board is simply uncomfortable with the *penumbra*, to borrow a term from the Great One. Nothing you can do about it, except to be simply aware and conduct yourself accordingly."

To this Porbus gave no perceivable ground.

Houdon continued: "Perhaps more practical is the larger relation you have developed with Frenhofer, for the board looks upon that with a bit of unease. Your own biography and critical analysis of the fellow is in a state of suspense, given the old academist's inability to complete his novel. Hence you have been pressing him to make the final brush stroke. On the surface, understandable. . . ."

"On the surface? Now what is going on?"

"The board has the sense you want Frenhofer to complete his work for a far different reason: Publication of the work in its incoherent state will ruin his reputation and clear the way for your own coronation as the paramount novelist."

"Really! Have people in general now become deranged?"

Houdon emitted an indescribable appreciation. "Well, this is the sensation at the present. Who knows whether it will all be forgotten in a year's time? Quite likely it might."

Porbus changed course. "I suppose you know that Frenhofer is still sending me his helpful letters."

"He speaks highly of you to me."

"Highly, indeed, if his usage of the term is to be accepted. He can't get off that kick of his, that I should write more in a way which expresses the inexpressible—that is, that reveals the secret code to the puzzle of that he calls the '*interpretive palimpsest.*' This would require writing in a style that, he says, resonates with an 'aura of the primal lyre.' How can anyone make anything out of that—making the novel into a poem, perhaps? He has one way of looking at the novel—look where that has got him, by the way—and he simply lacks the insight to perceive that I, in common with many other people, may have a different point of view. And for this he places the blame—in some perverted twist of logic—upon me, and doesn't mind letting the public know." He paused. "His arrogance is insufferable."

Houdon took this in with pursed lips. He said at last: "Frenhofer is a challenge. He bothers people." He paused and considered. "I have an idea. Why don't I arrange a meeting of the three of us?"

"Will he attend?"

Houdon smiled. "I think the two of you might have a good chat—clear up some of the fog that has settled over the landscape." He rose from his chair, gave a departing glance to the fire, and picked up his coat. "What do you say I ask him?"

Porbus rose to take his guest to the door. "Suits me." He paused. "I'm amazed you can stay friends with him. Hasn't he accused you yet of stealing his ideas, or trying to sell your knowledge of him to the press?"

Now it was Houdon's turn to give out a series of guffaws. "Not without a subsequent scene of dramatic solicitude, filled with earnest entreaties for forgiveness. The man and his paranoia are quite at odds."

They reached the door and entered the outer world, its crisp air infused with the cold light of the afternoon sun. "Oh, and if I am good enough to bring out the secrets of Frenhofer,"–Houdon paused and poked his host in a good natured way–"you must surely reciprocate by showing me your wonderful manuscript."

Porbus recovered himself, recalled his indiscretion, and gave an equally collegial smile. "Perhaps I have started a new tradition: Each Christmas Day the department head shall call forth the student body and read most injudiciously from an academic paper."

Houdon gave a brief bow of exaggerated gratuity and turned to go. Just then he noticed some footprints in the snow. This caused him to stop in a remembrance, turn back toward his host, and glance at the mailbox protruding from the door. Reaching out with his walking stick, he poked the device with a loud crack that caused his host to start.

"Read your letter."

CHAPTER 23:

The First Letter

Porbus,

What a long time! News of your amazing novels has been coming my way for so long that I can well imagine your memory of your poor old school chum has quite faded away, lost in the shadows cast by the bright shine of your readers' applause. So much production—you are a machine! Sometimes I think you have a workshop of little elves churning out books to order like hot cakes.

For my part, rest assured I have not forgotten the intellectual stimulation, the many conversations we had about art and writing, extending long into the wee hours over cold cups of coffee. I don't mind saying that I long for those days when we had the time, the proclivity, and the inspiration—wasn't Frenny a hoot?—to consider whether the severe line or the exuberance of chiaroscuro was the superior material for rendering a living subject. Hah! Weren't you the one who drew their parallel with proposition and metaphor? Or was it somebody else? Let's not get started, though. Weighty matters they are indeed, and ones, I fear, engaged in by few young people at the university today.

By the way, I hear you are writing a biography of Frenny. Is he really agreeing to tell you anything? I can't imagine him sharing his precious secrets with anyone. Has he accused you of stealing his ideas yet? Hah hah. . . . He must be ripping mad that you are writing popular novels after sitting through his lectures on the power of complex sentences.

Speaking of students today, I know Nicolas is in your class. I don't imagine I need tell you I am disappointed in his progress. He is not keeping his work up; I know he is not giving his studies the attention they need. Little wonder his grades are terrible. The issue I lay certainly on his shoulders. He does not apply himself as you and I did back in the day. He seems less interested in working than in a kind of dreaming about fame—as if someone were to simply hand it to him as an entitlement. I'm afraid he spends all of his time strumming a guitar rather than studying. Nothing wrong with music, I tell him; indeed I still encourage him to master the instrument—but he also has to keep up his studies. And he has a taste for the young ladies as well. I understand you are familiar with his current paramour, a young lady named

Gillette, who, apparently, he met in your class. I hope she is a good influence on him. In which case, I thank you for bringing them together. In any case, please do not give him any special breaks because he is my son: that kind of unfair treatment will do him no good. I know you will do the right thing, what is best.

Anyhow, I am writing to you about a completely different matter. You know I am up to my neck in wattle and daub—architecture, to recall another Frennyism, has much in common with writing and painting. And what do you think? I've been building a house for a colleague of yours named Houdon. He bought some land close enough to Newmarch so he can enjoy the benefits of being near the academy—but far enough away that he can avoid the commotion of a college town. As it happens, we have been running into considerable difficulties putting in the foundation, which we are building rather deep. As you know, this area is riddled with history and there's a good deal of old buried construction still about. As a result, we have had to clean out quite a conglomeration of junk. We have been able more or less to plow our way through the ruins—all of which are rather mundane, and similar to the other excavations in the area—but the fact is that last week we discovered something completely unexpected. At some depth we ran into a conglomeration of stone in a box shaped roughly ten feet square. We were able to lift the thing out of the ground using our crane. Curious as to what it might contain, I had our men crack it open with jackhammers. The operation took quite a bit of time, I'll tell you: It seems like whoever created the thing was frantic to make sure no one found what was inside. And that was pretty strange, too: a large box constructed of some kind of metal. The edges were seamless. Once again, of course, the question arose as to what was inside that. So our metalworkers did their duty. Again, it was not an easy task, but we succeeded through sheer bullheadedness.

As for what was inside—that's the amazing thing, and that's exactly what got me thinking about my old school chum and what resources you might have at the academy. What we discovered was just this: a virtually life-sized statue of a young woman. She is posed in a rather withdrawn fashion, her eyes downcast, her arms held close together before her. And she is covered in nothing except what looks for all the world like a shroud. Furthermore, the entire thing is cast in bronze, and quite heavy. Isn't that extraordinary?

I'm at a loss. Houdon let me set it up at home in our den, and I don't mind saying that it seems to have a life of its own—it has quite taken over the room in the sense that when you're there you can't do much else but stare at the thing. To tell you the truth, it is giving my wife the creeps. I was sitting in front of the statue last night, musing about the strange look on the young lady's face. And you know what I couldn't get out of my mind? Old Frenny's dictum that he must have told us a hundred times: "Find in the image a meaning to give it value." Hah hah—I still have nightmares about that one. I wonder if our professor can figure out a meaning in this image.

So I'm writing to ask you: Can you take a look at it? Do you know anyone at the academy who might be able to figure out what this thing is? I'll have it sent over to you if you like. Maybe you can write one of your famous novels about it!

In any case, when we are done with this house you are invited over. Tell you what—let's invite Frenny and his wife to stay too. The location is inspiring enough that you might be able to wheedle enough information out of him to finish the biography. Come to think of it, the atmosphere might help him finish his own work. How long has it been since his last novel—ten years?

I've taken enough of your valuable time, chum. Let me know about the statue.

Henry

P.S. Eh . . . might best to burn this letter. It's got some delicate stuff in it. Burn, burn!

CHAPTER 24:

A Voice from the Sculpture

"Please try to recall as much as you can about the girl. A detail, seemingly inconsequential on its surface, may by implication provide for her disappearance the resolving key. Do you feel, in these quarters,"—the man made a vague gesture toward the walls of the room—"free to speak?"

Those were the words of a gentleman who had, no more than a few minutes before, arrived with solemnity at the door of Mary Frenhofer. The woman's response came in the form of a remonstrance—that being her certainty, communicated while her visitor accepted with grace an offer of breakfast tea, that her husband would be the best source of information, untarnished as his words would be by the dimming filter of the secondhand. For which the visitor had but to play the ace: An opening foray in that quarter had been advanced, rebuffed, and the brave soldier returned to the rear.

That rout, in turn, had brought the gentleman to the lady's parlor where he would continue his entreaty with these terms: "You will perhaps agree with us that the girl's story, even as early as its prelude which I shall this morning relate, is unusual. Since her arrival at the monastery as an infant, we considered Gillette a special girl, one blessed with a remarkable gift for creation but not with the correlative skills of prudence and judgment. She has always been guided by high emotion rather than cool detachment."

Mary Frenhofer nodded. "And as such she entered my husband's study as an acolyte. She was enthusiastic, honest. As for her remarkability, I do not attempt to judge. Her creative talents were submitted to the control of my husband—from him you will obtain the clearest assessment, as I have indicated. If you like, I shall attempt to bring him round."

Father Rachel, however, seemed more prone to the straight line. Giving a grateful nod at his hostess and accepting the proffered tea, the priest sat back in his chair with an accommodative air. "Perhaps you will dash off the rough strokes of a quick sketch, then—one for which Dr Frenhofer may later provide the requisite *chiaroscuro* of full meaning."

Accepting this presupposition as a sufficient straightening of cross-purposes, Mary collected her thoughts. Then she opened from within them a parenthesis, breaking forth with these words: "How much do you know of Gillette's life with my husband in this house?"

It would not be out of the ordinary to suppose that those words had upon the old priest the effect less of question than of revelation—had indeed something of the puff and clank of an old train pushed onto new track. As for his response, in the physical sense it was modulated to a degree commendable, for he had but brought together his fingertips in a tent characteristic of the individual who had accepted the inevitability of the need to balance the competing intentions of a weighing of evidence with the requirement in terms of a dialogic companion to answer the age-old question, "What next?" As for the verbal manifestation of the visitor's momentary confusion, it amounted to but a weak recall of the common appeal to "Turn the page."

Mary stared directly at her interlocutor. "We were naturally delighted when we heard about the offer of this charming house,"—here she gestured with her eyes to her surroundings—"provided for the use of Joseph by an anonymous benefactor, for the completion of that novel which has remained in its raw form for a decade. Our only surprise was the channel of communication—that being through Franklin Porbus, our husband's biographer."

"Certainly it would make sense for that gentleman to provide the grounds suitable for his subject's success, given that it is upon that very wheel upon which his *own* success rides."

Mary nodded carefully, as this had been the reason proffered for what could only be understood as an act of kind intercession. "Nevertheless, I could not accept that as the only force in play, the history of my husband and his biographer being what it was—that is, not characterized by the most gracious air."

"And the other forces—the ones possessing, I presume, a less savory flavor—what were they?"

"Suppose the creator should spectacularly fail?"

Father Rachel took this in. "And in so doing, propel his rival to the summit?"

Mary, as if taking this conclusion as a given, appeared stolidly not to have heard, but trimmed a new branch: "And then there was the other matter."

Father Rachel waited.

"It came to me some months after we had moved in, after the girl had come here with the sculpture. Both had been delivered to us by way of Porbus. And both brought considerable disturbance to Joseph. In fact, they seem to, mentally, have set him off."

"The sculpture?" responded Father Rachel, having understood but half of what had been presented.

"That is really the nut of the matter. Gillette had been here no more than a week before she began to promote a certain bronze as a source of inspiration for Joseph. It was a work she had first seen in the library of Porbus, where she had taken a liking to it. As it later turned out, her liking had the taint of a rather more severe condition—one I would with greater certainty signify as an obsession."

"And she was successful, I understand, in convincing Dr Frenhofer of the work's value?"

"She seemed to possess a power of her own over my husband. The two would spend hour after hour together, going over their manuscripts, engaged with the analysis of the relative merits of competing metaphors, determined to resolve the mysteries of rival potencies of alternative patterns of confused allusions—in brief, resolved to engineer the most productive engagements of complex sentences. It was as though she understood something of my husband that I never could—something that was beyond my ken.

"It was through her entreaties that Joseph finally agreed to accept the sculpture into his study. I remember the day of its arrival. It took four men to haul the huge thing in—it must have weighed several hundred pounds. We gathered in Joseph's studio around the object, standing as it did some six feet tall, wrapped in brown paper and bound round and round with twine as if the person who secured it were trying to keep something from escaping. As my husband began unwrapping the thing, I stepped back, scarcely knowing what to expect beyond some vague reference the girl had made to the work being that of a woman, and her enthusiasm that the statue had been so finely done that it seemed to have a life of its own.

"As Joseph removed more and more of the paper, the sculpture was gradually revealed. I observed first the side of an arm clinging to a waist, and as the paper fell away, I saw what appeared to be a great cloth wrapped around the body of a human being. Joseph pulled away the paper from the lower part of the creation and a pair of womanly legs came into view. Finally, the entirety of the cover was removed and we stood in awe before a life-sized statue of a woman, huddled inside a shawl of some kind, her head down and her arms clasped around herself. She was the very vision of coldness, the essence of the winter season, a raw emotion infused into a bronze of a human being fending off the deathly embrace of the frigid.

"Joseph and Gillette stood before the sculpture, their eyes fixed to the bronze vision. I could but ask myself silently, *What variety of woman is this?* In an attempt to answer, I stepped forward, advancing to a place immediately before the creation where I could stare upward into its eyes, hidden as they otherwise were by the covering shawl.

"At first I could see nothing of interest—the mind of the bronze woman seemed to be elsewhere and she seemed to be unaware of my existence, or indeed, of anyone else's. *Could she be so cold?* I asked inwardly, referring to her spiritual rather than her physical state.

I determined to look closer, and I squinted my eyes, shading them with my hand so as to block out any of the light that might obscure the nuanced lines that I was sure the sculptor had impressed into the founding block. Even so—nothing! I stepped still closer, bringing my face as near as I could to the face of the cold woman, and stared deeply into her eyes.

"Then, as I continued to concentrate, the face of the bronze began to quiver and the woman's eyes emanated a dim red glow. Finally, I heard it: a woman's voice. At first I thought it was the creation of my imagination, over-activated as it might well be by the stress of what had transpired recently in my husband's life and study. The sound was just vocal enough to make me start—and I hoped that my movement had not been observed by my husband or Gillette. I screwed up my face in fierce concentration, stood as close as I could to the bronze creature, and listened. And then, after a bewildered minute, I again heard the woman's voice—but not so much heard as simply sensed as one might sense a breeze passing through the forest leaves, or—better—understood, as one might apprehend the distant call of a primal lyre. '*Please,*' the voice said to me, '*Return me to life.*'"

Mary Frenhofer, who had uttered this story in a voice of increasing intensity, at once stopped, sat back in her chair, and stared at her visitor as if to invite interpretation.

And how, indeed, *would* Father Rachel interpret this? For his part, the priest, who had quite forgotten his tea, collected his thoughts and determined the best way to forge from them a shield of the spoken word, one strong enough to project the necessity of advance but embellished enough to prevent unnecessary battle. Luckily, Father Rachel's counseling history was as the training of Hephaestus, forger of the strong Ocean River upon the shield of Achilles. And so Mary's interlocutor offered but these words, common in form but remarkable in meaning as they projected a communicable sympathy in league with the very essence of non-commitment: "An *extraordinary* event." He then nodded soberly.

Her companion's words having their intended effect, Mary proceeded with her story. "I kept these words in my heart, knowing that the others would not believe them, but also knowing that both Joseph and Gillette—each far more sensitive than I to the celestial song of the antique aura—would not take long to hear words of their own. And so it was. As the days passed, my husband and his companion devoted more of their attention to the sculpture that stood in the middle of Joseph's studio as—what seemed to me, at least—a sentinel of death. The girl, especially: I was troubled to see her sit before the bronze hour after hour staring into the woman's eyes, engaged in some kind of communion. From time to time she would pause and retrieve her diary, into which she would jot what I presumed to be notes on what the bronze was telling her.

"As for Joseph, he took an active interest, continually measuring the sculpture and engaging in a kind of formal analysis. His adventures seemed to resolve into a hopeless puzzlement, and he would retire with words such as, 'In the statue there is something missing,' and, 'Something is wrong; there is a section missing.' Even with these caveats, he seemed to inherit from the girl an obsessive faith in the sculpture. 'There is a secret of life in the bronze,' he once told me. 'If only I could discover it. With that secret in my hand, I can finish my novel. I can make of Catherine Lescault a living, breathing woman.' And all the time he would be continually urging Gillette to continue her work recording the words of what she heard from the statue. 'The sculpture's words are a vital code,' I heard him tell the girl. 'They will reveal the key to the lock of the *hesitational conflict*.'

"Here, then, was his mission for Gillette: discover the secret of the bronze. Commune with the woman within; tear from out of the bronze the secret of creation, record it in her diary, and present it to the master of the studio. Gillette was quick to agree, but it was apparent to me that the girl had no real interest in the work of Joseph, or, indeed, in her own nascent writing—or, indeed, in any kind of demanding art at all. Instead, she was content to devote all of her energies to her engagement with the bronze sculpture, to what I can only describe as a bringing forth from the bronze the spirit of the woman herself as a living being." Mary paused with a knowing look at the priest. "And so, you see, Gillette and my husband were engaged in a kind of commingling of purpose, an obsession with the creation of life which they shared, and which seemed to grow in force as they fed off each other." The speaker paused. "Until at last the obsession became all-consuming."

Father Rachel pursed his lips in thought. "And Porbus—the designer of the arrangement—where was he?"

"He was content to wait it out. Knowing of my husband's distaste for him, he remained behind the scenes of the drama he had created, hence allowing the sculpture to perform its magic unhindered." Mary paused. "Only one time—at the very end—he came to see my husband. And that caused a row. And it was after that row that Gillette disappeared."

Father Rachel suddenly lifted a palm in the sign of denial. He rubbed his chin thoughtfully, frowned in thought, and turned over the details of the story in his mind. "Wait," he finally said. "Wait. Before we come to Porbus. Something about Gillette." He considered. "I don't doubt she could become addicted to the sculpture. It was her nature to possess an extraordinary sympathy with matters of creativity. And yet I was also told of a paramour. A young man. . . ."

"Nicolas."

The priest gave a quick nod. "Nicolas Poussin. Where was he while all of this was happening? And how in the world did he ever agree to allow Gillette to live with an older man?"

CHAPTER 25:

Winter Light

Mary Frenhofer, it so happened, possessed a womanly knowledge of the heart of the young man whose name had been mentioned—a knowledge tarnished, it was to be hoped by her interlocutor, neither by the wifely terror of a loss of the husbandly bind nor by that dark angel's pendant: the spite of a rejected woman toward her nemesis. "Nicolas," Mary simply said, "came to me with romantic concerns—ones not so much centered about a male rival—for my husband, despite his virility, was in the Phthonusian arena a trusted sword. Rather, it was to the mind and the heart of his paramour that Nicolas paid heed. Gillette, he told me—and of this you are surely more informed than I—was prone to concentrated enthusiasms, puzzling and erudite communications, and distant wanderings. Often Nicolas would wake to her screams—reactions to her constantly repeating nightmare of falling into a deep canyon. Gillette, in brief, possessed a mind of particular softness for the intrusions of insidious forces.

"Nicolas, then, was concerned about Gillette's life with my husband, but solely because of the latter's influence on the more extreme facets of the girl's natural proclivities. If Gillette were to become mesmerized, would not Joseph's own fascination with the bronze creature embolden its spell? What would keep the engine of enchantment from building in force over time until the young girl found herself in a situation of serious danger?"

Mary Frenhofer had learned of Nicolas's fears from a most direct path. "The young man had come to me for the assistance that a wife might provide in tempering the influence of her husband over a young acolyte. The day before his first visit, Nicolas had discovered a diary maintained by Gillette, and, seeking to read it, could make nothing of what he saw. 'It appeared to be a series of codes,' he told me. 'And they were composed of letters, numbers, and even symbols that reminded me of nothing save rubrics on the stones of the ancient Egyptians. My heart sank as I saw page after page of these meaningless symbols—entered in a small, tight, careful hand, the extent and detail of which could only come from a mind energized by the concentration of an all-consuming monomania.'

"'And moreover,' the young man continued, 'these codes themselves seemed to have been entered over page upon page of previous writings, the faint outlines of which I could barely discern. I turned the pages one by one. Why, I wondered in my heart, was so much text erased—or almost erased—for its bare outlines could still, for one sure of eye, be discerned? And further—don't think that any of the material on either level was simply entered as a daily routine, only to be forgotten. No! For at various spots in the text Gillette had taken care to enter small numbers above the lines—numbers which, witness as they be to an intensity of intellectual power, seemed to refer by implication, if not, from time to time, by direct angled interconnecting lines entered in the book, to places in the diary where the topic at hand—whatever it might be—was dealt with in a manner supposedly deeper and fuller. From these cryptic marks, I could reach but one conclusion: Here was a work of mighty mastery from a maiden's tender hand. And how could my concerns be any less than many? What could the entries mean? For whom were the words created? Whither would the massive effort lead?'"

Mary Frenhofer paused in her recitation and eyed her visitor. Father Rachel, for his part, stroked his chin as he turned these matters over in his mind. He finally said: "The diary, I take it, was inspired by what Gillette heard from the sculpture. Did our young man confront his paramour with the discovery?"

"Indeed he did," said Mary. "At first he put the book back into its secret place on the shelf, intending not only to give the matter of his approach to Gillette some thought, but also to seek my counsel on the best way to break the news of his broken faith—broken, that is, not only in the sense of his distrust of the mental condition of his paramour, but also in the intrusion of his eye into a book of privacy—the horn of the male in rude rupture of the feminine dome.

"His plan, however, was thwarted. The next day, Nicolas, deep in thought over a challenging text, suddenly felt the presence of his paramour. Glancing up, he saw standing before him the figure of Gillette—holding forth the volume from which he had received such discontent. Before he could express surprise, the girl broke forth: 'You have read my private diary.' Think not, though, that Gillette expressed vulgar surprise or anger. Nicolas saw nothing in the girl's eyes other than the simple reflection of a young girl holding before her, for the edification of her companions, a seashell plucked from the sand. 'My book is not meant to be read,' she said in simple tones. 'It is not even meant to be known that it exists.'

"Nicolas expressed his sorrow at his intrusions, for he was ashamed he had broken the trust of his paramour. Gone from his mind at once were any misgivings about the nature of Gillette's writing. The work of a private hour, he now understood, was not to be questioned.

"Wonderment, then, was his next concern. Gillette seemed to ignore his apologies, or perhaps she was beyond hearing them. Instead, she opened her diary, turned to a page that she desired, then held the book outward toward Nicolas so that he could read it. She asked him this question: 'What do the words mean?'

"Nicolas's heart sank, for the text before him was no more comprehensible than the cryptic markings he had seen the previous day. The fact that Gillette did not seem to be expecting an answer—but was prepared to carry on her presentation absent dialogue—did not increase her companion's equanimity. She continued: 'My words are understandable to any person who will see. Look!' Here Gillette pointed to a few lines on the page she had selected. 'These I heard from the lips of the bronze.'

"Again, Nicolas peered at the page, but his attempt to understand the text was no more successful. Rather than confront the girl with his frustrations, however, he determined to communicate with her the best way he could. 'Your writing is beyond me,' he said, and then he followed with this invitation: 'Why don't you read the lines aloud?'

"Gillette nodded. 'You will soon see that anyone can understand.' Turning the book about so that she could read the page, she recited the following:

'Winter
For every night that cracks with bitter frost
Match you the warming wind of summer day;

Remember me, the one who silent lost
Her life and love and at my image stay.

At my image stay when life and love
And even sunshine leave your summer day;
May then your warmth release me from my
glove
Of frozen bronze that forms my overlay.'"

Mary continued her narration: "At the conclusion of her poem, Gillette gently closed her book, sat on the divan, and addressed Nicolas: 'Do you see? It is a matter not of deciphering but of becoming one with the Ideal. It is a matter not of the rules of art but of the laws of substance. Meaning does not arise from the decoding of a text but from a communion with the spirit infused in material.'

"Nicolas was about to issue a response when Gillette continued with this lucid speech: 'Let me tell you the story of my legislator. One day he and I were visited by Porbus, who had brought with him a copy of his latest book. The conversation immediately turned to the proper nature of the novel—that is, to its role as the Aeolian harp of the Three Graces—and there naturally arose the disagreement that always occurs between the two practitioners of the written word. Porbus, as you know, took the position that the novel—if not exclusively a medium for entertainment—is intended to communicate a moral lesson to the reader, or at a higher level to shape society into a better environment for humanity. Frenhofer determined that the novel is properly oriented in another direction: Its mission is to create a condition of cognitive value, a heightened state of sensitivity to natural forces, and in pursuing its task is as divorced from the petty concerns of the common person as a ship at sea from the waves of the shore. Back and forth the combatants parried, until the Old Master, tired of the battle, tore from the hands of his companion the offending volume, opened the book to a random page, and raising his pen high over the prose, made this pronouncement: "The words you have written are unfit for the page. They should be tossed into the *pulper* along with their maker." He then lowered his pen and began to edit, in furious strokes, the printed text. "*There!*" he shouted, his word plunging as a dagger into the heart of his audience. Again: "*There!* There is how you write so the gods of Olympus sing your words."

"'It was over in less than ten seconds, and just as Porbus began to protest what he deemed but the ravings of a madman, we—all three of us—were arrested by a sound that began to emanate from the bronze sculpture in the library adjacent to my legislator's study. At first the sound was so low that it could scarcely be heard, but within seconds it grew into a mighty roar. We rushed into the library to confront a thrilling sight: The eyes of the bronze had begun to glow and life seemed to emanate from its surface in a kind of miraculous aura. Dr Frenhofer and I raised our hands in praise.

"'Porbus stepped away from us, staring at us as if we had lost our minds. His assessment mattered not. Frenhofer, facing the statue in a kind of benediction, shouted, "Do you see, Porbus? Here, from the Divine sculpture, has come for the living principles of our labors the sacred rage! Here has come to us, from this extraordinary bronze, the principle which for our power of creation shall be the willing, masterful, and fecund talisman."'

"With this, Gillette's story came to an end. The young woman appeared to be drained of energy. Her face pale, her posture stooped, she gently closed her diary and turned to go. 'I seek rest,' she said weakly. In a moment she had disappeared into her room."

Mary Frenhofer settled back in her chair and peered at her visitor. "Who could fail to understand that Nicolas—presented with such a scene as I have just described—now understood the necessity of seeking my assistance, for he had come to the realization that his own powers—in terms of their ability to save Gillette from the most severe effects of her monomania—were insufficient?

"And so, the following day, Nicolas came to me. Upon hearing the story that I have just repeated to you, I told the young man there was no time to lose. For the safety of Gillette, we must quickly put in place the plan I had already determined as the best course of action for the girl. Indeed, we would take action that very evening."

CHAPTER 26:

A Woman in Full

Two gentlemen were engaged in a spirited conversation. The first—who seemed considerably more at home in the room than his companion—sat hunched over a writing desk littered with empty coffee cups and stacks of manuscripts. From his lowered eyes he stared evenly at the second, who sat facing the desk in a chair which—despite or perhaps because of a preponderance of worn cushioning—did not appear to be among the most comfortable. This second gentleman was toying absently with the head of a walking stick, the lower end of which he tapped from time to time on the floor, his maneuverings perhaps providing him with an aid to reflection.

The man at the desk was attempting to open—by force of will—a desk drawer. "Is the entire house against me?" he asked in a tone of frustration. "Shall I find no peace in my own home?" He finally relented his efforts, resting his elbows on his desk and burying his face in his hands.

"Where is your household help?" asked the visitor, whom I might as well identify right now as Houdon.

He glanced from the great bookcase on one side of the study to its pendant on the other as if expecting a servant to rise as if by magic from the thick dust.

"Fled."

"I see." The guest paused. "And does it not strike you as odd that they should disappear like that into the darkness of the land? Those who, I mean, have been so loyal over the years?"

"I suppose you, too, are questioning my sanity," the man said dully. He added: "Porbus did it."

The visitor ignored this sally while imagining the pending advent of a more determined advance. He shifted his gaze from the seated man to the study's old grandfather clock, the pendulum of which swung patiently back and forth with muffled clicks, providing the room's only ambient sound. "Your relationship with your biographer is a complex one. He, after all, if I am not mistaken, is responsible for your residence here."

"Porbus has mixed motives. Whether he shall continue as my biographer remains to be seen." The tone here was dark, the evenly spaced words testifying to a balance: the subject of the conversation was more than suspect in his intentions, despite his seeming generosity; the individual in the cushioned chair had the considerable advantage of carrying with him an overwhelming aura of trust, while having a sense that his dispensation—that is, an allowance to remain in the great writer's study—was but provisional. Houdon, welcome as a trusted sounding board, must toe the line or risk exile. The speaker—he was Joseph Frenhofer—rested his mouth behind his clasped hands and stared at his visitor.

Recognizing potential in this new line, the man with the walking stick determined to draw upon the first component of Frenhofer's statement while allowing the second—fraught as it was for a danger perhaps unperceived by its creator—to drift. Motives, it appeared, comprised a topic both safe and productive: "Why do you suppose Porbus was so anxious that Gillette come here?"

"Porbus is a conniver." Again the same even tone as the speaker glared at his visitor. "On the surface, he believes Gillette will help me in the completion of *Catherine Lescault*. In this, I am in full agreement."

"That is good, then," said Houdon helpfully.

Frenhofer glanced down and gave his desk drawer one more mighty pull. It flew open, resulting in a great rattle of pencils and staples. "Do you see this book?" He reached into the drawer and pulled out a covered volume, raising it in the air for the edification of his guest, who raised his eyebrows in anticipation. "This is the diary of Gillette. It holds the secret to facility—to the creation of life itself."

"The diary that Father Rachel encouraged the girl to keep," said Houdon in noncommittal tones. "And where does a young girl of her age obtain this wisdom?"

"From the bronze."

Houdon allowed the lure to float for a time unsnatched as he tossed a new line. "The board has been speaking of you, I must tell you, and asked that I come to make sure you were in good health. They have not heard from you for a while. They are concerned that you have been overworking."

Frenhofer ignored the statement, preferring to remain with what was, to him, a more fraught topic. "Porbus, of course, has much to gain from my success. How much better a selling environment for a biography if its subject has produced one final great achievement. And that achievement–*Catherine Lescault*–what a creation it will be." He peered intently at Houdon and pointed an index finger. "You will not see just words printed on pages, Houdon. You will see a living, breathing woman."

Houdon gave a nod of acknowledgement. "And the work, then, is progressing?"

Frenhofer reached out with two hands, holding two fingers inches apart. "I am so close! So close! Thanks to Gillette and to the bronze which speaks to her." The Old Master reached down and tapped the cover of the diary. "Everything is recorded in here. No more hesitation! The novel will be finished in a matter of a week."

Seeing an opening, Houdon decided to coast. "That is excellent news. Good lord, man, I don't see why you have an issue with Porbus. It would seem you owe him a great deal of thanks."

Frenhofer returned to his previous defensive pose, staring at Houdon now at a bit more of an angle. "Unless, of course, the man has an alternative agenda." He paused as if to assess his companion. "Why does he laugh at me?"

"He laughs so?"

"You have read it, have you not?"

"The parody. Perhaps it was an unfortunate thing to do. But it is an honor to be so treated. . . ."

"By an honorable person."

Houdon conceded: "Of course."

"Is it honorable to call me an 'old academist' to his friends, and to say I am determined to send the literary world back to the age of the beaker and the test tube?"

Houdon nodded his head to the side, a universal gesture of non-commitment and an invitation to continue.

"Is it honorable to call me a kind of giant elephant, reaching about with my proboscis, attempting for all the world with all my effort to twist myself into a position where, at the cost of my literary dignity, I might pick up a pea for the edification of my readers? Do you call that honorable?"

"I call it imprudent. But you know, you have given the man rather a hard time in your reviews."

"My work is legitimate. I do not call the man, for example, an elephant. I maintain my ship on its true course: The man's prose is written as if hacked from rock with an axe. It would be unprofessional for me to allow to pass unmarked what is so obviously meant not to harness thunder from the mountain but to ring the flea market's cash registers."

"He has a different idea of the novel."

"He has, rather, subsumed the novel to a different thing. A person such as he possesses a desire, you think, to see the greatest work I have ever done come to light?" Frenhofer shook his head. "More likely—yes, more likely—he wants to see me fail, that my work, arising from the germinal mist before it is ready, should pave the way for his own advance in the ranks of the greatest of the world's creators."

"And you feel, then—or think it likely, at least—that he is deliberately rushing you to publication? But after ten years. . . ," he added weakly.

Frenhofer, though, simply continued. "Yes, the key to the *hesitational lock*—Gillette has learned it from the sculpture, which she was wise to beg Porbus to bring here." Frenhofer paused. "I only fear Porbus." He then appeared to withdraw into his thoughts as he wrung his hands and stared vacantly beyond Houdon. Just as his companion was about to break the silence, Frenhofer spoke these words slowly under his breath, as if to no one in particular: "Porbus is the rage of the beast. Yet Porbus is I."

Houdon tucked away the utterance for further reflection and attempted to return the Old Master to the present. "And Gillette—what does she gain from all this?"

"Gillette is a pure soul," Frenhofer said easily. "She is a young woman of great potential. One can see that from her communion with the sculpture and from her work. She is destined for greatness. She need only obtain from me the base materials—the principles of the mastered word, the laws of the text infused with the Ideal. The life-giving fire she will obtain from the bronze."

"And Porbus—he is so willing to risk the loss of his laurels to an attractive beauty?"

Frenhofer adopted a darker visage. "Porbus has a history with Gillette."

This was a matter of some alarm. "History? Take care, Dr Frenhofer. It is one thing to be a rival in the world of belles lettres, another to state false witness. Recall I answer to the board. I am familiar with the rumors, but investigations have been made and files closed. We must be fair even to those people we do not like." Conscious of a pang of condescension, Houdon nevertheless felt he possessed sufficient reserves—given his history with Frenhofer—to survive what he instinctively determined was, for his current audience, passable.

A shrewd glance from Frenhofer informed his companion that the old master had quickly detected, processed, and assimilated the complex of forces that had traversed Houdon's consciousness. Frenhofer placed his elbows on his desk and rested his chin behind his folded hands. "Porbus writes a short story and includes a real human being," he stated. "What happens to the soul of the person who has been absorbed in the kind of trivial scribbling to which the mind of Porbus is attuned? Does the person not die?"

"And this, then, is what happened?"

"Porbus feels guilt. He must return Gillette to the living world. It shall be done."

"Just how?"

"*Catherine Lescault* shall redeem her. You see: Porbus and I have a complex relation."

"And by what means can a novel save a young girl?"

Frenhofer was just about to answer when he was interrupted by a loud crashing noise from the back of the studio. Houdon sat up in alarm, then stood and turned to see a young man rushing breathlessly into the room from the back door. "Dr Frenhofer!" he shouted. "Dr Frenhofer! You must not let the spirit come out of the sculpture."

Frenhofer scowled at the intruder: "What are you talking about?" He then turned back to Houdon. "Did you know this malapert was coming?"

The young intruder advanced into the room until he was at the side of the Old Master's desk. "I saw what is happening in your house, with the sculpture. It is wrong. You must allow Gillette to escape this place."

"Nicolas," said Houdon by way of introduction. "Gillette's paramour."

Frenhofer narrowed his eyes and stared directly at the young man. He repeated: "What are you talking about? What have you seen—or imagine you have seen?"

"Last night I was in the vestibule late at night, after speaking with your wife. We were able to peek into the library through a hole that had been drilled behind one of the old portraits that line the walls."

"Trespasser!" shouted Frenhofer. "Spy! Get out!"

"I will not leave without Gillette!" the young man continued. "What we saw was this: Gillette was sitting so close to the sculpture—so close that her lips were nearly touching those of the bronze. I held my breath and tried to see clearly in the dark, to determine what she might be doing. What I saw was not something that any person would believe possible—unless the girl had gone insane. For the fact was—" Here the young man turned to Houdon as if for support, or as if seeking a reasonable audience for his recitation. "The girl was speaking with the sculpture, in a voice so low we could barely hear it." The young man spun away from the desk and would have rushed into the adjacent library with its resident sculpture and scholar—had the door not been clearly bolted. Frenhofer made a daily habit of securing the entrance against the intrusions of barbarians.

The young man was about to continue when Frenhofer spoke. "Gillette is a sensitive individual, attuned to the higher aesthetics, and is hence to the creation of my masterwork an essential helpmate. I will have you know that she is 'speaking'—as you put it—with a respectable work of art. To put the matter another way, she is in a state of high sensitivity to the principles that enliven the work's constructive materials. The bronze creation, like many others of similar import, possesses secrets which are priceless to the higher realm of the fine arts—and to my manuscript in particular. Your puny mind is too undeveloped to interpret what you have seen in any way other than by bottling your conjured images into banal man-in-the-street propositions. But by interjecting yourself into a delicate aesthetic dynamic, you are threatening my life's work—indeed, the completion of the greatest novel I have ever written."

Nicolas, however, would have none of this. "You crazy old man! No one cares about your stupid novel. You are threatening the sanity of a young girl who is already on the edge, who wakes up in the middle of the night screaming from her falling dream, who scribbles nonsense in a diary that no one can possibly make any sense of. Shall I tell you what I heard her say to the sculpture? She said these words, in a voice that was like something from a disembodied spirit: 'Come forth, come forth, from the bronze.' And then I heard the response of the sculpture, 'Come to me, come to me . . . what lives within lives forever.'"

Frenhofer, who had become enraged at the charge of insanity, raised his fists in the air. "Get out! You have the soul of a snail and the mind of a toad. You imagine something out of thin air—some speech from a deaf and dumb statue—and then try to use it to turn everyone against me. You and all the others!"

With this pronouncement, the Old Master took an imprudent step toward his intruder—an event which inspired Houdon to cash in some of his personal capital. He walked behind Frenhofer and embraced him gently to keep him from committing an unwise attack, then simultaneously gestured just as gently to the young intruder in a universal gesture to back off. "Now is not a good time to approach Gillette," he said in even tones, the words intended to calm both sides of the altercation. He glanced meaningfully at Nicolas. "Let me speak with Dr Frenhofer alone for a bit. I will reason with him on your behalf. Soon we will come to the aid of your young lady."

CHAPTER 27:
A Locked Room

Tea arrived with salutary dispatch, sugar and lemon were provided, and Frenhofer's guest settled back into the same chair he had occupied the previous week. Unlike the earlier meeting, however, Houdon was now accompanied by two other gentlemen—one being Franklin Porbus. Aware that the brush of this gentleman upon the cusp of the host might create something more incendiary than smoldering embers, Houdon, who had promised the academy to attempt a reconciliation between the antagonistic authors, had also brought along Father Rachel in recognition of the holy man's talent for mediation. Houdon had also been informed of the details of Father Rachel's conversation with Frenhofer's wife. These disinterested parties recognized that neither of the authors at odds was prone to attach to the other's neck any but the shortest of leashes, the careful watch maintained by such security being deemed, under the strained circumstances, but minimal prudence.

And so it was that the two literary combatants took stock of each other with jaundiced glances. The younger writer could not but notice a particular aura of gloom that seemed to envelop his host. "Well, master," opened Porbus, a keen eye at work. "Are the metaphors stale? Are the characters stubborn and prone to balk at their duty? Or is it perhaps the plot—does the story insist on sailing north when only a southern clime offers sufficient breeze?"

Frenhofer slumped forward at his desk, passed a weary hand over his forehead, and peered glumly at his visitors. "I had a terrible dream. I had died, and my spirit was stumbling through a series of old, dark rooms—it was some kind of library—and I met writers from the past, telling me all kinds of things of which I was already aware." He glanced at Porbus. "Gillette was in the dream, also. She seemed to be floating somewhere up above, and she was beckoning to me. She said something about returning her to life. I don't know. It was all rather dismal." He paused and glared at his visitors. "The thing quite drained me."

Porbus took this in, then turned to Father Rachel. "Well, that's in your line of work, Father, is it not? Our old genius has had a vision—doubtless one that will make its way into his great novel."

Father Rachel adopted a noncommittal visage, perhaps loathe to say anything that would cast the conversation in the wrong direction. All he finally said was this, which, as it happened, was quite enough to advance everyone's agenda: "Dr Frenhofer has been working very hard on *Catherine Lescault*. I believe he has some good news for us."

Porbus gave an expression of surprise and eyed the Old Master closely. "You have made progress?"

Frenhofer, in his characteristic manner, set his elbows on his desk and rested his chin behind his folded hands. His eyes shifted uneasily to each of his guests, and then he stated in even tones: "*Catherine Lescault* is completed."

The words all had been waiting for, when finally heard, caused at first nothing less dramatic than a kind of shock. Porbus was the first to speak. "Well, well, old fellow!" He broke into a broad grin. "I never thought this day would come. The greatest novel you have ever written—finished." Then he began to beam even more broadly. "And after ten years. What do you say?" He reached out with a thumbs-up signal, his countenance adopting that collegiality often seen among those sharing a common drinking schedule. "Are you going to admit that you owe it to me? Confess! It was the sculpture and Gillette—both my gifts to you at your request—who inspired you to complete your life's work."

The Old Master, however, seemed to have little inclination to thank Porbus for his assistance. Instead, he stared at the younger novelist as glumly as before, then reopened a former wound. “You have stooped to my level, then. You have agreed to assist an old elephant with a swollen, grabby proboscis. Very fine of you. Nothing in it for you, of course.”

Porbus responded immediately by raising his hands and making sounds of protest. Father Rachel attempted to ease the sudden tension, raising a pedagogic index finger. “Now, now, Dr Frenhofer. Let bygones be bygones. Let the errors of the past be forgotten—”

“Yes, errors,” broke in Porbus. “Errors a thousand times, Dr Frenhofer. A thousand times I have regretted what I wrote. It was the tension of the academy; the pressures all of us have been under.” Then he adopted a submissive and honorable position: “Please accept my apology for what was a stupid and foolhardy prank that reflects more on me than on you.”

Father Rachel and Houdon emitted some murmurs of agreement and encouragement. For his part, Dr Frenhofer seemed to loosen a little. He sat back a bit in his chair, lowered his arms and pushed himself slightly away from the desk. “Very well,” he said, casting at his visitors another shrewd glance of appraisal which, if it had warmed a bit by their efforts, nevertheless maintained a more than sufficient degree of prudent chill. “Now you shall see perfection.”

The three companions glanced at one another as Dr Frenhofer stood and walked to a file cabinet on the side wall. He opened the top drawer and retrieved what appeared to be a large manuscript—a work, as it happened, which was divided into sections with large clips. He began to leaf through the parts and muttered under his breath while examining several: "*The Hidden Beam . . . Across the Moors . . . Christmas Eve. . . .*" He then walked back to the desk, and, in a few curt businesslike movements, handed each of his guests a section of writing. "Three chapters, gentlemen," he said, eyeing each potential reader in turn. "Read! Read and understand how an artist creates a living, breathing woman."

His three guests bowed their heads as obedient schoolboys and began to peruse the text for which the academy had waited a decade. Houdon was excited to be among the very first to read what for all the world promised to be the greatest work of the man who, for Newmarch, had been nothing less than the personification of the intellectual paradigm. One would do well, then, given the state of Houdon's mind, to refrain from a hypercritical assessment of his reaction as he absorbed the text before him.

And what, in brief, *was* his reaction? One of incomprehension. The fact was that the sentences he was reading were, to his eyes, unintelligible. As he grappled with this reality, he felt a pang of emotion—an amalgam of embarrassment, fear, confusion, and—to be sure—a rising component of pity. He felt his cheeks begin to flush—a condition he had not experienced since grade school days. He began to glance furtively at his companions, who, he realized with a mixture of relief and dread, were exhibiting expressions of individuals struggling with similar indignities. As for the author of the chapters in question—how can he be described? One can only imagine, or try to imagine, a beaming father in a delivery room, proud of his work and delighted that his audience, after such a long wait for delivery, could at last experience and savor the victory of an accomplished master whose work, mind, and pen were at the peak of their powers.

Houdon was just about to formulate an opening statement to what for all intents and purposes would seem to promise a disastrous conversation when the master suddenly began to shout, his voice causing his guests to jump in their chairs. "Aha!" he exclaimed. "You did not expect to see such perfection. You were looking for a mere description, a mere exposition, a mere—shall I say it?—popular entertainment that Porbus here"—he made a dismissive gesture in the direction of the younger writer—"has been spoon-feeding the masses. Well, instead you are seeing reality—not a mass of simple text but the complex spirit of a woman. Does not Catherine Lescault—in her parts, mind you, for you must read the entire novel to get the whole woman—rise before your eyes as Venus rose from the sea? But wait, wait."

Here Frenhofer interrupted himself, raised a cautionary hand, and walked back to his cabinet to launch another search, allowing the three critics a brief respite to exchange whispers. Father Rachel leaned to the side and, pointing down at the pages in his hand, spoke in low tones to his colleagues: "Can you understand a word of this?"

Houdon could only shake his head dumbly.

Porbus, for his part, lowered his eyes and glanced furtively over at the master, then back at his companions. "It is nothing but a conglomeration of abstraction," he whispered. Then he added in a still lower rasp: "This work is the gibberish of a raving lunatic."

By this time, however, Frenhofer had returned. To the amazement of his guests, the man had become transformed—almost young again. His cheeks were flushed with life; his eyes sparkled with the delight of the creative temperament; gone was any taint of the old anger and resentment. "Here's more!" he fairly shouted, as if handing out candy to clamoring children. "Look at this vision in the scene by the old stone manse, for example—" Here he eagerly shoved more pages at Father Rachel. "And Porbus, my good man, just see if you could render an afternoon tea scene—and its effect on a visiting gentleman, of course—with the clarity you see in this little gem of a paragraph." But by the time Porbus had accepted the proffered sheets, the old Olympian was running off one more time to his sacred cabinet.

"Ah!" a mystified Porbus suddenly exclaimed. "We are mistaken, gentlemen—here, look—this paragraph does show a certain clarity." The others leaned over and looked eagerly at Porbus's text. "You see, this is a quite charming tea scene—and, yes, how lifelike seems the conversation between the courtesan and the King." The other readers nodded to one another. Porbus added: "There is indeed a woman beneath."

By the conclusion of those desperate endorsements, Frenhofer had become lost in a kind of creative ecstasy. He stopped at his sacred cabinet, turned again in the direction of his guests, held his hands behind his back, rocked back and forth on his heels, and then began to speak to an unknown presence in the air. "You see, gentlemen, that creating life is not a matter of wishing, or of drawing the outlines of a subject as a novice might trace the outline of a mushroom. No! Creating a living work of art means achieving a state of high sensitivity, then infusing the text with spirit—and that can only be done after a lifetime of labor."

As he was going on in this way, Houdon felt the gentle hand of Father Rachel rest on his shoulder. "You know, gentlemen," the priest suddenly pronounced in an elevated voice, turning to each of his fellow critics, "in Dr Frenhofer we see a very great author."

The path being blazed by the good priest was easily spied, and his companions set upon the trace. "He is even more a poet than an author," offered Porbus in a loud voice.

"Beyond a certain limit in art, the work loses itself in the world of spirit," Houdon enjoined. "The Old Master has exceeded whatever limits we have perceived with our dull eyes."

Frenhofer had ceased his speech to peruse his own text, smiling deeply to himself and nodding, seeming to have disappeared into a world of his own making. It occurred to Houdon that he might not even have heard the strained accolades. Porbus leaned toward Houdon, speaking in a low voice as he glanced furtively toward the master. "Of course," he whispered, "sooner or later he must discover that his writing is gibberish."

"Gibberish!" exclaimed Frenhofer. He looked down at his manuscript and then back up at Porbus.

"What have you done?" Houdon muttered, turning to the young author.

"Porbus!" shouted Frenhofer. "Are you making a fool of me?" He turned to Father Rachel. "And you—tell me, have I ruined my work after all?" Again his attention changed as he shifted ground. "Houdon!" That man began to demur but the Old Master shook his head quickly, holding out the palm of his hand. "Houdon! You are the only man I can trust. Tell me. What do you read in my work?"

Houdon wanted to say something positive, but could not lie to his friend. Looking down at the chapter he held in his hands, he paused a moment, lowered his eyes, and then placed the pages gently on the desk of the master.

Frenhofer stood silent. His face fell into the old pattern of aged resentment. He sat back heavily into his chair. "So I am a madman," he uttered. "I have no talent." He shook his head in quick jerks as he gazed at the far wall of his studio. "I am a rich man who works for his own pleasure. That is all I am."

The three visitors began to make noises of reconciliation, but Frenhofer had clearly understood the truth. The babble of words seemed to pass over his head as he sat with eyes wide, head bowed.

Suddenly his countenance changed. He raised his arms and began to wring his hands together as his face darkened and he peered at each of his critics in turn. A light—a powerful one—began to rise in his visage. He stood from his chair and seemed to tower over the room. "By God, you are all jealous of me. You are trying to convince me I am a failure because you want to steal my technique." He raised the sheaf of papers in his hand and tapped on them with one index finger. "This is a breathing Catherine Lescault!" he cried. He shook the papers. "You fools do not see her because you have never really seen a living woman."

At that moment, the discussion was interrupted by a creaking sound emanating from one side of the study. As the visitors turned toward the source, they witnessed a sobering sight: the gradual closing of the old oaken door that led into the library. The squeak of its rusty hinges sounded as the cry of a dying soul—a cry that was followed by a dull click.

The door had shut tight, enclosing in the library's gloom the scholar and her sculpture.

"Gillette!" cried Father Rachel.

By this time, however, Frenhofer had recovered himself, standing before his cabinet with a new attitude, staring suspiciously at his guests much as a merchant with a fine collection of gems might glare at untrustworthy customers. "Gentlemen!" he pronounced. He held one hand palm up toward Porbus, a gesture that wordlessly demanded the return of the sullied pages. After Porbus complied, Frenhofer subjected his two other visitors to similar treatment.

"Dr Frenhofer," Houdon could only say, "I am sorry." The Old Master looked at his guest with suspicious eyes, then turned away and gathered together the scattered remnants of his masterpiece, assembling them into a single stack of papers which he moved efficiently to replace in the file cabinet. He then closed the drawer with a sharp click, turned the key in its lock, and with a contemptuous look and a series of supercilious gratuities ushered the traitors from his studio. As the gentlemen mingled dumbly outside the door of his house, Frenhofer stood in the threshold and bade them farewell. "Goodbye, my young friends." He gave a final suspicious glance, then turned and closed the door behind him.

None of the guests liked the sound of that last farewell. They all knew Frenhofer was living on the edge. But at the same time they knew he would accept no assistance—indeed, in his mind the three critics, and the world entire, had become his enemy.

The next morning, Father Rachel went to the old man's home to see if the light of a new day might inspire a spiritual refreshment. But he was too late. Mary met the priest at the door, her eyes red with weeping: During the night Frenhofer had burned his manuscript along with Gillette's diary, and then he had died.

Attention turned at once to the young woman. The key to the library was not to be found. When calling through the old bars of the intervening door, Mary received no response. By this time Porbus and Houdon had both arrived and determined immediately that the police must be called. No call, however, needed to be made for they were already arriving on their own, led by a frantic Nicolas who had been informed of the tragedy. When Nicolas himself received no response to his pleas to the sequestered girl, three of the burliest of the group's men threw themselves against the library door to break it down. Once . . . twice . . . still they made little headway beyond a small splintering. Finally, on the third try, the door caved in and everyone rushed into the library.

The bronze sculpture was standing alone in the middle of the room, facing the door and surrounded by a choir of old volumes. Was the bronze woman welcoming her invaders as Pluto welcomed the dead? Perhaps she was welcoming the living, for every person in that brave party later spoke in hushed tones about what they had seen: a living presence which seemed to pulse and glow with some form of inner life, and which seemed to see with inhuman eyes what no lifeless material of earth should divine.

Gillette had vanished. As soon as it was confirmed the girl was not in the room, Nicolas begged everyone to help him search the surrounding forest. Of course they complied, as did many subsequent volunteers from the town. The search went on for a week but not a trace of the girl was found. Many days later, Father Rachel could be seen attempting to console Nicolas as the authorities dragged the lake—considered the likeliest resting place for the girl. That final effort also failed. To this day no one has discovered the fate of Gillette.

CHAPTER 28:
The Rambling Cottage

If you take the time someday to travel down the winding road that leads west from the Newmarch academy, you will eventually arrive at a height of land covered by a rough scattering of pitch pine and scrub oak. On this windswept spot stands a charming old cottage with a design more helter-skelter than you will likely see anywhere, for the structure's confusing pattern of porches, pergolas, sunrooms, dormers, and other oddities had been added willy-nilly over the years by a series of owners cultivating idiosyncratic enthusiasms unhampered by blind faith in architectural coherence.

Local natives with a knowledge of history will tell you that the original sections of the house—their roots in a distant past discernable by their antique cedar casts—had been constructed as a residence for a brotherhood, the leaders of the contemplative order having looked favorably on the lonely hilltop as one agreeable to prayer. With the passage of years, however, the members of the order dwindled, and—the remaining acolytes having blended into rival organizations—the house was set for sale.

While the building enjoyed a rest, eventually its elevation and the surrounding crisp pine-clean air attracted the interest of astronomers who determined to view the heavens from an angle different from the building's earlier residents. If the new tenants found the environs perfect it also remained true that time, as it so often does, continued to pass. Eventually the scientists—now subjected to the indignity of a snub on the part of a civilization that had emerged onto a broad expanse of the ineffable and grown disenchanted with the heavy tread of fact and formula—found themselves tracing the same sad path of the forgotten monks.

Once again the house's rooms were able to stretch, yawn, and enjoy a comfortable slumber. If they were disturbed by the occasional crowd of schoolchildren scrambling about the acreage in challenge of a popular conceit—did the house adopt a different visage when viewed from different angles, or shift in position and change configuration at random intervals?—they never complained. When the gleefully frightened children ran screaming back into the safety of town the structure shrugged off the incident as the price requisite for a presentation to the public of a personality idiosyncratic.

Then, one more time, came a rebirth: a "For Sale" sign attracted yet a third tenant: a sculptor who delighted in the soft glow filtering through the building's frosted skylights. His domain—that of the fine arts—was not all that different, when you stop and think about it, from the structure's predecessors. Each, after all, created value by isolating and delineating natural forces while filtering visions through characteristic first principles and engineering paradigms. And did not each discipline determine an artifact—whether *object d'art* or cognitive impress—shaped from the world by human hand?

Shortly after his purchase of the building, the sculptor determined its size to be barely sufficient for the display of his growing body of work. He therefore began to construct a companion residence a few hillocks over. This required the excavation of a good deal of land that through the ages had accumulated the debris of former civilizations. The result, after an impressive number of antique items had been uncovered and cataloged, was a classical structure, the towers of which peeked, elflike, over the treetops at the atelier.

Despite the artist's seeming need for privacy, he possessed a welcoming personality. For many years, therefore, visitors would stop and chat with the amiable man while viewing his many works that had become known around the world for their uncanny resemblance to living things. I might as well tell you right now that the sculptor's name was Jean-Antoine

Houdon, and that I was one of his many visitors. And I would be less than honest to say that in my visiting I did not have a motive ulterior to the pleasant viewing of the man's mature works. For the manuscript that the professor had read to us students that Christmas Day so many years before—the gist of which in this work's previous chapters I have redrawn as close to its original visage as I deemed prudent—was intriguing but nevertheless left hanging a matter of import. And it was for the dissolution of the shadow which a communicative lack had cast over this matter for which I was determined to ask the old professor the favor of a light.

Before I broached the matter, however, there arose the rather delicate requirement of my revelation. I don't mind saying that I was nervous. Would my presence, after all, be deemed an intrusion? The man had not taught for many years, was in a state of comfortable retirement, and there was no way of telling how happy he was that he had revealed a bit too much about his view toward sculpture as the queen of the arts.

As for the subject of sculpture in general, it happened that day that he felt quite at home and evidently in a state of expansion. As he escorted me through the many rooms of his hodge-podge atelier, my host explained his philosophy of creation: "An artist must know not only how to make works that live, but must possess the willingness to attempt the *miracle germinal*," he said. I recognized at once the tone of the professor pacing before the fire in my student days. "Otherwise it is impossible to give meaning to the mental image. And if one does not from the springboard of image leap into meaning, one fails to create value."

These matters, so familiar to me in style and import, also struck me, as I looked up from a close study of a work titled *The Three Graces*, as to the point of my mission a happy accompaniment. To gain his goodwill, I began with a little flattery: "You make it sound very easy, Dr Houdon. I daresay many artists would give their lives to learn your secrets for creating living works. These three ladies here, for example–charm, beauty, and creativity. They all seem to be stepping forth from their pedestal and walking around the room. You have been able to harness natural forces and exploit them in a manner that cannot be explained with a few propositions."

Houdon gave the tolerant smile of an artist who had heard such praises before. "Look over here at this one," he said. "It is my *Head of Balzac.*" He gave his visitor a sly glance. "Does he not seem ready to speak to us? Perhaps to narrate one of his stories?"

I gave the work a bit of a nod, my noncommittal visage, to my mind, endorsement sufficient of a favorable assessment which the artist seemed to have adopted easily enough without the benefit of outside assistance. I, instead, took a deep breath and turned a corner: "If you don't mind my saying so, your greatest work is not on display in these rooms."

Houdon stopped and turned. "My greatest work?"

"I am embarrassed to say that I must reveal myself as something of an intruder. You know, I am perhaps one of the last individuals who recalls a certain Christmas Eve before the fireside, and a charming day following, in which a great professor read for the edification of his students a treatise that illustrated just why sculpture is the queen of the arts."

Houdon stopped and stared at me with a startled eye, and then, to my relief, emitted a small chuckle of surprise. He pursed his lips, clasped his hands behind his back, raised his eyebrows and nodded. "Ah, the *famous* reading," he offered in a tone of self-denigration. He again chuckled softly, paused and considered the matter. "So you have come back for more punishment—or perhaps you fancy that you have found me out?" The sculptor peered at me and broke into one of his characteristic sly grins. I immediately thought of a similar sidelong glance that had so disconcerted me years before.

"Certainly not the latter. If anything, your story has rather haunted me over the years. Only one matter has stayed with me as a part of the picture unfinished. The matter of the resolution of the extraordinary work around which the narrative revolved. And so I have come here with the hope—most cheeky, I admit—to view the work which played such a great role in your life and in that of Dr Frenhofer."

Houdon bowed his head in thought. He then bid me follow him to a small anteroom—one which no one save he who had a firm grasp of the building's rambling pattern would have realized even existed. And what a charming space it was, surrounded with glass walls which allowed easy vistas across an expanse of pines. In one direction the visitor could see the charming towers of the sculptor's residence peeking over the treetops.

A table set for tea was bathed in a cheerful light. Houdon, bidding me sit, ordered refreshment from the kitchen. We then entered upon a long chat, sharing fond memories of our days at the academy. As the rollicking controversy about the greatest of artistic media was not neglected, the conversation naturally arrived at that topic which for my visit had been top of mind.

"You see, over the course of my life I devoted myself to many forms of expression," said Houdon. "All I was trying to communicate that Christmas Day was the manner in which the bronze sculpture had forced my decision toward the plastic art as superior. Why? For the simple reason that the work was able to fully contain the dynamics of a living human being—something that I had never before been able to do with the written word or an oiled portrait. Hence you see the works that I have created, and here, in this atelier, presented for the view of the public. They live; for that reason they create value."

I assured the master of my agreement. But he demurred: "I don't know, now, that I was entirely correct. We artists tend to be self-centered—what is true for us, we believe, is true for all. I have proven the case to myself—or have I? Perhaps I simply prefer to surround myself with a certain set of false principles." He gave me another one of those disconcerting smiles. "In any case, I have not *proven it* for others." He paused. "As for the little narrative I entertained you with that morning—interpret it as you will."

"Little narrative!" I protested. "It was hardly a simple entertainment. It is not the only work of yours that has changed lives."

Houdon gave me a shrewd look. "You have grown older and wiser," he said. "And I am older still."

As I absorbed this pronouncement, Houdon pushed aside his tea cup, rested his forearms on the table, and leaned toward me. He gazed at me with a piercing look. "Now, about the sculpture."

I held my breath in anticipation.

Houdon seemed to turn some matter over in his mind. "There is something vital to consider: the young lady."

"I have not forgotten her. I believe Gillette was never found."

"She disappeared. But how did she disappear? Do you recall the suitor? The young fellow?"

"Nicolas. Yes."

"Do you know what happened to him?"

"No."

"He went insane."

I sat back. "Good heavens."

Houdon pursed his lips and lowered his eyes. "As you already know, he became distraught at the disappearance of Gillette and engaged the entire town—whomever indeed he could convince—to assist in finding her. He insisted that the authorities continue to drag the lake and when he was told nothing more could be done, he threatened to sue. Well, a lover's duty transmogrified into an obsession. Everyone understood that the matter had gone beyond the simple grief of a man for a woman and had entered a different stage—one of mental unbalance. He was abandoned by his helpmates, even his friends. Yet he maintained his search, sometimes spending entire nights wandering in the forest, searching for her body."

"What a tragedy."

Houdon took a deep breath, as if about to embark on a part of his tale that required some courage. He gave me a piercing glance. "Then he began to insist that the sculpture was to blame."

"The sculpture?"

"He maintained that the girl had disappeared into the bronze; that the work had consumed her."

I was speechless. I tried to absorb the implications of this. I am sorry to report that I simply sat with my mouth agape.

Houdon went on: "Nicolas began to roam the streets of the town, collaring everyone he could and telling them that the sculpture was an evil presence. Then things took a turn for the worse. He began to wander into people's homes at night. People would awake to see him standing at the foot of their beds. As soon as they opened their eyes, he would start blabbering about how Gillette had been captured by the sculpture." Houdon paused. "Well, it was not long after these events that Nicolas was contained."

"I see."

"You can probably understand why I felt very uncomfortable keeping the bronze sculpture here at my atelier. As a matter of fact, Nicolas had on more than one occasion attempted to gain entrance to this studio. I had to obtain a trespass warning against him. Later I had to consider that his story might gain credence among the public, with the result that thrill seekers would crowd in here to see the work. I would not like my studio to be the venue for a long parade of individuals—mind you, I judge them not—who would likely come here to gawk at a weird spectacle. I therefore determined that the best thing to do was to donate the sculpture to the Metropolitan—with the stipulation that it not be displayed until I have given my permission."

My heart sank, although I understood the man's motivations. I could but again say: "Ah. I see."

Houdon continued: "So the sculpture is in storage, crated up, out of harm's way, in the basement of the museum." Houdon gazed through the windows at the sunlit pines. "Someday I shall give my consent to the work again coming to light—when? I cannot say right now."

"I do hope you shall!"

Houdon leaned back and gave me another shrewd glance. "Nicolas, I understand, has recently been released from the asylum and is on medication. It seems that he has forgotten about his monomania—or perhaps it is no longer as strong. So perhaps the time has come to return the sculpture to life." Houdon gave a tight smile. "We shall see."

Hearing the story of Nicolas had created a mixture of emotions in me—not only sorrow for the young man but also a deep shame that I had disturbed Houdon, and had caused him to recall such unpleasant memories—all for what now seemed to me to be a feckless mission. I half feared that the old professor looked upon me as a rather impertinent example of those many tourists who might come to gawk at the sculpture, looking upon a tragic story as nothing more than a monstrous spectacle.

Given the somber state of our conversation and the lateness of the hour, I expressed my apologies to my host and bid him farewell. I flatter myself that my departure, during the course of which my host accompanied me to the threshold of his door, was graced with a greater portion of goodwill than Houdon and Father Rachel had received from another artist so many years before.

CHAPTER 29:

Returned to Life

"Have you heard the tragic news of Dr Houdon?" The messenger from the *Scuola Grande di San Rocco* had preceded his interlocutory with a modest bow, one reflective of his employer's commendable regard for the sensibility of an individual who—having long accepted the wisdom of effecting upon one's soul the delights of morning coffee on an old *campo*—had just begun to engage the delicate process of accepting the damp, the stone, the seaward view, which for the larger Venetian wisdom provides a refined sheen of the *antique penumbra*.

"We received word, for our part, this morning from the academy," the gentleman continued, his rather mundane pendant appropriately framed by my gaping mouth and staring eyes. This secondary information I barely registered, for the man's opening words had ushered me into a world where past stimulants in their recall held sway.

My better social graces, I must add in my defense, quickly rose in response to my dumb appeal as I recognized in the gentleman's fierce gaze a knowledge of the regard I had long held for the master of Newmarch. I responded with this simplicity: "I thank you for informing me." The tone here, if I may leap anew to my defense, communicated more than the words' signification. Rather, I intended the gentleman to realize that my sadness was genuine; that death's messenger had been sensitive and good to grant me the honor of my emotion's anticipation; and that, finally, the news so communicated and its attendant train of sorrow was for the morning's engagement sufficient.

Sufficient, however, was not a word I would grant appropriate to the images which passed through my mind that morning under the Adriatic sun. The sculptor's demise stimulated many memories. Among them were the lectures on the fine arts, the Christmas Eve celebration with my colleagues, the reading of the unusual narrative the following day, and my shame at possibly being perceived as nothing but a feckless tourist at Houdon's final atelier. But the story of the passion of creation by Dr Frenhofer and the tragic results of the involvement of Houdon and the young girl Gillette in the completion of the old man's novel cast into high relief the most dramatic of all of the images which were called to mind: *the bronze sculpture of a woman in a shroud.*

Would the institution which had accepted that creation now reveal it to the public? I knew the answer was *yes.*

Before many days had passed I saw the announcement: The Metropolitan would honor Houdon with an exhibition of the full array of his works. How can I explain the surge of excitement that rose within me? It is no exaggeration to say that I could think of little else in the few weeks remaining prior to the opening, and, indeed, found myself haunting the museum in advance, roaming about the hallways and casing the approaches to the exhibition room where the great man's works were to be displayed. I began to wonder: *Would it be possible to catch a glimpse of the sculpture before the public viewing?*

My years of work with institutions of preservation, my knowledge of their springs and pulleys, was of inestimable assistance in helping me to infuse nature with my ideal. I am embarrassed to admit that the day before the opening, I found myself, rather like a thief, creeping down the access hall behind the Houdon exhibition room. By carefully analyzing the habits of the guards I was able to secrete myself in a cubby hole created by a chance arrangement of moveable panels. I stood thus in this shadowy otherworld scarcely daring to breathe lest I announce my presence.

Peering through a crack in the panels, I saw in the center of the room a large wooden crate upon which had been stenciled the following words: *Houdon. Woman in Bronze*. It was no more than the matter of an hour when workers appeared to reveal the work that had been the center of such drama. Did they realize what they were doing? Was the bronze just another object to them?

While I was sure the answer to the latter question was *yes*, I had no chance to reflect further on the matter, for the men were laboring with professional efficiency. Down with dispatch came the four walls of the wooden crate. What was now before the eye was a surprise: The work had been covered with a brown canvas, and that fabric wrapped round and round with twine. *How odd*, I thought to myself. *It is almost as though whoever packed the sculpture wanted to keep something captive inside rather than to protect the work from exterior damage*. The workers stepped back and gazed at what was exposed. I strained to hear what they were saying: It seemed they were expressing a surprise of their own at the unusual packaging.

The final work was the matter of a few moments. The twine was clipped; the canvas torn away; the woman exposed to view. At last I could see what for so many years had been only a myth: Before me, returned to the world after so long imprisoned, was the bronze around which had revolved so much human pain. I squinted to get a better look, but the dimly lit space, the downward incline of the woman's posture, and the angle with which the work was displayed all conspired to keep from me the full embrace of a view which would have to wait until the following day. It was with this realization that I heard a voice, a rasping, low pitched one—was it man or woman?—coming from I could not tell where, uttering these words: "*It is she.*" The sound caused me to start, and for a moment I despaired that my untoward motion would reveal my spy work. No one, however, seemed to take heed. I turned over what had occurred. Had I really heard a voice? Was it perhaps my own—had my excitement caused me to speak aloud without conscious knowing? And if not, whose voice could it be? As I considered these matters, I heard a sullen breath near me. My heart stopped and I strained to listen. Then sounded the voice anew: "*It is she.*"

Alarmed, I glanced around furtively for a hidden companion. There was none. As I peered back into the presentation room, I saw something that arrested my attention in another way: The workers gathering the packaging material were acting in what I can only describe as a subdued manner. I saw them pause, stare a bit at the work they had uncovered, and then leave the room without saying a word to one another.

I heard the click of a switch. The light had gone out.

My view, for the day, was over. I glanced about to make sure I was not under surveillance, then assumed a professional posture and made my way back down the access hall to the main gallery. To my despair, I walked into the path of a guard who was about to roll a security gate over the access hall entrance for the night. A professional nod—my years of gallery work came in handy—accompanied by a brisk "Good evening," and I had negotiated successfully what might otherwise have been a rather embarrassing incident.

I had just passed beyond the hall into the main gallery when three uniformed figures rushed in my direction. My trespass, then, had been discovered. I was about to launch into an outrageous explanation of my behavior, when, to my surprise, the officers ran past me. Their target was not I, but the gallery just behind. They were running to the room containing Houdon's bronze sculpture. What did that mean? I noted bitterly it was too late for me to turn back—the guard had locked the access hallway. If only I had remained in place! All I could do was return to my hotel and ponder.

That night I slept fitfully. I dreamed of a young man roaming through the woods in the darkness, searching for a lost love, wandering into the town and entering people's bedrooms, begging everyone for assistance.

The following day, I skipped breakfast and was among the very first to arrive at Houdon's exhibition. As the crowd was larger than I expected, Houdon's reputation as a magic-wielding Pygmalion serving to bulk up the public interest, the museum personnel were keeping people at some distance to allow sufficient room before the displays. I was thus unable to maneuver my way to a vantage point close enough to see into the woman's face—that visage that had been so frustratingly elusive the previous day.

I had just begun a conversation with a fellow enthusiast about the importance of the exhibition when I sensed what seemed to be a flash of light, or some kind of rapidly moving object, enter the exhibition room from a side door. I scarcely had time to register the image before it distilled into that of a young man rushing toward the bronze sculpture. As he approached his target, he began to shout these words: "Gillette, come forth from the statue! Gillette! Come out to me."

A chill went through my bones and I found myself stating aloud the name of a young man about whom I had long been troubled: "*Nicolas.*"

The security officers went immediately into action, rushing after the intruder and grabbing hold of his arms. As Nicolas put up a furious fight, the assembled audience began to emit a mixture of sounds expressing a mixture of outrage, surprise, and sympathy. "The poor man," I heard one woman say. "What could possibly be wrong with him?"

Nicolas was no match for the well-trained men who easily dragged him across the floor and through an adjoining door. "People!" he shouted as he was removed. "Gillette has been taken into the statue! Help me get her out of there! Help me save her." And that was all that we could clearly hear, for now he was escorted through the side door of the building.

The scene had affected my nerves, making me feel so lightheaded that I staggered away from the crowd to a seating area in the back of the room. Several guards came to my assistance, helping me to a chair, expressing concern, and offering refreshment. I raised a tentative arm in denial of the last, assuring my interlocutors of my good health. After the guards departed to engage with others, my breath started to come easier and I began to stretch and stand. It was then that I felt a small pressure on my right elbow. "*Stop*," a voice whispered to me. "*Stop*."

At first I thought this was another helpful individual attempting to ameliorate my panic, and I was about to protest, when—turning my face in the direction of the voice—I spied a fellow definitely not of the protective order. Dark-browed, fedora jammed down upon his head, the man was staring intently at me with a conspiratorial grin. "*Stop*," he said again. I attempted to pull my arm away, but his hand, despite its lightness, kept me in a vice-like grip.

"Who are you?" I asked. I felt some consternation, and would have feared the man a robber save for the presence of so many witnesses.

The stranger gave a brief shrug and smiled good-naturedly. He nodded toward a room behind us. "I came forth from a painting. I came to see her. As did you."

"See her?" I feigned ignorance, but I knew exactly what he meant.

"Stop," he said. He peered more closely at me. His eyes narrowed in appraisal. "You went to see Houdon."

At that remark my alarm grew more intent. I glared at the man. "See here. How do you know I went to see Houdon? Who are you?"

"I saw him too. He told me. Did he tell you?"

"Tell me what?"

"Did you see her?"

I frowned. I was starting to feel some anger and frustration. "See who!" I tried to pull away my arm, but again the strength of the man's grip surprised me.

"See her." This time it was a statement. He glanced over at the bronze sculpture, then back at me. He took on a wistful air. "Now she is among the living. If they had destroyed the painting—frail vessel as it was—she would have been happier. Am I sorry for what I did? Yes. Would I do things differently? No."

"What did you do?" My voice was rather weak.

A loud voice suddenly boomed in my ear from the opposite direction, causing me to start. "Are you feeling better, sir?" It was a guardian angel returning to check his invalid. As I was offering assurances of my good health, the man in the fedora took the opportunity to depart. I turned and watched him disappear into the room from whence he came. "Better not," I whispered to myself, in response to an urge to follow and discover his destination.

By this time, the crowd had dissipated and the noise had diminished. I realized that I was finally alone with Houdon's bronze. I stood and approached the work, each step bringing me closer to a clear view of the figure's face. At last I stopped and stared upward into the woman's eyes. What I saw was—nothing. The frozen form, the dull eyes, the solemnity of a visage detached—all such details seemed more the work of an artist's hand than traces of a woman's soul. I stepped closer. Imagining that a guard might take my conduct as perverse, I adopted as best I could the professional air of a connoisseur attempting to discern by close inspection the creative secrets of a master artist—which critical process, I suddenly realized with a shock, was my true intent. I continued to stare into the woman's eyes, and after some time passed, I began to sense a tremble, a kind of undulating tremor, arising from deep within the bronze. I gasped and the entire sculpture seemed to come alive before me, pulsing and breathing with a kind of energizing life. It was then that I began to view the bronze as something more than a work of art: The sculpture had become a living, breathing woman. As I gazed at the miracle before me, I wondered: *Could the ravings of Nicolas be true?* I screwed up my courage and stepped closer still, holding my breath lest any small sound obscure a message from the bronze. Then I heard what I had inwardly desired and dreaded: the voice of a woman so soft, so raspy and low that I could scarcely determine her words. But determine her words I did, and they were these: "*Release me.*"

In the years that have passed since I first heard that voice, I have returned as often as I can to commune with Houdon's sculpture. For some reason—don't ask me why—I feel as though my visits make the woman feel less lonely. I even feel a pang of guilt when my duties keep me from the museum. And business travel does detain me—a recent gallery opening in Rome, for example, has required more attention than anticipated. At other times family issues intervene: A troublesome daughter has recently provided more problems than I can handle. I sent her a bitter and destructive letter—the mailing of which I immediately regretted. Now I must spend time making amends and helping her cope with what seems to me to be a less than desirable marriage.

More than once the thought has occurred to me that I should inform the museum about my knowledge of the sculpture. I realize that would be the rational thing. I am held back by two things. First, people might well believe I have followed Nicolas upon his dark path. And who could blame them? I often wonder if what I am experiencing is a figment of my imagination. All that keeps me from giving that possibility more credence is, oddly, the man in the fedora who accosted me during Houdon's opening exhibition—I am sure *he* was real. And then I must admit the statue speaks to me erratically. On some visits, as I stare into the woman's face, I hear distinctly the same two words with which the woman first addressed me. It is just when I am determined to tell everyone what I know that I make one more visit—just to be sure—and the bronze falls silent. Can there be within the work an intentional pause, that old hesitation between brush and canvas? During my most recent visit I was surprised to see the sculpture had been moved to a far more visible, permanent location on a pedestal in a bright courtyard under a great overarching glass ceiling. And to my amazement the work had been given a title—the wording of which rather caused me to reel. I stopped dead in my tracks—what did these changes mean? *I wonder,* I thought to myself. *I wonder.*

In any event, I can only do so much. Although I'll keep going as long as I can, I confess that in recent years my visits have grown less frequent. Why? I can answer that question no better than I can explain my initial compulsive interest. Houdon's work presents to this day nothing but a series of questions. All I can say for certain is that the sculpture is for all the world an object which if it does not exist in the world, ought for that very world to serve for the sake of every artist a caution, for the sake of every critic a censor, and for the guiding light of every human being, in my imagination at least, a talisman.

The End

BIBLIOGRAPHY

In English:

Ashton, D., *A Fable of Modern Art* (Berkeley: University of California Press, 1991).

Balzac, H. de, *The Unknown Masterpiece*, intr. by A. C. Danto; trans. by R. Howard (New York: NYRB, 2001).

Gervais, D., "The Master's Lesson: Balzac and Henry James", *Cambridge Quarterly*, 33/4 (2004), pp. 315-30.

Gilman, M., "Balzac and Diderot: *Le Chef-d'œuvre inconnu*", *PMLA*, 65 (June 1950), pp. 644-48.

Kear, J., "'Frenhofer, c'est moi': Cézanne's Nudes and Balzac's *Le Chef-d'œuvre inconnu*", *Cambridge Quarterly*, 35/4 (2006), pp. 345-60.

Robb, G., *Balzac* (London: Picador, 1994).

Wingfield, M. S., *Art and Artists in Balzac's "Comédie humaine"* (Chicago: University of Chicago Libraries, 1937).

In French:

Balzac, H. de, *Le Chef-d'œuvre inconnu* (Paris: Poche, 1995).

Bonard, O., *La Peinture dans la création balzacienne: Invention et vision picturales de "La Maison du chat-qui-pelote" au "Père Goriot"* (Geneva: Droz, 1969).

Guise, R., Introduction to *Le Chef-d'œuvre inconnu*, in H. de Balzac, *La Comédie humaine*, ed. by Pierre-Georges Castex, 12 vols (Paris: Gallimard, Bibliothèque de la Pléiade, 1976-81), vol. 10, pp. 393-412.

WALTER IDLEWILD

Walter Idlewild lives in New York City. His studies on the creative process began with *Form, Restriction and Power*, a thesis submitted toward an MA in the Humanities from California State University, Dominguez Hills, and later expanded into *The Aesthetikon*, a critical study of the components invigorating a variety of artistic media. He completed his undergraduate studies at the University of Notre Dame and holds a DA in the Humanities from Harrison Middleton University.

DR ANDREW WATTS

Dr Andrew Watts is Senior Lecturer in French Studies at the University of Birmingham. He has written and edited numerous books and articles on nineteenth-century French literature, focusing in particular on the works of Honoré de Balzac, Gustave Flaubert, and Victor Hugo. He is the author of *Preserving the Provinces: Small Town and Countryside in the Work of Honoré de Balzac* (2007) and co-author (with Dr Kate Griffiths) of *Adapting Nineteenth-Century France: Literature in Film, Theatre, Television, Radio and Print* (2013). He has recently completed work on *The Cambridge Companion to Balzac* for Cambridge University Press, and is currently preparing a new book entitled *(Re)Writing "La Comédie humaine": Balzac and the Practice of Literary Adaptation*.

ROCÍO DE JUAN BAYARRI

Rocío de Juan Bayarri is a Spanish artist who earned her Bachelor's Degree in Arts from the University of Murcia. A recipient of scholarships from the University of Seville and the Florence Academy of Fine Arts, she exhibits her paintings and drawings at the Venice Art House and Palazzo Ca 'Zanardi, where she participates annually as resident artist.